GOODBYE FOREVER

GOODBYE FOREVER

Bonnie Hearn Hill

severn
House

This first world edition published 2016
in Great Britain and the USA by
SEVERN HOUSE PUBLISHERS LTD of
19 Cedar Road, Sutton, Surrey, England, SM2 5DA.
Trade paperback edition first published
in Great Britain and the USA 2016 by
SEVERN HOUSE PUBLISHERS LTD

British Library Cataloguing in Publication Data

Hill, Bonnie Hearn, 1945- author.
  Goodbye forever.
  1. Women radio talk show hosts–California–Fiction.
  2. Missing persons–Investigation–Fiction. 3. Detective
  and mystery stories.
  I. Title
  813.6-dc23

ISBN-13: 978-0-7278-8586-9 (cased)
ISBN-13: 978-1-84751-656-5 (trade paper)
ISBN-13: 978-1-78010-749-3 (e-book)

All Severn House titles are printed on acid-free paper.

Severn House Publishers support the Forest Stewardship Council™ [FSC™],
the leading international forest certification organisation.
All our titles that are printed on FSC certified paper carry the FSC logo.

Typeset by Palimpsest Book Production Ltd.,
Falkirk, Stirlingshire, Scotland.
Printed and bound in Great Britain by
TJ International, Padstow, Cornwall.

For Ann and John Brantingham,
with love

ACKNOWLEDGEMENTS

As always, I thank Laura Dail for her excellent editing suggestions, advice, and inspiration as my literary agent. I'm also grateful to Larry Hill and my critique family: Jen Badasci, Ann and John Brantingham, Hazel Dixon-Cooper, and Christopher Allan Poe. Every writer needs a strong support team. Thank you, Cyndi Avants, Ted Badasci, Brandi Bagley, Stella Barberis, Anne Biggs, Meredith Booey, Jeani Tokumoto Brown, Gayle Taylor Davis, Jeannie Groves Erdman, Fred and Stephanie Gonzalez, Elbie Groves, Lisanne Harrington, Rochelle Kaye, Kara Lucas, Rome Lucas, Stacy Lucas, Brenda Najimian Magarity, Alice McCord, John Milburn, Barb Moen, Janice Noga, Bob and Carol O'Hanneson, Toni Raymus, Dee and Jon Rose, Dianne Swain, Sylvia True, Unni Turrettini, and Anne Whitehurst.

PROLOGUE
Three years earlier: The camp

Wyatt's screams have died out like the fire in the cage. Even though Jessica's blistered knuckles burn, her teeth chatter in the cold. She pulls her jacket tightly around her until she feels the seams threaten to burst. Now, only an occasional whimper rises above the murmurs of the other kids. Poor Wyatt, his only sin being weaker than they pretend to be.

The broken shadows of redwoods loom over them. Hidden here, with smoke still clouding the night air, she can smell the ocean. Jessica breathes it in and tells herself that they really are going to be able to leave. Dr Weaver said only fire, flood, or blood would cause him to cancel his so-called study, and they have given him two of the three.

'Are you all right?' Lucas whispers. 'You're shivering.'

'We almost killed Wyatt,' Jessica tells him. 'You almost killed Wyatt.'

'Thanks to you, that fire was out practically before it started.' Lucas pushes a wisp of his pale hair over his ear, and even though he is only eleven years old, he speaks deliberately, the way Dr Weaver does. 'He'll be all right, and now the Weasel will be forced to let us go. You intervened too soon.'

'Intervened? He could have died, Lucas.'

'At least that would have gotten us out.' She whirls around to look at him, and the little boy grins back. 'Just kidding. I only wish you would have waited another five minutes.'

'I couldn't.' She gestures toward the campground, where Weaver finishes bandaging Wyatt's arm. 'And what we did to him is a crime, isn't it?'

'We're minors.' Lucas chuckles softly. 'Disturbed children. Besides, you don't really think the doctor will risk admitting the truth about his pet project, do you? I'll bet he sends us home tomorrow – tonight even.'

Jessica wants to believe him. Even though he is the youngest in the group, she trusts him more than any of them. He is the one who pointed out that they're nothing but laboratory rats to Weaver. He is also the one who shoved the burning logs into the cage less than an hour ago, risking everything, even Wyatt's life, to free them.

Everyone except Jessica had scattered. Wyatt's shrieks stopped her, though, and as the flames burned her fingers, she yanked at the rickety bars and shouted to the others for help. Soon they were all tugging at the cage, except Lucas, who stood off to the side, watching, as Weaver ran out like the great rescuer.

Now, standing in the middle of the camp, his arm around Wyatt's shoulder, Weaver calls them back, as always, in the order of their ages. 'Ike, Theo, Angel, Jessica, Sissy, Lucas.' He speaks in a sing-song voice. 'You can come out now.'

One by one, they creep out from behind the trees and go back to the clearing – big Ike tense and ready for a fight, Angel and Sissy holding hands for once like good little girls, Theo nerdy and alone as always.

'You disobeyed me,' Dr Weaver says. 'Due to my quick actions, Wyatt will be fine, but you could have seriously injured him. Who started the fire?'

Silence. Only the ocean and the breeze through the pines.

Weaver's thin lips tighten. 'I'll ask you again. Who started it?'

Lucas, she can hear them thinking alone and together. *We have to protect Lucas.*

No one speaks.

'Wyatt?'

'I don't know. Couldn't see.' He looks down and then glances at Jessica.

'Jessica.' Weaver's voice is a command in the sooty air.

'Neither could I.' She forces herself to look right at him, into the weasel eyes that inspired his nickname.

'Yet you were the one nearest the cage. Hold up your fingers, please.'

She pauses, but then Lucas nudges her, and she remembers that the punishments get worse the longer they put them off. Silently, she lifts her hands, knuckles out, and Weaver squints through his glasses.

'They've been burned, have they not?'

She nods. 'I was trying to help, to get him out.'

'Then surely you saw who took the logs from the fire pit and shoved them in there.'

She shakes her head. 'I didn't see anyone.'

'If you tell me, there will be no reprimand for your earlier silence.' He moves nearer until he is close enough to touch her. But Weaver will not touch her, she knows. His punishments don't leave marks. 'Just a name. That's all I want.'

She stares at a blue-gray blob of smoke as the breeze breaks it up and blows it away.

'No.' Her voice trembles.

'All right, then.' Weaver watches, almost sadly, as the last of the smoke disappears. 'I have no choice but to call off the study. Your parents will be notified tomorrow. Wyatt, as you know, has permission to stay here until the paperwork is completed for his new foster home. There's a little ice cream left from dinner, and I'm sure you'll agree that he should have it.'

They mumble their responses.

'My work will continue, however,' Weaver says. 'We have enough parents who are interested. I'll meet you in the kitchen, Wyatt, and I'll see the rest of you in the morning.'

Their shoes crunch on the branches as they head back inside the barracks.

'One moment, Jessica.' She stops, and a chill runs up her neck. 'Come back here, please.'

Lucas starts to follow her. She gives him a quick shake of her head, and Weaver doesn't seem to notice. Lucas hurries to catch up with the others. Good. At least he is safe.

When they are face to face, Weaver rubs his chin and gives her a watery-eyed expression that he must think passes for concern. 'I'm not certain what part you played in what happened tonight, so I must blame you for ruining the completion of this current study.'

'You'd have to end it whether I told you anything or not,' she replies.

He clenches his teeth. 'Indeed I would, and that's what you wanted, isn't it?'

'I don't care.'

'You don't care, you say? Not about anything or anyone?'

'No.' Tears fill her eyes.

'I'm sorry to hear that, Jessica, and I wish I knew how to help you. Tonight, you will experience a little of what you put poor Wyatt through. Over there, please.'

He wants her to beg, to sob, to rat out poor Lucas, who is probably more scared than she is. If she doesn't, Weaver will make her stay out here all night in that stinky cage too small for any human, the cage where they had planned to burn Wyatt. God, would they have really done that?

'Jessica?'

'All right.'

'What did you say?' Weaver asks.

She stands straighter, tries to shut out the thought of what waits, and glares at him with all the hatred she feels. 'I said *all right.*'

Unable to sleep, not fully awake, she leans against the cold slats, drifting in numb pain.

'Jessie.' She hears her name, opens her eyes, and tries to move. 'I brought you a blanket.'

Lucas shoves it through the bars, and Jessica wraps it around her. 'God, I'm freezing. You'd better get back before he sees you.'

'He's asleep.' Lucas moves close to the bars, his eyes large in the hazy light. 'I didn't want you to think I was mad at you for putting out the fire too soon.'

'It wasn't too soon.' She breathes in the nasty smell of the cage and hears Wyatt's screams all over again.

'All I know is we'll get the Weasel for this, Jessie. I promise you.'

'I'll just be glad to get out of here. Don't know where I'm going, though.'

'You're going with me,' Lucas says. 'The next time we come back here, the Weasel will die.'

'I wish.'

'It's not that hard to kill someone. There's only one of him.'

'Sure,' she says, wanting only to calm him down so that Weaver won't find him out here.

'No. I mean it.' Lucas clutches the bars and presses his face against them so that all she can see are his eyes. 'I have a place, Jessie, and I have a plan.'

ONE

The day she learned of the girl's disappearance, all Kit Doyle wanted to do was sleep in. That was what people who worked all week did on Saturday. Sleep was an escape from what she had just gone through. It was a way of avoiding this reconciliation that felt neither all right nor all wrong.

Richard wouldn't get up early and drive her across town just to shop for vegetables, but she didn't feel like arguing. Six months before, Kit had lost her best friend and almost her own life while finding her biological mother. Now, she and Richard still lived in separate residences by day. By night, they stayed at Kit's house, lying in the bed that used to be theirs, watching films they had once loved, and reading from new books they wanted to share. They talked to each other. They listened. Most of all, they tried to cling on to what had brought them together in the first place. At its best, what they shared in that bed felt like hope to Kit, and, at its worst, like desperation. Although they couldn't seem to find what they had lost of their marriage, they couldn't let go of what remained of it either.

As they headed for the raw-food truck at a Sacramento farmers' market on that Saturday morning, Kit tried to feel like the wife she almost was, the wife she would sacrifice almost anything to be. The *almost* was the problem, and, even after everything she had gone through, it hadn't changed. Richard chewed on his lip, his thoughts clearly elsewhere.

'Something on your mind?' she asked, thinking she would just as soon learn his reason for this trip now as later.

'I was thinking about the quote I read you earlier by that Vietnamese monk. *If we look deeply at the rose, we see the garbage; if we look deeply at the garbage, we see the rose.*'

The point, Kit guessed, was how connected the ups and downs of people's lives must be. Or maybe just that no one should view anything as unchangeable. Richard could always find an obscure, indirect way to discuss any topic, and she both loved and hated that about him. 'Meaning that?' she asked him.

'I'm not sure,' he said, 'but thinking about it makes me feel good.'

They pulled in and parked in the dirt. Again, Kit wondered why he seemed both focused and distracted. The farmers' market stretched out along a seemingly endless strip of grass in what looked like an overgrown parking lot. Vendors peddled everything from jasmine rice pudding and local honey to homemade tamales and the healthy stuff Richard steered them toward. He put his arm around her as if sensing that she wanted to know why he had insisted they come here on her Saturday off.

'The ones with the green banners are the most sustainable booths,' he told her.

'No hotdogs? No curly fries?'

'Not today. You might like this, though.'

They stopped, and he handed her a paper cup of something the texture of hummus.

'Cashew *queso*,' he said.

Roughly translated, fake cheese made out of boiled nuts.

'Not bad.' Kit ate the stuff and then tossed the cardboard dipper into the suspiciously full trash barrel beside the food truck. 'Why did you really want to come here today?'

'To help you reconsider the way you eat, perhaps.' The warm autumn breeze tossed Richard's hair across his eyes. Farm-dog hair, she thought, silky and untamed.

'You're a vet, not a dietician.' She leaned against him and tried to figure out what he really had on his mind. 'I eat very well actually.'

'You *cook* very well.' Kit looked up into his eyes and guessed he was doing his best to hold back something. Maybe a secret. Maybe an emotion. Maybe even tears.

'Am I right in suspecting this conversation is leading somewhere other than the nutritional and political correctness of my sirloin tips in Marsala sauce?'

He seemed to force a smile. 'Remember my niece, Jessica?'

She felt her lips tighten. 'Your brother's daughter? You haven't mentioned her since we started seeing each other again.'

'Jessica's missing.'

'Missing how?'

'I'm not sure.'

'What do you mean you're not sure?' she demanded. 'What happened?'

'That's what I want to talk to you about.'

Without saying more, he led her to a booth with a sign that read *Organic plums. Last of the season.*

The unsmiling blond woman behind the counter offered them a tiny black lacquer tray. The thin golden plum slices smelled and tasted like spring. The woman watched Kit as if expecting a comment.

'These are wonderful,' Kit told her.

The blonde's expression didn't change.

'This is Sarah.' Richard nodded toward the woman with the gelled-back hair and long brass earrings. 'Sarah, this is—'

'Rich, I told you no.'

'And I told you Kit can help you.'

Kit's dad Mick would have called it a set-up, in this case a ploy to drag her into Richard's most recent attempt to fix someone's life the way he wished someone would fix his.

'Sorry.' Kit backed away so fast she nearly tripped over a display of pumpkins. 'Richard, I have to run.'

'Wait. I just want to introduce you two. Sarah is Jessica's mother.'

So this was the woman who had kept Richard's niece from him for more than fifteen years. She didn't look vindictive – just scared. 'I can't help someone who doesn't want help,' Kit said.

'That would be me.' The woman shook her head, and her earrings almost brushed her shoulders. 'You shouldn't have done this, Rich. You have no right.'

'I have every right.' He moved closer to her. 'I'm your daughter's uncle. You and Kit need to talk.'

The woman glared again, and Kit reminded herself that her job at the radio station was already stressful enough, especially now that she and Richard were trying to figure out a way to get back together. Still, she wanted to be polite. 'Nice meeting you, Sarah.' She put out her hand. Sarah didn't take it.

'Jessica disappeared Thursday.' Richard placed his paper cup back on the tray.

'I'm sorry,' Kit said. *Stop talking*, her dad would tell her right now. *Just shut your mouth or you'll be buying into the problem.*

'I already spoke to the police,' Sarah said.

'Sounds as if you've got it handled,' Kit replied in a fake-cheerful voice.

'I do,' she said right back.

'Besides, my blog and the radio segment focus on only old, unsolved cases.'

'Right. That leaves me out.'

'There's something else, though,' Richard said. 'Over the last couple of years, at least one other girl has gone missing from the apartment complex where Sarah lives.'

'How many?' Kit asked.

'I'm not sure, but you can find out, Kit. Farley can help.' Richard opened the vegan cheese container again. 'So can that ex-cop who's working with you now.'

'John Paul has other cases he's interested in,' Kit said. 'And Sarah has already made it clear she doesn't want me involved.'

'Don't talk about me as if I'm not here.' Sarah slammed the tray on the counter, and the one remaining cup of fruit bounced to the ground. They both ignored it.

'You haven't exactly been forthcoming,' Kit said.

'Because I don't want my private life used as entertainment for your radio audience.'

'Farley and I do a lot of good on that show.' Kit glanced at Richard. 'Surely you know about what happened with my biological mother?'

'Yes, and I get that you haven't had an easy time of it. But you don't have kids of your own, do you? You have no idea what I'm going through.'

That did it.

'I'm not inhuman, Sarah. I know how scared you must be.'

'That's not how you're acting.' Her dark eyes filled with tears. 'I keep thinking I should have done something, paid closer attention. I never thought Jessica would just take off without talking to me. I just never dreamed it.'

'If another girl also disappeared from the apartment complex, maybe Jessica didn't take off willingly,' Kit said.

'But who would harm her? Why?' She reached down like a woman in a trance, picked up the plum slices from the grass, and placed them into the trash can.

'Somebody knows something,' Kit told her. 'I understand that you think the radio show would violate your privacy, but if I put something – even a small mention – in my blog, someone might come forward. I'm no substitute for law enforcement, and I'm not pretending to be.'

'Kit does have a following,' Richard finished. 'Can you see now why I wanted you to talk to her?'

'I know you're probably trying to do the right thing,' Sarah said, 'but I'm scared. There has to be something else going on here. For all I know, she's in some kind of trouble.'

'Another reason you need to find her right away.' Kit saw surrender in Sarah's face and realized she had just convinced the woman to share her story.

Richard lifted the *queso* cup and something that looked like a potato chip. Kit took a bite and had to admit the taste was starting to grow on her. At his strongest, this man could convince her to attempt any task, regardless of how hopeless.

'So,' she asked him. 'If I look at this cashew patty long enough, will it turn into a cheeseburger?'

For the first time, Sarah attempted a smile. 'Jessica left a note,' she said in a harsh whisper. 'The police have the original. This is a copy.'

'Could I see it?'

She pulled a folded piece of paper out of her black handbag. 'It's her handwriting. Jessica's.'

Kit took it from her and studied the note. Just a few words, neatly written.

I love you.
Goodbye forever.

TWO

I *have a place, Jessie, and I have a plan.*

Jessica had never forgotten those words. They had kept her going through all kinds of hell. Now, as she sat at the counter of the Mexican restaurant, Jessica willed herself invisible. She had perfected that skill, a shutting down of self, a dimming of perceptions. Gray, inside and out. Background noise blended to a hum. She pulled the navy watch cap below her ears. Hair the cartoon color of hers attracted attention. *Paranoia*, Lucas would say, and had said when he was only eleven, and she was fourteen. *Pay attention to it.* No reason to advertise herself, especially when she was this close to freedom.

'Miss?' Jessica looked up at the woman on the other side of the counter. 'Are you all right?'

'I'm meeting someone,' she replied in a precise, staccato way that discouraged further questions.

'Can I get you something?' The black-haired woman, her soft skin lined with thin shadows that would soon be wrinkles, placed a red-plastic woven basket of tortilla chips in front of her. The heat lifted from them to Jessica's cheeks. God, she was hungry, but she couldn't spend her last dollars on anything until she knew she'd be back with the others.

'Just waiting for my friend.'

'On the house.' The woman went to the end of the counter and came back with a bowl of salsa. 'I make it myself.'

Jessica gazed down at the chips dusted with chili powder. Their scent made her mouth water. 'No, thank you.'

'Eat, child.'

The woman's apron was a disgusting shade of green, a cross between lime and moss that only accentuated her rotund shape. *Rotund shape*? That sounded like something Lucas would say, as if being geographically closer to him brought her closer to his mind. If he were here, he'd devour this woman's free food and compliment her on her parrot earrings and matching fuchsia lipstick. *Take advantage*, he would say. *Take what you can before they try to take you.*

Yet he had brought her a blanket that night in Weaver's cage. He risked his own safety to protect her.

Jessica lifted a chip from the basket, dipped it into the chunky sauce, and chewed it slowly. The flavors melted into her mouth, hot and sweet and so satisfying that, even as she chewed, she reached for another.

The woman smiled. 'That's more like it.'

'Hey, Jessie.'

A hulk of a guy in jeans, his hair cut close to his head, settled on to the stool beside her. She glanced over. Ike had grown both up and out. No more shaved head. No more black barely-there beard. In his red-and-gray jacket with 'Bulldogs' printed across the front, he could easily pass for a jock or at least a fan of whatever team sport folks got off on around here.

'I go by Jessica now, Ike. Good to see you. I've been waiting awhile.'

'A lot of trucks on the highway tonight.'

'The ninety-nine is always slow on Sunday,' the woman behind the counter said. 'Everyone heading south toward Los Angeles. Would you like menus?' Her eyes registered the expected answer, even before Ike spoke.

'Thanks, but we have to get going.' He grabbed a chip, dragged it through the salsa like a spoon, and expertly shoved the whole thing into his mouth. 'Ready, Jessie?'

'Jessica.' She didn't budge.

'Jessica, right.'

She could feel the woman watching her, as if trying to make sure this was consensual. As a couple, they didn't match. Ike was brought into the group for his loyalty and brute strength, as Lucas had pointed out from the start. Though tall for a woman, Jessica must have looked far more delicate than she was. Lucas didn't want her here for her height, though. He wanted her because of her brain and because they were like the siblings neither of them had ever had. That alone was reason enough to be sitting in this sad little restaurant with this slow-witted animal.

'Ready?' she asked.

Ike grabbed another chip. 'Whenever you are.'

'Let's go, then.'

They rose from their stools as the woman openly watched. Jessica dug into her bag, took out her last five-dollar bill, and placed it on the counter.

'Goodnight.' She met the woman's astonished gaze and gave her a smile. 'And thank you.'

Once they walked into the quiet, cold air outside the restaurant, Ike said, 'That wasn't smart.'

'Like you'd know smart?'

'Leaving that money, I mean. Lucas says we can't do anything to draw attention to ourselves.'

'You think taking free food wouldn't? I had to pay the woman.'

'Not trying to argue.' He opened the door of the truck, and she climbed in. 'I'm just pointing out what Lucas says. Come on. Let's get in the vehicle.'

'Do you think I really care what Lucas says?' She slammed the door. 'And why do you call it a *vehicle*? Are you trying to sound like a cop or something?'

'It's the way I talk.' He took his time coming around to the driver's side. Once he got in, he turned to her. 'I don't think Lucas would be too happy to hear what you think of him.'

'Do not presume you know one thing about my friendship with Lucas, Second Year.'

'Wait just one minute.' He warmed up the truck and began driving. 'We're here so we can finally have the freedom to be ourselves, remember? We don't judge each other, Jessie . . . Jessica.'

'No, we don't, so let's get going, all right?'

As the truck moved into the field and its narrow dirt road, she knew that she would have to make this trip several times before she could find her way. After weaving through dead vines, Ike parked alongside a tractor that was mostly rust.

'We'll have to walk the rest of the way,' he said. 'We've got a golf cart on the compound, but no one uses it.'

'Not a problem.' She slung her bag over her shoulder and was glad she had left almost everything from her past life behind.

'It's farmland,' he said. 'Dried-up now but rough.'

'I said I'm fine with it.' She forced herself to keep up with him.

'Snakes around here sometimes.'

'Really?' She was less fine with snakes. 'Don't they hibernate in weather like this?'

'Not out here. Foxes too. Lucas swore he saw a bear tear through the compound one night.'

'So,' she said, 'is that part of your job? To try to scare the crap out of me before we even get there?'

'Yeah, kind of.' His grin in the moonlight seemed too innocent for the rest of him.

'Why?'

'The part about the bear is true,' he said. 'At least, Lucas claims he saw one. Something sure tore the place up.'

'Ike.' She stopped, as much to take a breath as anything else. 'Whatever is out here, I can deal with, I promise you. Remember, I am one of the Originals.'

'So am I.' He stopped too, and, even in the dim light, sweat shone on his forehead.

'There are only six of us.' She counted them off on her fingers. 'Wyatt, Theo, Angel, Sissy, Lucas, and me.'

'Seven.'

'Lucas let you in the following year.'

Neither one of them spoke, and she knew Ike was remembering why Weaver had been forced to call off that second-year study. She glanced down at Ike's thick black gloves. He yanked them off and shoved them in the pocket of his jacket. The raised strips of scarred flesh on the back of his hands matched her own.

'Lucas says I'm an Original, and that's good enough for me.' He took off ahead of her.

'Fine, but just don't be trying to terrorize me before I'm settled in. We made a vow to stick together, and if you'd been a First Year, you'd know that.'

'I do know it, Jessica, but it had to be this way.'

'If you say so. We're all on the same side now. How much longer?' she asked him.

'Right over here.' He pointed. 'Look.'

Through the skeletal vines, she spotted a clearing dotted with small structures. She breathed in chilled air blended with smoke – not the dangerous kind, but fragrant wood smoke that came from logs on a fire. The compound.

'It really does exist?' she said. 'He didn't make it up?'

Ike stomped ahead of her, and branches cracked beneath his boots. 'If you thought that, why did you come?'

'I knew Lucas had something out here, and I believed his grandfather really had owned vineyards. But I didn't know . . . I wasn't sure there'd be real houses.'

'Four,' he said. 'If you count my tree.'

'You live in a tree?' she asked.

'A treehouse.' He folded his awkwardly thick jacket sleeves as if trying to protect himself from more than the cold. 'Someone has to keep watch.'

'Are we in any danger here?' she asked. 'I mean, no one would think of looking for all of us in one place, right?'

'That is highly unlikely,' he said. 'It's just best to play it safe, not take chances.'

'Agreed.' She hurried to catch up with him.

As the compound came into view, Jessica realized that it was everything Lucas had promised. Someone had built three small houses where no one would ever look for them. Even if one did look, no way could they spot this one-time hippie commune with vines surrounding it from all sides.

The temperature seemed to drop as they approached.

'I'm cold,' she said.

'He has a wood stove in the unit.' Ike went ahead and opened the door for her. 'Before me, please.'

'Someone must have taught you some manners.'

'Maybe once. These days, Lucas teaches me all I need to know. Inside, please.'

She stepped in and followed the stinging smell of wood smoke to a squat black stove in the kitchen. Next to it, Lucas stood, lifting a coffee mug to his lips.

Still short, he was no longer the brainy little kid who had commanded them around the Weasel's camp before they could make sense of who they were or what they believed. His hair, darker blond now, had been gelled to give him an illusion of height. When he saw her, he placed the cup on the counter and smiled. The cold inside here was nothing compared to what she had felt in Weaver's cage. Lucas had told her the truth that night. He did have a plan, and he did have a place.

'Finally.' The real power – what had differentiated Lucas from all of the older guys back then – was his voice: clipped, almost British, and by its very softness, its politeness, full of authority. He put the mug on the sink and took both of her hands in his. 'Welcome home, Jessica. I've missed you.'

She squeezed his fingers. 'Oh, Lucas, I am so glad to be here. How'd you know I dropped that horrid nickname?'

'Jessie was fine, but Jessica is beautiful,' he said. 'You must be starving. Pizza's on the way.'

Just then a pale blond girl came through the back carrying two large boxes. Jessica inhaled the scent, and her stomach growled.

Lucas smiled at her, took a box, and put it down on the long wooden table. To the girl, he said, 'Take that one to the others, Sissy. We won't need anything else tonight.'

'Sissy?' Jessica hadn't recognized her.

She seemed to pause for a moment, studying Jessica, and then, without a word, she left through the same door.

'She hasn't changed,' Jessica said.

'She can talk when she wants to.' Lucas opened the box and handed Jessica the first slice. Ike hovered next to her like a dog.

'Pineapple and Sriracha,' Jessica said. 'That's my favorite. How did you know?'

'Lucky guess.' He motioned to Ike. 'Help yourself, friend. After you eat, show Jessica to her room. Tomorrow, we'll all meet here for coffee.'

Ike dove into the pizza, and Lucas headed for the door. 'I have to take care of some business tonight,' he told her. 'You rest, Jessica. Everything's OK now.'

'Thank you.' Exhausted, she couldn't express more than gratitude and a need to fall into a warm bed for a very long time. Now she would be able to sleep without fear of being caught and taken back to that crazy woman and the nightmare she had lived for too long. Not just on the streets either. Now she could be with those who shared her gifts and her demons too, even though theirs were different. That's what family was all about – being different together, being free.

'Jessica?' Lucas stopped at the door. 'One more thing.'

'What's that?'

'Too bad the weather didn't cooperate, but I was hoping you'd wear that pink swimsuit.'

Heat filled her cheeks. 'How?' She nearly choked on the pizza. 'How could you possibly know about that?'

He looked back at her with that serious, straight-lipped expression that hadn't changed in three years. 'I have to look out for my people.'

THREE

Jessica's note had struck Kit with its simplicity and absolute lack of sense. How could anyone write both of those sentences in one message? *I love you* meant forever, or at least it should. So where did the *goodbye* part come in?

She thought about it most of the weekend. Once they left the farmers' market, Richard barely spoke to her. She was used to the way he examined his emotions before sharing them, and she didn't press even though she wanted to. Richard had driven up in front of her house, not into the driveway. He pulled her to him and said, 'Thank you for helping with this.'

'I'll do my best,' Kit told him.

'If anyone can find her, you can.' He could barely finish the sentence. 'I need to go. Do you mind?'

'Where?' Kit asked.

'I need to try talking to Sarah again. With Mark gone, she and Jessica are my family now.'

'Would you like me to go with you?' He seemed to hesitate. 'On second thought,' she said, 'it's better if you go alone. I have a lot of work to do.'

'If you're sure.' He kissed her before she could answer, and Kit told herself she should not resent a woman who had been involved with Richard's brother for fewer than six months. A woman whose daughter was now missing.

'I'm sure.' She pulled him into her arms and gave him a real kiss. 'And I love you, Richard.'

'I love you, Kit.'

Yet Sarah and her daughter were his family. Family meant everything to Richard, and Jessica was the only link to his brother. Kit knew little about her, other than that she had been rebellious from a young age.

That night was the first in a long time that Kit slept alone, without films, books, or conversation. Richard didn't come over Sunday either. Again, Kit didn't ask why. She had done too much asking, too much demanding when they were married. Questioning him about what he was feeling wouldn't bring her closer to him. It would only cause him to push her farther away – the way he had before, when she tried to discuss why he had wanted to start a family so soon after his brother's death.

The answer was as clear then as it was now, and it didn't do anything but make Kit question why she and Richard had married too soon. The least she could do was try to help him find Jessica. Farley would go along with anything she asked. She and her radio partner had been friends a long time, more than friends briefly, and trusted confidantes from then on. Farley liked to say how alike they were. Maybe that was why Kit had married Richard, who was nothing like either of them.

With that marriage and divorce hanging by a thread, she and Farley had fallen into a comfortable, no-expectations friendship that worked for both of them. Last week, he had told her he was 'half-ass dating'. She didn't call him on the euphemism for any number of reasons, including the fact that she was fine with whatever he wanted to do in his personal life. In any case, she could trust Farley as to what would or wouldn't work on the air. When she made him understand how important it was for Richard to find his niece, he would agree to devote their show to that search. But neither he nor she had the law enforcement connections that John Paul Nathan did.

As much as Kit wanted to avoid John Paul that Monday morning, she knew she would need his help on this one. He owned the last five minutes of their radio segment now, and that alone meant he might be willing to use his police department contacts, even though he had distrusted Kit in the past. When she looked up into his light brown eyes, she still felt as if she were trying to prove her innocence for a murder she had not committed. But, Kit reminded herself, that case had been solved almost five years ago, and the true killer had been found. John Paul was more like a co-worker now, if one stretched the meaning of that word. Besides, he thrived on any case that made him feel like a cop again.

John Paul's spotless silver pickup and Farley's freshly waxed black Corvette seemed to be silently dueling beside each other in the station lot that Monday morning. Kit parked in the shade she didn't really need this time of year, especially considering the storm clouds darkening the sky. Only after she got out of her car did she glimpse John Paul beside his truck. Immaculately dressed as always in a white jacket, matching open-collar shirt, and jeans, he pulled a phone out of his pocket and started talking. The month before, he had shaved off his short, gray-sprinkled afro, which made him appear younger than whatever he was – forty, maybe, forty-five. As she watched him standing there, the morning sun slanting down on him, Kit realized that he was actually attractive. His problem was attitude – lots of attitude.

'I'll do everything I can, Jasper. You know that,' he said. 'All I get is a lousy five-minute segment, but I have a plan, assuming I can make that Doyle woman listen to me for once. Got to go, brother. Bye.'

In one quick movement, he returned the phone to his pocket and focused his gaze on Kit. He must have sensed her watching him, and she felt like a stalker caught in the act.

'Hey,' he said, not quite dismissing her, which was friendly by his standards.

'Good morning,' she replied, her cheeks still burning. 'Farley said you're talking about one of your old cases today.'

'Not mine now. My buddy Jasper's. Just got off the phone with him, but then you know that.' His words were friendly, but his face held that lie-detector expression that always made her think of times she had just as soon forget. 'Missing wife. No body, no proof. But someone saw something.'

'Who? How do you know?'

'There's always someone, Doyle. You know that.'

'I'm not sure I do. Why's your partner so interested in this case?'

'Former partner, and, to answer your question, because Jasper had a relationship with the woman.' He sighed to make his point. 'Because it was our last case together before I . . . before I got shot.'

'I didn't know that,' she said.

'No big thing. That's my point. It's not about me. It's about the case. No one knows anything about it.'

'Get me the information, and I'll write it up for the blog,' she told him. 'I need you to do something for me as well.'

'Such as?' His eyes narrowed slightly, and she felt her mouth go dry.

'Such as use your connection with Jasper and the other officers you worked with. I met a woman. Her daughter disappeared.'

'Disappeared?' He rolled his eyes. 'You mean ran away? When?'

'Last week. Another kid disappeared from the same apartment complex a year or so ago. I thought maybe if you could get some details, we could do a segment.'

He started shaking his head even before she finished.

'Missing kids? You don't want to go there, Doyle, especially not after what you just went through with your own family.'

'I'm fine, and this doesn't have anything to do with that.'

'Then why are you so interested in this case?' He started toward the back entry to the station, and Kit realized he was trying to hide the limp she had noticed before. 'It doesn't work,' he said. 'Take it from me.'

'What doesn't work? And why the sudden concern for my psyche?'

He stopped and squinted into the cloudy sky. 'Do you know what happens to a cold case, Doyle?'

'Of course I know. That's why I started my blog.'

'With cold cases,' he said, 'our hands are tied. We can't do anything. That's what's going on with Jasper right now.'

'So you want us to focus our segments on his case?' she said. 'Missing wife. No body, no proof.'

'That's right.'

'Which, as you just explained, was your last case. Why didn't you just come out and say so?'

'I did.' A few raindrops fell. She wiped them from her face. 'You weren't paying attention.'

She wasn't going to stand out here and argue with him when she had to be on the air in a few minutes.

'It's late, and I'm cold.' She started for the door again.

'Here.' He took off his jacket and handed it to her.

'I'm fine.' Just then, the rain came down with more force.

She grabbed the jacket and said, 'Let's run.'

They headed for the back door, John Paul's limp more pronounced but not slowing him down.

Heart pounding, she rushed inside as he pulled the door shut.

Stepping into the station always calmed Kit, and she could use a change of scenery at the moment. Radio had changed and mellowed since her dad's disc jockey days in smoke-filled announce booths. Monique, the station owner's overbearing daughter, considered herself an interior designer, and the place had benefitted from both her touch and her father's money. An oasis of high ceilings, art-covered walls, and glass partitions, the lobby held a serenity that overpowered the caffeine-fueled debates that took place on the air.

'I want to talk to you more about that old case,' John Paul said. 'You have time for coffee later?'

That was a first. Kit glanced away from him at a new painting over the sofa, some kind of abstract in bright greens and purples. 'Only if you promise not to try talking me out of this missing girl story.'

'I'm not trying to talk you out of anything. I just want you to clear this story with Farley and get it on the air as soon as you can. It's a natural for you two.'

'Farley's my partner, not my boss,' she reminded him. 'I'm sure we can cover both, but Jasper's is a cold case, and we need to find this girl right now. I keep thinking about her mother, John Paul. I can't imagine what she's going through.'

'So that's what's really happening here. I knew it.' He walked over to the sofa and then turned to face her. 'You're trying to fix every other broken family now, aren't you?'

'That's ridiculous,' she said, but his words stung.

Just then, Monique came out of the announce booth lifting her phone. 'I just took a few of Farley,' she said. 'Can I get one of you two out in the lobby?'

Blond and brown-eyed, she had a flawless yet forgettable beauty and an earnestness that, fake or not, would be endearing if she were not so self-absorbed.

John Paul rolled his eyes in the condescending look of dismissal he had directed at Kit earlier.

Kit glared at him. 'Sure,' she told Monique. 'But we need to hurry.'

By the time Kit met Farley in the announce booth, she had put on a proper noncommittal expression.

'What's going on?' So much for noncommittal. Farley, the perpetual surfer boy turned rock jock turned talk radio host, could deal with anyone's catastrophes, especially hers.

'Nothing. I'll tell you later.'

'Lunch after?' He reached for a bottle of water. 'There's a new buffet at the hotel down the block.'

'It's raining.' She tugged at her damp hair. 'Want to go across the street?'

'Not really,' he said. 'Let's get away from this place.'

He seemed nervous, and she wasn't sure why.

She walked around and joined him at the curving desk. 'You get to choose because it's my turn to buy,' she told him.

He pulled his chair around so that they were eye-to-eye. 'You don't have to wait until then to tell me what's bothering you.'

'John Paul,' she said under her breath in case the mics were already live.

'He's not a bad guy.'

'He is to me.'

'I know you two have a history, but this isn't personal with him,' Farley said.

'A history?' Her cheeks burned. 'The man suspected me of murder not so long ago.'

'And he admitted he was wrong. Cut him some slack, Kit. He's just trying to be the cop he was before he got shot.'

'I'm fine with that as long as he doesn't try to interfere with what we're doing.'

'Actually' – Farley gulped his water, but not before he could hide the guilty expression – 'there's a case he wants us to cover. I think we should consider it.'

So John Paul had talked to Farley before her.

'Disappearing wife?' she asked.

Farley nodded. 'No body.'

'No proof,' they finished in unison.

'So he must have spoken to you about it as well,' Farley said, fighting a grin.

'I thought he was asking permission. Apparently, he went to you first. And Farley, as much as that pisses me off, there's another reason I don't want to work on his case right now.'

'It better be good,' he said.

'It is, believe me. Richard introduced me to the mother of his dead brother's daughter. The girl disappeared on Thursday from an apartment complex where one other kid has gone missing.'

'Kidnapped?' he asked.

'I don't think so. She probably ran away.' Kit could tell she had piqued his interest, but they had only a minute before they went on the air. Their chemistry would carry them through. 'Jessica left a note – pretty odd. I'll share it after.'

'What about John Paul's story?' he asked.

'That case will be just as cold once we find Jessica – if we find her. Come on, Farley. You know what we can accomplish together.'

'Then prove it, my friend.' He moved close to the mic. 'We're on.'

In spite of her concerns, she and Farley connected as they almost always did. By the time they finished talking about a missing teacher who may or may not have committed suicide, they were flooded with phone calls.

'You're the best,' she told Farley.

'No, Kit.' He squeezed her arm. 'You were right. We can accomplish a lot of good on this show.'

'So you're with me on the missing girl case?'

'Maybe. We can talk about it at lunch. Let's get out of here.'

They stepped into the lobby, where John Paul waited.

'Shouldn't you be on the air right now?' Kit asked.

'I've got a minute.' His stiff expression didn't change.

'So you're blocking our way because . . .'

'I'm not blocking anything.' He stepped aside. 'I do need to tell you something, though, Doyle. Against my better judgment, I might add.'

Farley nudged her ahead, but she couldn't move. 'Tell me,' she said.

'Not that I took anything you said this morning very seriously.'

'Spare me the disclaimers, John Paul.'

'This is serious.'

'I get that.' She forced the hostility from her voice. 'Go on, please.'

'OK, here's the deal. After you and I talked, I called Jasper back. And I asked him to check out those kids who disappeared.'

'What did you find out?' Kit tried to control her beating heart.

'Not good.' He shook his head and looked at her with an expression that held enough truth and pain to make her want to look away. 'The one kid who vanished from the same apartment complex doesn't seem connected, but the other girl you told me about – Jessica – she's not the first one who left a *Goodbye forever* note. Another kid went missing last year in Oregon. His name's Isaac – Ike. He left the same note, word for word.'

FOUR

Kit and Farley ducked into the hotel lobby as the storm raced them to the door. Farley shoved the damp hair from his face, and Kit tried to figure out what was different about him. His hair, always shaggy blond, seemed shorter around his ears, and the turquoise shirt that complemented his eyes looked new. Another time, she might have teased him, but there was nothing funny about the photocopied piece of paper John Paul had given them. In a perfect script, the seventeen-year-old boy from Oregon had written, *I love you. Goodbye forever.*

Kit held on to it as they tried to find a table, but the place was packed.

'What's going on?' she asked Farley.

He pointed at a sign in front of the hotel dining room. *Vintage Toy-a-Thon.*

'A convention? The last thing we need.'

Kit turned and spotted other signs.

Movie props.

Action figures.

Anime.

'There's room at the counter,' she said.

'Come on,' Farley told her, as if it had been his idea. 'And thanks for not making it my fault that we walked into someone else's party.'

Yet he hadn't wanted to eat close enough for people at the station to see them together. Kit could deal with that later – or not. Right now, standing at the counter while the only server was delivering sweet potato fries to the couple at the far end, Kit put down the photocopy John Paul had given her.

'What do you think?' she asked him. 'Farley, why would two teens use the same exact words before running away?'

'Look how perfect this Ike kid's handwriting is.' Farley squinted at the sheet of paper in front of him. 'It's almost calligraphy. Maybe Jessica and he didn't run away. What if someone took them and made them write the notes? Maybe even wrote the notes for them.'

'That's not very likely,' she said. 'At least maybe now John Paul will agree that our segment needs to focus on Jessica and not his old case.'

'Yeah, maybe.' Farley studied the menu on the wall as if he could find all of the answers there. Kit had to agree with his unspoken opinion. John Paul could be hard-headed when his causes were concerned. But then so could she.

'We'll figure out something,' Farley said. 'We always do.'

'I did research on runaways,' she told him. 'Kids, especially girls, are trading sex for a place to stay within forty-eight hours of leaving home. Survival sex.'

'The first step to prostitution,' he said. 'I did some research of my own. Richard must be sick over this.'

'You know how he is. It's killing him from the inside out.' Her voice broke, and she realized she was close to tears. 'Sorry, Farley. Richard won't say so, but I know he's blaming himself.'

'He's only the uncle. He couldn't force the mother to let him see Jessica.'

'But guilt's his demon. It always has been.'

Farley leaned closer to her. 'What can I do, Kit?'

'Just keep John Paul focused on Jessica's disappearance, will you?'

'I'm not sure I can do that, but I'll try.'

A screech of cheers rose behind them, and four characters in costumes Kit didn't recognize rushed into the restaurant.

'Let's get out of here,' she told Farley.

'Can't we just have lunch?' he said. 'I don't want to deal with the rain, and to be honest, I'm not sure I can deal with John Paul right now.'

'Why not? He has to know this case is more important than his cold one.'

Farley glanced down at the counter.

'What?' Kit asked. 'What aren't you telling me?'

He lifted his head and met her eyes. 'John Paul already has Monique on his side,' he said. 'She's pushing for a larger segment for him.'

'Where'd you hear that?' Kit demanded. 'From John Paul? You

might want to remind him that Monique is only the acting program director.'

'Acting for now,' Farley said.

'When she's not drinking wine and visiting art shows. I get that her daddy owns the station, but even he must know how clueless she is.' Farley seemed to shrink beside her. Heat flooded Kit's cheeks. This was the last thing she had expected.

Farley must have read her expression. 'What?' he asked.

'On the other hand,' she said, trying to repair the damage she had done, 'maybe Monique just needs more experience on the job. In fact, she's probably very nice once you get to know her.'

'Stop backpedaling.' Farley gave her an embarrassed smile. 'I think I mentioned to you that I'm half-ass dating.'

But with the twenty-one-year-old bimbo whose father owns the station? 'Right,' she said. 'Maybe you can explain to her that John Paul's case is a cold one, and this one is life-or-death.'

They both went silent for a moment, as if they were on the radio, dead air louder than anything in the place. Then Kit's phone dinged. She looked down and read a text from John Paul. *More about kids. Call when you can.*

'I'm sorry.' She passed the phone to Farley. 'I've got to talk to him about this now.'

'I'm going with you.'

'You stay here,' she said. 'I'll let you know what he says.'

Before he could say anything else, she headed for the door. Although she was still trying to get her head around the idea of Monique and Farley, Kit knew that he wouldn't let her down.

Besides, if John Paul had a lead, she had to find out what it was. At least the man never changed his patterns. She didn't need to phone him to know where he would be after his segment.

The gym reminded her of a bar at midday. A few strangers and part-timers scattered around, and the serious regulars, intent on their heavy lifting, gathered in the back. John Paul stood in front of the wall-wide mirror, clutching a heavy weight with both hands and doing bicep curls next to a tattooed guy who sometimes worked as a personal trainer. Sweat glinted on John Paul's arms and soaked through the back of his lime-green tank. Dressed like that, intent on the job at hand, he looked like a much younger man.

He met Kit's eyes in the mirror, and, without changing expression, lowered his weight to the rack.

'I should know better than to text you when I'm working out, Doyle.' He picked up a white towel from the bench and wiped it across his forehead.

'But you did text me. What's going on?'

'I'll show you.' He motioned her to the bench behind him and unzipped his bag. 'I found out something else. Another girl earlier this year. Same note. This time, we have a photo. And names.' He held out the photograph. 'That's Jessica.'

Kit stared at the three children who stood with forced smiles in front of a backdrop of pine trees. Jessica, who looked about thirteen or fourteen, towered over the other two. Like Richard, she had sharp, fine features and high cheekbones. Her short, multicolor hair was thick and straight. On either side of her stood a little boy and an even smaller blond girl.

'Who are the other two?'

'He's Lucas Tibbs.' John Paul pulled a black sweatshirt out of his bag. 'The little girl is Sissy Purcell. Her mother turned over this photo when Sissy disappeared. The note she had was word for word, just like Jessica's and the boy from Oregon.'

Jessica's eyes, outlined in thick Cleopatra-like kohl, avoided the camera as if staring at a spot just beyond the photographer. Kit knew that look. She knew the feelings behind wanting to disappear, to erase yourself.

'I'm going to find you,' she told that girl.

'She can't hear you,' John Paul said. 'Besides, taking a case personally almost always leads to trouble. What's really going on here?'

Kit hesitated for a moment. She couldn't keep deceiving him. 'John Paul,' she said, 'I should have told you this sooner. I meant to tell you.'

For the first time in almost a year, he looked at her with doubt. 'Then tell me now.'

'Jessica is Richard's niece – his brother's daughter.'

'Now I get it.' He exhaled slowly, glanced out the wall of windows into the streaming rain, and pulled the sweatshirt over his head and then down over his tank. 'If I had known that, I wouldn't have shared this with you.'

'What would you have done, then? Just let Jessica stay out there on her own? You know as well as I do where that leads.'

'You don't have to convince me of the urgency, Doyle. I was going to ask you to help. Now, though, I'll just keep trying. You and Farley can share the results on the air and on your blog.'

A polite way of telling her to butt out.

'I want to do more than just talk about this case,' Kit said. 'I have to.'

'Didn't you hear what I just said about personal involvement?' John Paul reached out for the photo, and she stepped back, knowing if she let him take it, she would be giving up more than just a piece of paper.

'It's not as if I know the girl.'

'You don't know Richard's niece?' he asked, his hand still out. 'Come on.'

'We weren't married when she was born, and he's seen her only a few times.'

'Why's it so important to you, then?'

'Because it's important to him,' she said. 'His brother and Jessica's mother weren't involved long, and their breakup was so bitter that the woman didn't want anything to do with the family. Other than that, it's just like any other case to me.'

'Which is the reason you were talking to that picture of the girl a minute ago?' He moved closer and lowered his voice. Before she could come up with an answer, he asked, 'Where's the mom now?'

'Living here and, until recently, trying to raise a kid alone.' She stared into his eyes to make her point and added, 'The way my adopted mother did.'

'My mom too,' he said. 'But you're too close to it, Doyle. Besides, you're not a cop.'

Neither are you. She forced herself to stop short of speaking the words, but John Paul cringed as if he heard them. 'I've written about a lot of crime cases,' she said. 'I also know that the police don't have the time to track down every runaway who leaves a weird note.'

'It's much more than that,' he said. 'Jessica got sent to some kind of camp for disturbed kids.'

'Her mother didn't say anything about that.' Kit's mind scrambled as she tried to figure out how she was going to share this with Richard.

'Doesn't surprise me. It was some kind of tough-love psychiatric study. Parents got a stipend, and the kids were supposed to be helped. That's where this photo was taken.'

'Tough love?'

He shrugged. 'Whatever that means. According to the psychologist Jasper spoke with, though, these kids were young and very disturbed. The doctor is reputable. He's done a lot of research on kids and antisocial behavior.'

Kit studied Jessica's photo again. She didn't look antisocial or disturbed. She looked as if she were trying to hide something, most of all fear.

'And you were going to ask me to get him to talk, right?'

He nodded. 'The doctor wouldn't take my calls, and I thought you'd have better luck. He's promoting the hell out of the success rate of his new program and probably looking for all the free publicity he can get.'

'I can still help you do that,' she said. 'What's his name? Where is he?'

'I can't.' He put his bag over his shoulder and headed for the door.

'Wait.' She caught up with him and forced him to look at her. 'If you don't let me at least try to contact this guy, and Jessica turns up dead, how are you going to feel?'

'Don't,' he said. 'I've already thought about that.'

'So what's it going to hurt for me to try, John Paul? What's the worst thing that can happen? That he will refuse to see me?'

He sighed and moved the bag to his other shoulder. 'Odds are that's exactly what will happen. I just thought it might be worth a chance.'

'It still is,' she said. 'If that fails, we just have to think of something else.'

'Oh, no, Doyle.' He shook his head. 'If that fails, we have to depend on law enforcement.'

'There's no time,' she said. 'I researched the homeless shelters around here. Wouldn't that be the first place a runaway would go? Two of them are for teens.'

'Not much of a lead.' He shook his head. 'They're protective of the kids and only call in the law after the fact.'

'I'm not talking about the law, John Paul. We need a way to get inside there and . . .' She caught sight of herself in the wall of the mirrors and stopped.

'What?' he asked.

'Look at me.' She pointed.

'Not bad.' He grinned. 'That jacket looks better on you than it does on me.'

She looked down and felt her face burn. 'I'd forgotten you gave it to me,' she said.

'I gathered that.'

'If it makes you feel better to tease me, go for it. But tell me, how old do I look to you?' She pulled up her hair and held back her bangs. 'I still get carded.'

'Don't even go there, Doyle.'

'Come on, John Paul. I'm almost twenty-seven, but how old would I look to you without makeup, maybe just some pale lip gloss, if you didn't know my age?'

'I said no, Doyle.' He turned away from her as if he could make that image of her disappear. 'No way.'

'I could pass for a homeless kid, an older one, at least. Eighteen, right? Maybe younger.'

He turned back to her and gave her the scrutinizing cop look she hated. 'You probably could,' he finally said. 'But you won't know where to go. You could get in a shitload of trouble.'

She had already thought about that. 'But I can go places you can't. You could be my backup, and you could help Farley and me with the story. I know you want more time on the air. This is your opportunity.'

'Not at the expense of your safety,' he told her. 'Let's just concentrate on Doctor Weaver for now.'

'Doctor Weaver.' She couldn't help grinning. 'So that's his name.'

'Yeah,' he said. 'That's his name.'

Kit glanced at herself in the mirror again and thought about Richard's niece alone on the streets. 'How do I get in touch with him?'

'If I tell you,' he said, 'do you promise you'll give up this crazy idea of yours?'

'All right,' she told him. *For now*, she thought.

FIVE

Wyatt arrived from San Jose the Wednesday after Jessica. Lucas allowed Jessica to go with Ike to pick him up at the Mexican restaurant. By now, Jessica had caught up on her sleep and eaten the pizzas, burgers, steaks, and pasta dishes that Sissy prepared and they all stole from a high-end grocery store in town. During her short time there, Jessica explored the property with Lucas, met with the others, and marveled that they had carried out the plan flawlessly. If they could do this, they could do anything. With Wyatt joining them, they would be a family again, for as long as they needed each other.

She had showered in the freezing water that morning and lined her eyes with what remained of her pencil. Wyatt used to think she was pretty; maybe he still would. Maybe, by now, Wyatt had been able to understand what happened that night the way she had. Otherwise, he wouldn't have come. Otherwise, she wouldn't have.

Wyatt stood in the restaurant's parking lot, hanging on to a large bag and looking up at something that must have caught his attention in the sky. His once tight black curls settled into soft dark hair over his ears.

Ike huddled into his gray sweatshirt and squinted through the frosty headlights. 'Dude's grown,' he said. 'Either that, or we got the wrong guy.'

'That's Wyatt.' She forced herself to stay in the truck until Ike parked. Then she jumped out and ran toward him. Stopped. Then walked slowly.

'Jessica. Wow, did you ever grow up.' Wyatt pulled her into his arms and kissed her hard. 'You're beautiful, girl.'

She touched his lips the way she would something tender. 'I'm glad you're here. So glad.' And because she realized she sounded too soft, she added, 'Did you bring your clubs?'

He lifted the bag. 'Knives. I've graduated.'

She felt a shiver and liked it. 'You said you would. But isn't it dangerous?'

'Yes.' He grinned. 'Let's go.'

The three of them shoved into the truck's seat and drove to the drop-off place. Jessica tried to include Ike in the conversation but understood that he had always been slow to warm up, if he warmed up at all. Once they parked, the three of them walked over the scrub she knew well now.

'Snakes out here sometimes,' Ike said over his shoulder.

'Hibernating snakes. Bears too.' Jessica squeezed Wyatt's arm through his soft sweatshirt and shook her head to let him know not to take any of this seriously.

Ike shot her a look she couldn't read. 'Just trying to warn him.'

'Thanks, brother,' Wyatt said.

Ike narrowed his eyes and studied Wyatt for a moment. 'You're welcome.'

As they walked into the darkness, Jessica remembered other situations with the three of them, all trying to be cooler, to be smarter, and ultimately to hide their pain more than the others. As disturbed and scared as they were back then, they might have killed each other if Lucas hadn't figured out what was really going on and given them a plan, a dream they could believe in. Now they were living it.

She smiled up at Wyatt and then at Ike. 'You boys behave. We're going to have some fun tonight.'

'How many of us are back here?' Wyatt asked.

'Everyone but Angel.' She glanced over at Ike and saw his lips twitch upward.

'Some latecomers,' Ike said. 'Good people. Lucas is making it happen, man.'

'The only one I hate more than that bastard is the Weasel,' Wyatt said. 'That's the only reason I'm here.' He put his arm around Jessica. 'That and you, of course.'

'Lucas is cool.' Ike pointed. 'Look over there at all the kids who showed up.'

The scent of barbecue followed his words.

'Wyatt.' Lucas stepped out of the shadows in a heavy jacket. 'It's about time you got here, man.'

'You're right about that.' Lucas extended his arms, but Wyatt stepped back from the hug.

'Time for dinner.' Lucas glanced at Sissy, who stood a few feet behind him. 'I've even picked out your dessert.'

'I've got my own plans.' Wyatt pulled Jessica close, and she wrapped her arm around his waist.

'Sounds good.' Lucas turned to Sissy, whose face had gone blank. 'We probably need dinner,' he said.

'The barbecue is ready. It's the closest we can get to the Weasel's fire pit.' Sissy started toward the smoldering charcoal and the black, charred structure that held it.

'I was thinking of some grapes to go with the meat.'

'If you want grapes, you go into the cooler,' she said.

'It can't hurt you.' Lucas seemed to toy with her, and Sissy bit her lip as if fighting a response.

'Then have Theo go. He doesn't mind.'

'Theo's busy.'

'I'm not doing it.' She glanced over her shoulder as if the cooler were stalking her. 'We all have our shit to deal with, Lucas. That thing's mine, OK?'

'Of course,' he said. 'I shouldn't have brought it up. But we are getting hungry.'

'Can I do anything to help?' Jessica asked.

Sissy whirled around and gave her the same scathing look again. 'You do what you came here for, and I'll do what I came here for.'

'Fine,' Jessica said. 'I came here to be reunited with my family. You do whatever.'

'Fine.' Sissy headed for the barbecue. Ike followed her.

'Jessica didn't mean anything,' he said.

'Leave me alone.' Sissy glanced past Jessica, to the main house. 'We have company. Please just stop being such an ignorant ass.'

Ike seemed to fade, as if he believed everything she said.

'Leave him alone.' Jessica let go of Wyatt and forced Sissy to meet her eyes. 'Ike's one of the reasons we even have this place. So am I.' She tried to think of what Lucas would have said. 'Get down off your high horse, why don't you? We're all friends here. We have to be.'

'And if we're not all friends?' Sissy placed her hand on the waist of her long skirt and tilted her hip.

'Then you need to talk to Lucas.' Jessica looked around but couldn't spot him. 'Until you do, let's try to take care of each other.' She heard a burst of conversation and looked though the house as new people entered.

'Finally.' Sissy seemed to freeze like a statue in ice. 'Now we have options.'

'That's the point,' Jessica said. 'It's the reason we're here.'

Sissy didn't seem to hear her because she had already rushed to the door, and the strange kids were streaming into the room. Jessica followed her, not only to prove she wasn't afraid but to see these people who might have once been children with her.

They laughed, talked, ate. As the night grew colder, they began to reconnect as they once had – easily, without expectation. Ten of them, eleven. Jessica wasn't sure of anything other than the safety she was experiencing, the first time she had felt this way since that year they all met.

A dried-up swimming pool had been filled in and now held a vegetable garden. Only a few peppers and tomatoes remained, and they would be wiped out once temperatures dropped to freezing. Beside it, right outside the back door, was the makeshift shower that didn't hide anyone's nudity. Someone must have installed it years before so swimmers could rinse off after they got out of the pool. Yet it seemed newer, cleaner. Farther back, to the right of the pool, stood a walk-in steel cooler, the kind a restaurant might have used. Pool, shower, cooler for liquor and maybe food. At one time, this little compound must have been a party place.

The brick barbecue in back seemed to blaze into the stars. Jessica sat between Wyatt and Lucas, which was the right place for her. The others scattered into a disconnected circle. Moving among them, refilling wine glasses and replacing beers, Sissy pouted, perhaps because Lucas had chosen her to serve, possibly because Wyatt paid no attention to her.

'The Originals are finally together again,' Lucas announced. The air filled with the sweet smoke of their fire. On the patio table sat a bong filled with a green substance. Jessica looked at the container beside it and realized it was Gatorade.

As the sun sank into the sky, Wyatt got up, dragged his case to the center of the circle, and took out his knives.

He stared directly at Jessica. 'It's been a few years since I did this. Be kind if I screw up, will you?'

She nodded and joined the others as they began to clap in a slow, expectant rhythm.

'All right. Here we go.'

The knives he juggled flew like starlight, like silver confetti. At first, Jessica worried that he wouldn't be able to catch them the way he used to with his clubs. But he had only grown taller and more skilled, and he was still Wyatt, the boy she had liked, the boy she had burned her hands trying to rescue from a fire.

Lucas walked into the unmarked ring beside him. Seeing him beside Wyatt, Jessica tried to calculate Lucas's age. Fifteen? Sixteen? No, she was seventeen and he had to be younger. He didn't act it, though.

Once he stood beside Wyatt, he put out his hands. 'This is one of my best friends.'

Everybody applauded.

'He's one of the six Originals.' He glanced over at Ike. 'Seven Originals.'

More limp applause, except from Ike, who slammed his hands together as if intent on drawing blood.

'This is not just a typical reunion, however,' Lucas said. 'It is, most of all, a *union*. Let's go around the fire, and, if you feel like it, share with us your gift, and why you're part of us right now.' He smiled over at Wyatt.

'I'm here because I'm one of the Originals.' Wyatt lifted a knife in each hand, as if trying to stab his way into the sky. His face, framed by dark curls, glistened. 'And my gift? You just saw it.' He grinned at the gleaming blades and then touched the scar that crept above his turtleneck. 'Because of what happened to me, we got out of that prison.'

Laughter and applause filled the air.

'I don't like the way it happened, though,' Wyatt said. 'I don't like anything about what happened that night.'

Lucas nodded his approval and glanced at Theo, who sat cross-legged on an old camp chair. 'Go ahead.'

'The Weasel called me a follower.' He shook his long, dark hair, and in the light of the fire, his glasses looked like the fiery eyes of an animal. 'All that means is I'm smart enough to obey orders.'

A few murmurs came from the crowd, and Theo grinned as if that was all he expected.

'And you, Ike?' Lucas asked.

Ike sucked down a hit from the Gatorade concoction Sissy had passed him and slowly exhaled. 'I'm here as an Original.' He pushed up the sleeves of his sweatshirt and flexed his biceps. 'The idiots who analyze us say I'm a sociopath, but it's not true. Sociopaths are supposed to be stupid and from low-class families. I've studied it all.' His eyes gleamed. 'I'm not a sociopath. Far as I can tell, I'm a fucking psychopath and proud of it.'

More clapping and shouts of laughter.

'Sorry, Lucas,' he said. 'Pardon my French.'

'I didn't hear you speak French,' Lucas told him. 'Pardon your English. And your gift is . . .?'

'That isn't enough for you?' More applause. He flexed his muscles again. 'Brute strength. How's that? All any team needs is brains and brawn.'

When the laughter died down, Lucas said, 'Sissy? Welcome.'

'Glad to be here.' She shook her pale hair from her face and turned to look at Wyatt. 'I came in at the end of the first year, so I'm an Original. I was there that night someone tried to kill Wyatt.'

The others murmured the way they had that night, and then Sissy's little grin became victorious. 'Next?' She glared at Jessica. 'What can you do?'

'First of all, I'm the one who saved Wyatt. You, he, we all know that.'

'If you say so.' Her words were clipped, and Jessica remembered when Sissy couldn't or wouldn't talk at all.

'Lucas and I are friends,' Jessica said. 'We understand each other. One time when the Weasel gave us a Bleeds because Lucas was late, I flushed the Weasel's tie down the toilet.'

Laughter exploded around her.

'I remember that,' Lucas said with a grin. 'Those stupid Bleeds, where we all got punished the same if one of us did something wrong.'

'But what can you *do*?' Sissy demanded.

Jessica stood. 'I'm smart,' she said, and then smiled at Sissy. 'That's why I'm sitting where I am, not serving the food.'

'I don't mind serving.' Sissy jerked herself to her feet. 'Who's next?'

'You don't like Sissy, do you?' Lucas walked with Jessica back to the big house through a cluster of trees in the back after the rest of them had finished with their speeches.

'I don't care about her one way or the other.' Not a lie, exactly, but not the truth either. 'I'm more comfortable with Wyatt – and you, of course. We forced the Weasel to end his study. We saved the rest of them in a way.'

'But remember that everyone here went through much of what we did.' His voice was so soft and gentle that she could barely hear him. 'Besides, we need more than just us to make it in the real world.'

'We have each other,' she said. 'And we all have different skills. You're smarter than all of us, and you can convince anyone to do anything.'

'And why is that?' he asked her.

'Because you can mimic anyone's emotion. If I told you my mother died, you would cry on the spot.'

'That's what I did,' he said. 'When my own father died.'

'Your father. I remember. In a fire.'

'Wouldn't you light that match if you had the chance?' he asked.

'Of course not,' she said. 'But you did that night. You would have killed Wyatt.'

'We had to get out of that place. It was the only way.'

'And we did it. Thank you, Lucas.'

'Still, we need more than First Years, or we'll be a compound with no followers.'

'Why do we need followers?' she asked.

Lucas gazed into the distance and then back at her. 'Every leader does.'

SIX

As much as Kit hated to admit that John Paul was right about anything, 'truth was truth', as her mom always said. *Trying to fix every other broken family*, John Paul had accused her, and she had denied it. Maybe he was right, though. It didn't matter. Richard had been there for her when they found her mom in time to save her life. And now Kit would do whatever she could to help him find Jessica. She owed him that.

When she told him that the girl had spent time at a camp for disturbed children, he went silent, and she knew he was wondering if he could have done something to prevent it if he had pressed harder to spend time with his niece.

So now more than ever, in spite of what John Paul Nathan might think, Kit had to find Jessica. If she didn't at least try, she would always wonder if she could have done something more to give Richard the family he had been denied. If the psychologist wouldn't talk to her, she would try Plan B and attempt to pass herself off as a runaway teen.

But Dr Melvin Weaver did take her call, and he did agree to an interview, with what he called 'restrictions'. He told Kit in advance that he would only talk about current patients and his current program.

'In the interest of anonymity,' he had said in flat doctor-speak.

Richard insisted on driving her that Saturday. Although she had hoped the drive would bring them closer, she could feel Richard's detachment. Even as they spoke about how to deal with Dr Weaver, he seemed withdrawn, and she knew he was trying to protect his feelings. After reaching the Bay Area, they turned off and followed the winding roads three hours to Mendocino. Finally, after the Route 1 coastline became as rocky and dangerous as it was exhilarating, they drove into Fort Bragg. On the way, they discussed how to approach the doctor, who had made it clear that he was happy, even eager, to discuss his current program. Yet it was worth the drive to get his reaction to seeing Jessica's photo.

Fort Bragg came on in waves of sight and sound – a botanical garden along the sweep of coastline to their left, the bark of a seal through the open car window. Although it wasn't even four o'clock, the moon was already out, a ragged, translucent shape that might have been torn from a cloud. Under any other circumstances, she would have felt drawn to this serene little city. Now, she just wanted to get the confrontation with Weaver over with.

'How are you doing?' Richard asked.

Kit's stomach felt as twisted and hopeless as the road ahead. 'Three of the missing kids were here. I know he has the answers.'

She heard the fear in her rising voice and forced herself to lower it. 'We just need to get him to talk.'

'What if he won't?' The expression on his face reminded her of how it used to be with them back when they were a team and could almost read each other's minds.

Kit wanted to talk to him about her other idea, about posing as a runaway, but he had always been more cautious than she was, and he was already worried enough. She squeezed his arm and said, 'Let's just hope for the best.'

Dr Weaver's camp wasn't visible beyond the trees. They drove on a narrow path toward an assortment of portable rustic buildings. The one in the center looked like a small condo. To one side of it, a patio area held a battered metal fire pit at least four feet wide. They stepped out of the car, and Kit breathed in a mixed scent of pine and ocean. This place seemed peaceful, yet she kept remembering John Paul's words. *Some kind of tough-love psychiatric study.*

Weaver stood with his back to them, in jeans, a light yellow shirt, and a gray vest that matched his hair. He waved at the SUV and van pulling away and paused when he saw Richard and Kit. Then he hurried to them, all business.

'I see you made it, Ms Doyle.' His boyish smile didn't seem to go with his paunch, and his brusque, practiced handshake had just enough pressure to be friendly and not enough to offend. 'I thought you'd be coming alone.' Although his tone was pleasant enough, his gaze lingered on Richard.

'If I had,' Kit replied, 'I never would have found this place. This is Richard McCarthy, my . . .'

'Husband.' Richard stepped closer to the doctor. 'Jessica's my niece,' he said.

'Jessica McCarthy? Your niece?' Dr Weaver gave Kit a polite smile that carried no warmth. 'Perhaps I should have been clearer when we spoke. I explained to you that I can't reveal confidential information.'

'Not even to Jessica's uncle?' Richard glanced over at the fire pit. 'They let you burn this thing in the forest?' he asked.

Kit shot him a frown.

'The kids like it.' Dr Weaver answered in a clinical voice, as if he had been asked the question many times before. 'There's not much out here this far except a furniture-manufacturing place in an old lumber mill and a bunch of pot farmers. We all respect the land and each other. And no, not even to her uncle. I'm happy to speak with you, though, Ms Doyle, about what we're doing now.'

'Why now and not then?' Kit asked.

Dr Weaver leaned against the back of a weathered picnic table and crossed his arms.

'Because the parents now agree to share the information from the studies before we as much as start. I have significant findings to support my theories.'

Kit wasn't sure if he was boasting or attempting to dodge their questions. 'Why was Jessica sent here?' she asked him. 'How old was she when she joined your camp?'

'Thirteen, fourteen, I think. Again, I cannot speak to you in any detail about the patients prior to those in this new program.'

Richard's face flushed. Kit resisted the impulse to take his hand and turned toward Dr Weaver. 'She's disappeared, probably run away. You're aware of that, aren't you?'

'How could I possibly know that?' He shifted as if the table had suddenly become uncomfortable.

'She isn't the only one of your patients who has disappeared.' Kit reached into her bag and took out the photo. 'This is the girl you worked with, right?'

His skin paled. 'I can't really tell you.'

'The police have this photo,' Kit said. 'The other girl's mother gave it to them.'

'I know. I spoke with a detective on the phone, but he didn't tell me they were missing.' Dr Weaver shook his head slowly. 'Believe me, I know nothing about that. I've been out of contact with those families for three years.'

In spite of his composed tone, he looked ready to bolt, and Kit knew she had to keep her voice calm. 'But you did treat the kids?'

'Clearly. However, that's all I can say. When we started, we didn't have parental permission to share information. We worked from a different model.' He stood up and straightened his vest. Kit realized that he looked strong in spite of his slight build. 'I'm doing good work here now. I'm doing ground-breaking work, actually.'

'But what about Jessica?' She tapped her finger on the photo. 'What about Lucas and Sissy? All three of them are missing. Don't you care what happens to them?'

Weaver sighed, and his façade crumbled behind the beads of sweat on his forehead.

'Nothing I can tell you about them will help you find the girl,' he said.

'But they were friends.'

'Dormitory friends, I call it. They created their own group within a group, and Lucas Tibbs was the leader.'

'Do you know what happened to him?'

Weaver shook his head and waved them away. 'You're not hearing me. It's highly unlikely these young people ever saw each other after they left here. Friendships never amount to anything after the study is over, and everyone goes home.' He pulled a handkerchief from his pocket and wiped his forehead. 'I hoped I could interest you in my current research, but this is obviously a family matter.'

'A family matter?' Richard took a step toward Weaver, and Kit grabbed his arm. 'A girl's life is in danger. Maybe all three of these kids, for that matter. You can at least tell us why they were here, and what happened to them when they were.'

'I have no intention of doing that.' Weaver held his ground and glared up at Richard. 'If you don't leave right now, I'll have to call for assistance. A security officer is just a few minutes away.'

A soft breeze moved across Kit's face, and she realized that she was sweating as well. 'Do that,' she said. 'Maybe you should call the detective you spoke to in the first place. I believe his name is Jasper.'

'Don't try to threaten me.' Still, he walked over closer to Richard, who stood to her side, hands clenched. 'I'm sorry about your niece,' he said.

'Ms Doyle asked you a question.' Richard's voice was so low that Kit could barely hear it. 'She asked you about that boy – Lucas.'

'Lucas Tibbs? I'm not certain.' Weaver's expression went blank.

'Lucas came back the second year, I believe, as most of them did. As you probably already know, we had to end that study too early.' He pointed toward the empty road where he had waved at the departing vehicles earlier. 'We've had many success stories – children whose lives have been changed, maybe saved. That's what I had hoped we could focus on.'

'And Lucas wasn't one of those?' Kit asked.

'I'm not sure. We lost touch with the family.'

'What about Jessica?' She didn't dare meet Richard's eyes.

'I'm not currently connected with any of the first- or second-years,' Dr Weaver said. 'We didn't have staff for that back then. I had hoped you would help me spread the word on our work here as others in the media have.'

'All I know,' she said, 'is that at least three of these kids you treated are missing.'

'And I told you there's nothing I can do about that. I'm sorry.' He spoke slowly, but Kit could detect a tremor in his voice. 'The grants I receive go to helping antisocial kids. I learned a long time ago I can't help them all.'

'But Jessica, Sissy, and Lucas were young when they came to you for treatment,' she said. 'How can you just cut yourself off from them?'

'I'm not cutting off anything. But focusing on the ones I couldn't help won't improve the chances for the next group or the one after that. What we're doing here now is cutting edge.' He sank back against the wood picnic table again. 'But you're clearly not interested in that, and you really should go now.'

Richard seemed planted in one spot, and Kit knew she had to give it one final try. 'The word is out to law enforcement that you were running a tough-love camp.' He went pale, and she moved closer, into what she hoped was his comfort zone. 'What was tough love back then, Doctor Weaver?'

He seemed to sink into his shoulders like a beaten man, and Kit had to ask herself, *beaten by what?*

'They're free to investigate. I did nothing without parental permission.' He went over to the table and picked up a phone. 'Have a safe trip back, Ms Doyle. These hills can be treacherous at night.'

*   *   *

'That smug bastard.' Richard gripped the steering wheel. 'I'd like to show him treacherous.'

Kit glanced out at the sea below them. For a moment, it darkened and seemed to close in around her. She felt as if she were being smothered.

'What's wrong?' Richard reached out for her hand, and she forced herself to shake away the feeling.

'It's desolate out here. That's all. Yet all of a sudden, it feels claustrophobic. That guy just sucks the oxygen out of the air, doesn't he? Maybe something that happened to Jessica at that camp caused her to run away.'

'But that was three years ago,' Richard said. 'If I had been there for her then, maybe we wouldn't have to be trying to find her now.'

'You tried.'

He turned his attention back to the road. 'I didn't try hard enough.'

Her stomach sank, and she tried to fight off the feeling of hopelessness. 'Because you married me.'

'Don't blame yourself, Kit. I chose to give up after Mark died.'

'Because you hoped we could have a family of our own,' she said. She almost added that she was sorry she had been opposed to the idea, but that would not be true.

'You made it clear that you were too young.'

'Let's not go over it again,' she said. 'We've had a rough enough time lately.'

'Right,' he replied in the way he did when he meant something else entirely.

'I'm going to find her,' she said. 'And I have a plan.'

'You've done your best. We both knew this was a long shot.'

'Richard,' she said, 'I'm going pose as a runaway.'

For a moment, he didn't reply. She turned away and pretended to watch the sweeping landscape of ocean and forest.

'You can't.' Richard glanced over at her, and then back at the road. She knew he was trying to figure out if she could actually get away with it.

'I already talked to John Paul about it.'

'You did?' He sounded annoyed. 'He can't possibly think this is a good idea.'

You could get in a shitload of trouble. John Paul's words echoed in her head. 'He can fill in for me on the air if he needs to, and I can't see what it will hurt for me to spend one night homeless.'

'Are you saying he's going along with it?' Richard asked.

'I'm sure he will.'

'Don't lie to me, and don't even think about doing something I'm sure your cop friend has already told you not to do.'

'Former cop. And, Richard, she's not his niece. She's yours.'

'But you're my . . . I mean, as much as I want to find Jessica, I don't want to risk your safety.'

'It's just one night,' she said. 'Maybe I'll get a lead. Most kids do stay there at first if they can get in.'

'I wonder if you could just interview someone from the place,' he said.

'You know that won't do it, Richard. I have no choice.'

'Then neither do I. At least take some pepper spray. I'll bet you haven't thought about that, have you?'

'I could get searched. They'll probably just confiscate it.'

'Kit.' He took the turnoff and stopped abruptly at the stoplight. 'You do not know how to fake being homeless.'

'Newly homeless, and John Paul will give me plenty of tips.'

The look he gave her carried a mixture of anger and something else. Fear, maybe. 'You'll run into predators in there. You know that, don't you?'

'No, I don't, and neither do you. Besides, there's safety in numbers.'

He started driving again into the weather—wet and gray, a blur of headlights. Kit felt as if some kind of force pulled them forward. Yet this ride and this conversation felt safer than anything she had experienced in Dr Weaver's remote camp.

She settled down into the seat and once more thought of Richard's niece and where she was at that moment. In spite of the cold, she cracked the window a bit and gulped air until her breathing caught up. 'Let's give it twenty-four hours,' she told him. 'Between the two of us, maybe we can find out where kids go when they leave a shelter.'

'Give *you* twenty-four hours, you mean.'

'For now, it's the only way. Are you with me?'

'I don't like it.' His voice broke. 'I don't like any of this, Kit.'

SEVEN

After an initial argument, John Paul didn't try to stop Kit from carrying out her plan. He even offered to drive her. Maybe he felt guilty because he was taking her place with Farley on the air, or maybe this was just his way of helping. Either way, his presence comforted her. That he kept his opinion to himself for once pleased her even more.

This was the first time she had ridden in John Paul's truck, which smelled strongly of citrus. Then she noticed the little yellow lemon-shaped cardboard air freshener hanging from the mirror and wondered if he had purchased it for this occasion. Although she never wore much makeup, she had put on only sunscreen, and she hoped the very real uncertainty she felt was reflected in her face. The teal knit headband, more suitable for a teen, would add to the deception or at least keep her ears warm.

'Sarah turned over Jessica's computer,' John Paul said. 'It's not completely clean, but what's there is in code. "Meet you for cheese enchiladas on Wednesday." That kind of thing.'

'So at least there's one other person involved in her disappearance.'

'Don't assume anything,' John Paul said. 'Just be safe.'

'I did buy some pepper spray.'

'Good, but keep it hidden.' He pulled up close to but not in front of the shelter and handed over a pack of cigarettes. 'These will buy you a world of information.'

'A world, huh?' She had been naïve to assume that all of the facts she needed would be handed over.

'Don't worry,' John Paul said, misreading her expression. 'Because you're coming through Sacramento PD, your processing will be easy. No one is going to search you.'

'I'm not worried about that,' Kit said. 'It's the cigarettes. My dad smoked for years, and I don't want to contribute to someone else's habit.'

John Paul rolled his eyes. 'The only health I'm worried about right now is yours, Doyle. They'll come in handy, believe me.'

'So I just walk in the door?' she asked.

'You're already checked in as law enforcement referral,' he said. 'It will save you some questions.'

Sitting beside him in the truck, she felt herself shiver.

'Second thoughts?' John Paul asked, in a voice that conveyed it would be just fine to stop before she started.

She shook her head hard enough to make her point. 'If we don't find her . . .'

'All I meant was that you don't even know this girl. No one would blame you for changing your mind.'

'I'll be safe, John Paul.' She opened the truck door. Freezing wind rushed in. 'I guess this is it, then.'

'You look cold,' he said. 'You sure you don't want my jacket again?'

At first she thought he was mocking her, but the tone of his voice was as serious as that damned air-freshener lemon dangling in front of her. 'My coat's fine, and so am I. And you and Farley will be perfect on our shift.'

'Take these.' He reached across her, rummaged in his glove compartment, and then handed two small bags of pistachios to her. 'My buddy Jasper's family markets them. No telling what the food's like at that place.'

'Thanks.' She shoved them in her pocket, hopped out, and ran inside the building.

The chilled air seemed to move indoors with her. Maybe it had just settled into her bones, or maybe that was how unacknowledged fear expressed itself. She paused at the check-in area and wondered what Jessica felt when she first stepped into this place – *if* Jessica had stayed here, *if* she had entered the world of teen runaways by choice. This was a more likely destination than the city's homeless shelters, and it felt friendlier than Kit had expected, although hardly a place one would linger for long.

As John Paul had promised, no one searched her, and the woman at the desk seemed to take Kit's word when she said she had no money.

'Because of the storm, we're out of beds,' the woman told her. 'We're setting up cots in the kitchen.'

The zippered clear-plastic pouch the woman handed her contained a toothbrush and a towel worn thin by too much use, too much bleach, or both. Because of the law enforcement referral, Kit escaped the euphemism called 'processing' and was led directly to the kitchen. After the shelter worker returned to the front desk, Kit transferred her money and cigarettes from her jacket pocket to the pouch. 'They'll steal clothes right off you if they're desperate enough,' John Paul had told her. Kit was still close enough to him to hear his words of warning. She looked around the room.

It bore little resemblance to the smiling photos on the center's website. Long wood dining tables had been pushed to the walls to make room for the chaotic assortments of cots. They looked like little ironing boards and were probably no more comfortable. Girls in various stages of dress guarded their possessions as they huddled over their phones.

Whatever drove Jessica must have made those institutional taupe walls and thinly blanketed beds tolerable. The cot Kit would call home that night was functional and with sheets that smelled clean.

A pale-haired anemic-looking girl in a wool cap strutted up to her.

'You new here?' she asked, all attitude.

'Aren't we all?' Kit tried for a shy laugh.

'Some of us go through more than once.' The girl looked her over as if evaluating Kit's level of street smarts and finding it lacking. 'Not you, though.'

'I was supposed to leave with my friend. Her name's Jessica. We got separated, and I'm trying to find her.'

'Here's the way it works,' the girl rasped. 'This is a processing place, and we're like pieces of meat. You either land in the reject pile, the freezer, or they grind up your ass for hamburger.'

The two girls standing behind her chuckled obediently, as if they had heard all this before.

'Meaning?' Kit asked.

'They either send you back where you came from, put you in foster care, or, if they decide you're screwed-up enough, the appropriate facility. And believe me, there's a facility out there for anything that's wrong with you. Most of us, though, we just want a bed and a meal before we leave. You wouldn't happen to have a cigarette, would you?'

'They told me it's not allowed.'

The girl slammed a hand on her hip and looked back at her two friends with a shake of her head. 'Remember what I said,' she told Kit. 'To them, you're a piece of meat in the processing plant. The rules are for them, not you. Doesn't stop us, though. I got money. I'll pay you.'

Which meant she had hidden that money from the people at check-in. 'Where'd you stash it?' Kit asked.

'Honey, you don't want to know.'

The husky girls on either side of her moved closer. No wonder she was bold. One of them had red hair, shaved on one side, and blackbird tattoos that disappeared down her neck into her jacket. The other had large eyes beneath a wide afro.

'You managed to hide the cash,' Kit said. 'You should have hidden the cigarettes too.'

'I did.' She coughed out a laugh. 'Already smoked them, didn't we, girls?' They smiled but remained silent.

'If I could help you out, would you tell me if you saw my friend?'

'Help me out?' she demanded. 'Who do you think you are to try to bargain with me? I'd kick your ass right here and crush the cigarettes before I'd play games with you.'

The other two girls exchanged looks, and Kit glanced around. The kitchen noises weren't loud enough to bury a cry for help if she needed it, and two security guards stood just outside the door. Besides, most bullies were cowards.

'I'm not trying to play games,' Kit said. 'And what's wrong with bargaining anyway?'

'Because you assume we're on the same level.'

'If you know anything about Jessica, believe me, we are on the same level. If not . . .' She shrugged.

A dark-skinned girl in a red plaid shirt stood up from her cot. Kit wasn't sure whose side she was on, and she could tell the blonde wasn't certain either.

Just then, the blonde turned away from both of them and called into the dimly lit kitchen. 'Who the fuck has a cigarette in this place? I'll do anything.'

'Shut up, will you?'

'Go to bed.'

'I'm trying to sleep.'

Moans and curses echoed through the overcrowded room. Somebody began humming a song about getting high and touching the sky. Somebody else began clapping.

'Keep it down, ladies.' A pleasant but firm female voice broke through the chaos, and a uniformed security guard stepped into the room. 'You get one warning. Don't push it, all right? Lots of people out there would like to be in your places tonight.'

The girl in the red shirt moved closer to Kit. 'I'm Virgie, and I got the last bed. It's a bad night to be on the streets. We're lucky to be here.'

'I'm looking for my friend,' Kit said. 'Her name's Jessica. I'm Katherine.' That surprised her. Until that moment, she hadn't even considered using her legal name. 'We were supposed to leave together.'

'No fun being out here alone,' Virgie said.

The blonde came back. 'I don't know any Jessica,' she told Kit. To Virgie, she said, 'Got any cigarettes?'

'Afraid not. I haven't even eaten today, and the kitchen's already closed. Any of you girls got some food stashed?'

'Just suck it up until breakfast,' the blonde told her. 'They put it out early. You'll live.' She glanced to the right and the left, as if to call attention to her shabby posse, and Kit realized she had gotten herself into some kind of a standoff with this girl.

Kit reached into her pocket and pulled out the pistachio bags John Paul had given her. 'Take these.'

'Thanks.' Virgie tore at the wrapper of one of them.

'Well, ain't you Mother Teresa.' The cold way the blonde said it settled in Kit's back, and she shivered.

'Virgie wants to eat. You want to smoke. What's the difference?'

The blonde looked like a dark shadow against the dimly lit images of cots and kitchen appliances. 'Difference is, she got her food, and I'm still waiting for my cigarette.'

'I'm warning you, girls.' Kit looked toward the doorway and saw the shape of the security guard outlined by a laser beam of light. If she had held a megaphone, her message couldn't have been clearer. 'Lights out, all right? I know it's difficult with the storm. Don't make it any worse.'

'Screw all of you.' The blonde flopped on to the cot beside Kit's as if fighting with someone, even though she was the only one there. Kit guessed most of the battles in these cots and this place were with internal enemies. She thought about the one time she had tried to run away from the expectations and equally rigid deceptions of her own home. She had soon figured out what a bad idea that was.

'I'll try to get a cigarette for you,' Kit said.

Nothing, and then a sigh. 'How?'

'Please shut up, you two,' a female voice whined.

The girl patted her cot and whispered, 'Come on over.'

Kit hesitated and stared into the thin light outlining the shapes and surfaces of the room. The blonde could have a hidden weapon. John Paul had already drilled those warnings into Kit's head. On the other hand, the girl could be just that – young and scared. And she definitely knew far more than Kit did about where homeless kids went to hide, even if she hadn't met Jessica.

Kit put her hand in her pocket and clutched her canister of pepper spray. Then she walked over and crouched down beside her. She had seen pain before, but she could not remember meeting anyone who embodied it the way this girl did. In the room's dim institutional glow, her eyes looked like shadows, and her long, pale fingers gripped across her chest as if trying to protect something that had already been taken.

Kit spoke as quietly as possible to keep the entire room from waking. 'I have a cigarette in my bag.'

'What do you want from me?'

'I'm alone, and I need to know where to go from here,' Kit said.

The girl shrugged as if addressing a much younger sister. 'In case you haven't noticed, we're all alone. Unless you've got some guy, who's going to bail on you anyway when you don't have a cot and a blanket even as shitty as those in here.'

'I do have a guy who will help me,' Kit said. 'Maybe we can help you too.'

'Yeah. For the price of a threesome or whatever else you have in mind.'

'Nothing like that. I'm new at this. All I want to know is where to go once I leave.'

'That's what we all want to know.' The girl turned over on her side, her thin back facing Kit. 'Let me know if you decide to part with that cigarette. Maybe then we can talk about the other stuff.'

'If that's the way you want it.' Kit started back to her cot and then stopped. John Paul was right. She needed to use what she had. 'So I give you the cigarette, and you give me some idea of where I can go next.'

The girl's back stiffened even more. 'I told you, I don't bargain.' Her raspy voice wasn't convincing.

Kit returned to her bed and reached down for her pouch. John Paul had given her this stuff for a reason.

She turned and walked back to the girl's cot.

'One more thing,' she said.

'Leave me alone.' She didn't bother to turn.

'I have what you asked for.' The girl rolled on to her back, and Kit gave the cigarette to her.

'Thanks.' She yanked it out of Kit's hand. 'Took you long enough.'

'Let's talk,' Kit said. 'You have the smoke, and I need to know where to go.'

'Tomorrow.' The night shadows made her eyes larger and brighter. 'Don't bother me anymore tonight, or you're going to piss me off more than you already have.'

'I can get more cigarettes,' Kit said.

'I don't care if you've got a carton stashed under your cot. Just get out of my face.'

'Jessica.' Kit backed off, but she continued speaking. 'That's her name.'

'I'm not deaf. I already told you I don't know any Jessica. Why do you care so much anyway?'

'She's a friend.'

'Maybe not. Maybe she don't want you to know where she is.' The girl crouched on the edge of her cot, cupping her cigarette with her hand and waving the smoke away with short strokes in the air.

'I told you, we were supposed to leave together,' Kit said. 'I screwed up, left too late.'

'She's better off without you slowing her down.'

'You know as well as I do that two people have a better chance than one. Please tell me where I can go.'

'Depends on what you want.'

'Wherever she's likely to be. Where do most kids go when they leave here?'

'We get out.' Kit could barely hear the words.

'Tell me.'

'We get out of town. It's a no-brainer.'

'Is that what Jessica did?'

The girl jerked on to her stomach and pulled the pale blanket over her head.

If Kit asked for more, she would get only cryptic answers or nothing. As much as she hated waiting, morning was only hours away.

The covers rustled. Kit didn't look over.

'That's more like it,' the girl whispered. 'We'll talk once we get some sleep. I'll try to think about some of the girls I met in here. Maybe there was a Jessica, and I just forgot.'

As the smoke of the sneaked cigarette stung Kit's nostrils, she thought about Richard and how finding Jessica might restore him to the man he had once been. She thought about Jessica, who had run away for reasons Kit did not yet understand. And she thought about John Paul. She wondered what he had experienced that taught him how to give her those cigarettes, the only currency next to money that mattered in the place. He had tried to protect her even though he opposed her coming here.

Every moment, she grew closer to finding Jessica, and only that possibility made getting through this night possible. That alone made her disregard the twinge of uncertainty about taking this chance. With only the night-time sounds and the unfamiliar blanket, Kit waited for morning more than sleep.

Noises drifted in and out of her head. Voices. Movement. She dreamed of coffee, bacon. Kit stirred in bed and opened her eyes just in time to see a face close to hers. The blond girl.

'Hey.'

Kit tried to kick and realized her legs were pinned to the bed. Fully awake, she swung at her. 'Help,' she shouted. 'Help me!'

'Shut up.' The blond girl pointed a kitchen knife at Kit's throat. 'If you say one word about this, you're dead.'

Kit realized the two girls who had stood behind this one earlier now held Kit tightly in their grip. Slowly, the boot on her right foot was dragged off. And then the one on her left. John Paul had warned her about bringing in valuables. She had forgotten the boots her mother had bought for her.

Kit lifted her head to get a look at the girls removing them. The blonde's knife pressed deeper. Her gaze didn't waver. 'Be glad we let you keep your feet,' she said.

'What the hell?' Virgie, still in her red plaid shirt, faced them. 'Help, somebody,' she said. 'She's got a knife to this girl.'

Lights flashed on. The knife clattered beside the bed, and the out-of-focus kaleidoscope in Kit's head faded. She pulled herself up, kicked off the covers, and lunged to her feet.

'You OK?' Virgie asked.

Kit touched her throat. Blood covered her finger. The cot beside her was empty, the girls nowhere to be seen. 'That girl stole my stuff,' Kit shouted. 'They did. Stop them.'

'Stop.' The shouts of the security guard echoed back.

'Come on,' Virgie said. 'You need to report it.'

Still dizzy, Kit wasn't sure whether or not she should.

'Come on,' Virgie repeated. 'The guards will anyway.'

'Let them. I don't want any trouble.'

'Honey, it's OK.'

Kit looked into the dining area. If the people who ran this place figured out who she was, she'd be back where she started. In the meantime, Jessica would get that much farther away.

'I just need to get out of here.'

'Not that you asked for my opinion, but you're not cut out for this life.' Virgie pulled a scruffy knit cap over her hair. At closer glance, Kit spotted the dark blotches that stretched like shadows under her eyes.

'And you are?'

'Some of us handle this shit better than others. That's all I meant.'

'I get that.' Kit looked into her dark eyes. They gleamed with something she couldn't identify. Amusement, maybe, or sadness. 'If you hadn't been on the next cot, I don't know what that girl would have done to me,' she said. 'Thank you.'

'You're welcome. And thank you for giving me those pistachio nuts. I guess we saved each other in a way.'

'I guess we did,' Kit said. 'Good luck out there, and if you run into a girl named Jessica . . .' She wasn't sure what to say next.

Virgie sighed. 'Pretty girl, right? Stayed here for two nights?

Short hair almost as black as mine except for all those dark-red streaks in it? Big eyes?'

'That sounds like her.' Kit said. All this trouble, and Virgie had known who Jessica was all along. 'Why didn't you tell me sooner?'

'Not everyone in here has the right intentions.' Virgie picked up her backpack. 'You gave me your last food. It *was* your last, wasn't it?'

Kit felt herself smile. 'You were right in the first place. I'm not cut out for this.'

'Ought to consider going back – maybe not where you came from, but to somewhere they'll take you in.' Virgie inhaled deeply. 'Looks like they started the bacon frying. Come on. I'm so hungry my belly button's pushing on my backbone.'

EIGHT

As she and Virgie went into the kitchen, Kit, wearing only her socks, realized how lucky she had been to find this young woman. Finally, she might be able to learn more about Jessica. Even with the close call, she had been right to come here.

Once they sat with their food, Virgie seemed to savor the pieces of bacon on her plate. She ate the scrambled eggs slowly. Then she swallowed some coffee and dabbed at the corners of her lips with a paper napkin in such a natural refined manner that Kit had to wonder about Virgie's background.

'You ain't hungry?' Virgie asked in a tone that didn't match her gestures.

'Sure I am.' Kit faked interest in the muffin she had put on her tray. 'Just thinking about what almost happened to me.'

'Girl, every night out here is an almost happened. That's why you ought to get out while you can.'

'I will as soon as I find Jessica. I'll go to as many shelters as I have to until I do.'

'All right, then, if you insist.' Virgie frowned as she studied her. 'Here's what you got to do. First of all, hide that hair of yours.'

'Do you mean with a cap?' Kit asked.

'Vaseline first. You need to look like a guy. Wear a ball cap. Talk to yourself. Scratch yourself all over, and, most of all, act crazy.'

Even thinking about Virgie's words made Kit's skin itch.

'If I do that, no one will talk to me.'

'Not right off maybe, but you'll stand a better chance of not getting raped or killed. You still want to go looking for your friend?'

'I don't have any choice,' Kit said.

'Here's something else, then. When you're a runaway, everyone wants to get you into their system. A runaway don't want to be in no one's system, though. That's why we're out here.'

That was what Jessica had to deal with, whether on the streets or in the marginal safety of a shelter. Although she had never met the girl, Kit understood her more than ever after just one night in this place.

'Do you have any idea where Jessica went?' she asked.

Virgie shook her head. 'Sometimes you just have to take care of your own self. You, for instance. You ain't got any money, yet you gave me something you could have sold. Stupid, right?'

'What about what you did for me?' Kit asked.

'That was a thank you, and so is what I'm telling you right now, and that is this. When you go on the streets and ask for loose change, there's a way to do that.'

'I'd never beg,' Kit said, before she thought better of it.

'Don't be so sure, Miss High and Mighty.' Virgie looked at her with a mixture of pity and contempt. 'When you get out there, here's how you do it. You go up very polite and all. You say, "Pardon me, ma'am. Would you have any spare change?"'

'And if they tell you to get lost?' Kit asked.

'You're already are lost, so that don't bother you. Just go to the next person and say the same thing till someone bites. And then – and this is real important. Then say, "Thank you, ma'am. Bless you." I don't care what their faith is or isn't, but they all like that "bless you" part.'

'Man coming through,' someone called out.

Kit looked toward the commotion and spotted John Paul heading toward them in jeans and a black jacket.

'Looks like you're covered,' Virgie said. 'I'll be going now.'

'No, wait,' Kit said, but Virgie was already heading out the same door that John Paul had just walked in.

He came closer, and Kit noticed that the women were deserting the table as if a cop, even a former cop, carried an odor that everyone could smell.

'Come on.' John Paul towered over her, and she tried to figure out what she had done to anger him. 'Let's get out of here.'

Once they were on the sidewalk, he took a closer look at her. 'What happened to you, Doyle? Where are your shoes?'

'I screwed up. The girl next to me asked for a cigarette. I felt sorry for her.'

He touched her cheek as if it might burn him. 'Did she hurt you?'

'When I woke up, she had a knife to my throat, and her friends were taking off my boots. I feel like a fool.' Inside the socks, her feet felt numb on the cold sidewalk.

'Don't worry about it. I have a lead.' His eyes gleamed.

'What kind of lead?' She felt as if she were negotiating with the cold, letting it take just enough of her to make its presence known, but not enough to slow her. A police car crawled slowly by, black and white in a world of neutrals.

'We probably look like hustlers,' Kit said.

'Be glad they're patrolling.'

'I am. So what's your lead?'

He walked with her to the corner and watched the car disappear into the fog. 'I knew this wasn't going to be easy, but I hadn't counted on you being attacked your first night.'

'Please tell me you aren't using that as an excuse to back out,' she said.

A guy on a bicycle pedaled slowly in their direction, his features hidden by the hood of his bulging jacket. Something about the way the streetlight hit made him appear enormous. Kit shoved her hand in her pocket and clutched her keychain.

'I've got my pepper spray,' she whispered.

'And what do you suppose he has? Don't make eye contact.'

The bike swerved down a driveway into the street and passed them. Kit's heartbeat quickened anyway as if her brain hadn't sent the message of safety to the rest of her. They reached the street corner. As she started to cross, John Paul pulled her back. 'Wait a minute.'

Kit breathed in the street air. It felt as overcast and as dark gray and indifferent as their surroundings. She would answer his question once she had a chance to figure it out, but not now. Not with every shadow on their path reminding her of the guy on the bike, the girl with the knife, or worse.

'Come on.' He motioned to his truck. 'Let's get you some shoes.'

'Thanks.' The only feelings in her feet were little needles of pain. 'You warned me about valuables. I just didn't think it through. At least I found one girl who had seen Jessica. I just don't where to go next.'

'After what happened last night? Nowhere.' She started to protest, but as he pulled out of the parking lot on to the street, he said, 'The shelters are just the starting place, Doyle. The kids team up after that. Or they don't.'

'Because they don't want to be in the system, right? I already learned that. They didn't run away just to be sent back.'

'Exactly. And most shelters, however well meaning, are conduits to one or more systems.'

'Doesn't sound that bad compared with what could happen.' Feeling began to return to her feet, and she tried to squeeze away the pain. 'You weren't supposed to come back early this morning, John Paul. What happened?'

'Some runaway kids were talking about a Mexican restaurant several hours from here.'

'What?' Kit asked him. 'They live at a Mexican restaurant?'

'I don't think so, but the two guys I talked to had heard of it. They didn't sound as if they were going there, though. More likely, it's another conduit – one outside the system.'

'Cheese enchiladas.' Kit pulled her jacket closer, even though the chill had come from inside. 'Remember the stuff on Jessica's computer? I'm going to find that restaurant.'

'Not alone,' he said.

'Richard will help me.'

John Paul's hands seemed to tighten on the wheel. 'The man's not equipped to help you. Don't involve him in this. I'll do what I can as long as it doesn't interfere with law enforcement.'

This wasn't the time to decide if she would involve Richard or

John Paul to find the restaurant. Or neither of them, for that matter. At the moment, she would have promised him anything. 'I'm just not sure where we're going.'

'Neither am I,' he said. 'But here's the deal. Someone meeting Jessica's description was spotted hitchhiking near Fowler.'

'Fowler?' she asked.

'You never know.' He gave her a look she couldn't figure out. 'It's a small town. At least, there can't be that many restaurants there.'

NINE

W hen John Paul dropped her off at her house, he had said he would pick her up Monday after they got off the air. But when she shared her plan with Richard late Sunday afternoon, he insisted they drive to Fowler right then.

'It won't harm his efforts,' Richard said. 'Besides, we might get lucky and find her right away.' The hope in his expression was enough to convince Kit.

As they drove down Highway 99, Kit savored the stream of air that warmed her feet in Richard's car. Except for the gaudy neon sign along the highway, the tiny agricultural town between Sacramento and Bakersfield was one she had barely noticed in the past. The sign, which was in the shape of a hand, advertised the local palm reader who had been telling fortunes there longer than Kit had been alive. According to their research, the town had fewer than a dozen restaurants that were not fast food. They could go through all of them that evening.

She had spoken to her mother that morning and had lied when her mom asked if she was all right. As always when they ended the call, Kit had to fight tears. This woman, both innocent and wise, both amusing and serious, could have been hidden from her forever. Had it not been for Kit's persistence and a great deal of luck, they would have lived separate lives, unable to know what they had lost. Many conversations lay ahead for them, more confessions and disagreements even. But now Kit had what she had always needed, and realizing what she had after all these years, she didn't fear much else – certainly not a road trip a few hours away.

Tule fog, indigenous to this place and this time of year, had risen and clung like translucent ghosts. It reminded her of frosted glass that let only the light pass through and distorted the forms beyond. Richard turned on an NPR station, which had been their background music.

'I used to drive this highway with my dad when I was a kid and he worked in LA radio,' she said. 'It brings back memories.'

Richard glanced over at her.

'What?' she asked.

'Want to discuss the elephant in the car?'

'What elephant?' she said. 'Stop trying to be the therapist, will you? I don't know what you're talking about.'

'Your insistence to go into these places alone.'

'I've got my phone,' she said. 'It will be all right.'

'Even though Jessica was seen near there? Kit, you don't know what you're walking into.'

'After what we've just been through, I'm not worried.'

A Mexican restaurant just before the city limits sat off from the freeway. 'Richard, look.'

'We won't get anywhere here,' he told her. 'It's too obvious, too close to the mainstream.'

'If you were a runaway, wouldn't you want something like this?' she said.

'This close to the freeway, it's the first place people would search for you.'

'Not if they didn't know what they were searching for. And not if they had no idea the kids they were trying to find had headed this way.'

'All right, then. Let's look at the other restaurants first.'

She entered and left two cafes, both Spanish-speaking only, and, after them, something calling itself a Mexican delicatessen. 'Let's go back to the first one,' she said.

Richard agreed. As they pulled into the drive, the restaurant came into view, even smaller than it had appeared from the highway. She wished the two of them could walk into that sorry-looking place together, arms locked against the world, but once they did, they would be viewed as a pair, and she would appear less vulnerable.

'Let me go in first,' Richard said.

'You can't,' she told him. 'You've got to agree that a girl on her own just might have a better chance than two people walking in there tonight.'

'But they can look out and see the car in the parking lot,' he said.

'Good point.' She felt nervous again, and she started to feel the darkness closing around her. But that was nightmare stuff. This was as real as daylight, and lately Richard worried more than he should. 'Why don't you drive around?' she said.

'While you go in there alone?'

'It's a restaurant, Richard, and too small to be housing even one runaway. Besides, there's a side road right over there.'

'Looks like a driveway to me.'

He might be right, but she wasn't about to admit it. 'Well, check it out. I'll text if things get weird. Otherwise, give me fifteen, twenty minutes.'

'I don't like it, Kit.'

'I like it better than my other destinations this far. Don't you?'

That got a smile out of him. 'John Paul probably knows the cops out here. Think I ought to call him?'

She opened the door and turned to meet his grin. 'He's not going to be happy that I didn't wait for him to drive me. Don't call him unless you have to.'

He sighed in that way that meant he agreed with her even though he didn't want to, and he pulled her in for a kiss. 'I won't be far away.'

Kit watched his car leave the parking lot and realized he was right about potential danger. But how dangerous could this place be? She could count on Richard. She could count on John Paul. Kit opened the single door of the restaurant.

As it closed behind her, she stepped into warmth and smelled a mixture of scents from heavy to sharp. Peppers, oil, heat. The dim lights cast shadows on the crudely plastered wall. The T-shaped restaurant ended at a long bar made out of wood so polished it seemed more suited to an upscale place. To Kit's left, one couple sat at a side table. The bar was empty. As Kit approached it, an attractive older woman, her dark, clipped-back hair lightened by silver, entered from what must be a side kitchen.

'Good evening, Miss.' The woman glanced at the clock and back at her, taking her in as if they had met before. 'We'll be closing soon.'

'That's all right.' Kit looked down at her hands, pretending fear, as if she didn't dare to meet the woman's eyes.

A basket of chips and salsa appeared before her on the bar.

'On the house. I made it fresh today.'

Kit looked up at the woman's face and knew the gesture had been too automatic to have been a first-time response to a hungry-looking kid.

'Thank you, but are you sure? I don't have any money.'

'That's OK.' The woman glanced to the front door and then to the back. 'You need to eat fast, though.'

She motioned to one of the round leather stools, and Kit sat.

The chips, tortillas cut into long slices and deep-fried, tasted as hopeful as the woman appeared to be. 'I'm looking for a friend of mine. She's about my age.'

'I can't help with that.' The woman turned her back and headed into the kitchen. 'I do what I can with food,' she said over her shoulder. 'That's it.'

'My friend's name is Jessica.'

'I don't ask names.' Yet the woman stopped on her way back from the kitchen.

'You've never seen someone by that name in here?'

She leaned against the counter. 'You want some coffee? A soda, maybe?'

'Thank you, but I want to hear about Jessica. You stopped when I mentioned her name. Please help me.'

'Maybe I did see her. I can't remember right now.' The woman headed for the coffee pot, poured it into a turquoise-glazed mug, and handed it to Kit. 'Drink this fast. We're closed.'

She went over to the door and, with a rattle of the blinds, turned around the sign in the window.

As if taking it for a signal, the couple at the side table rose and left.

'When was Jessica here?' Kit asked, once they were alone.

'I already told you, I'm not sure.' The woman reached down, placed a towel on the counter, and began wiping it. 'If I remembered everyone who passed through here, I wouldn't have room in my head for how to make all this food. You drink your coffee, and then we'll leave.'

Kit looked down at the laminated menu. 'It says here that you're open until nine o'clock on Sundays.'

'Not tonight.' She poured the rest of the coffee into the sink behind her. 'If you're like the rest of them and don't have a place to stay, there's a homeless center about ten miles from here.'

'I don't want a homeless center,' Kit said. 'I just got out of one.'

'These people seem OK. I have a card.'

'I'm all right,' Kit said, but she took the business card anyway. 'I just want to find Jessica. I have a photo of her.'

'Don't want to see it.' She stared down at her towel and swept it over invisible crumbs. 'If I start worrying about you kids, it will kill me.'

Kit took out the photo of Jessica and the other two kids anyway. She placed it on the counter. 'Please.'

The woman glanced down at it and seemed to reel back. 'How did you get this? Who are these children? Why are you looking for them?'

'I think you know more than I do.' The woman had said *children*. She recognized more than one of them.

Kit touched Jessica's face on the photo. 'Do you know her?'

'She looks younger here, but not any happier.'

'So you *have* seen her,' Kit said.

'How do I know you really want to help?' The woman stepped back, eyes so hard they had to be covering something. 'How do I know you don't wish her harm?'

'Look at me.' Kit rose from the barstool. 'Do you really think I would come here for any other reason than to find this girl?'

'You're very young. I don't know what you would try.'

'She's my friend,' Kit said, and felt as if she were telling the truth. 'If I don't find out where she is tonight, I'm not going to be able to sleep. I've got to find her.' She glared at the woman, silently demanding the response she knew was there.

'Probably she's all right.' She turned and began cleaning the spotless counter in exaggerated gestures.

'What about the other kids?' Kit said.

'They may be all right too. I hope so.'

'Because they're together, aren't they?'

'That's none of my business.' She smoothed the towel over the edge of the stainless-steel sink behind the bar. 'As you said, not everyone trusts the shelter. Besides, it is not my job to judge.'

'I'm not asking you to judge,' Kit said. 'But Jessica shouldn't be out here on her own, and I think you know where she is.'

'I swear I do not.' The woman glanced back at the door again. 'You must leave now. I need to go home.'

'You're not hiding her?' Kit asked.

'Of course not. I can barely take care of my own. You do have to go, though. The fog here gets too thick to drive.'

The front door swung open, and the guy who stepped inside filled the doorway and the room so completely that Kit felt a wave of claustrophobia.

'Hey, Juanita. Why shutting down so early?' The grin that spread across his face reflected innocent friendship along with something darker. 'You know I'm meeting someone here tonight.'

'The fog,' the woman muttered. 'I cannot stay open.'

Then the guy's gaze drifted to Kit. 'Well, hello,' he said, and walked over to where she sat. 'Looking for some cheese enchiladas?'

The words she had been waiting to hear.

'Cheese enchiladas,' she repeated, forcing the words out. 'Yes, I'd love some.'

'You wouldn't be Angel, would you?'

Kit thought about lying but realized something was wrong. She needed time to figure it out.

'No,' she told the guy, 'and I'm just leaving.' She caught the look of relief on the woman's face.

'What's your hurry?' he asked.

'The place is closed.'

'Juanita won't close until Angel gets here. 'He reached into his pocket and took out a handful of cash. 'Will you, Juanita?'

Without answering or even looking at his money, the woman turned and hurried into the kitchen.

'I can see now that you're not Angel, although your hair's the same,' he said. 'You're prettier.'

Kit tried to match up this guy's features with the photograph, but nothing about him resembled the smiling little boy. This one must have been huge even as a child. With the hair cut close to his head, he would have passed for ordinary except for his mismatched eyes and goofy grin.

'Who's Angel?' Kit asked.

'Who are you?'

Although most with his features would have been unattractive, maybe even freakish, he had a friendly voice and a way of smiling that reminded her of those dolls that were so ugly they were almost cute.

'That's not important.' She glanced at him as if he were a co-conspirator and not someone who might have the answers she was seeking.

'Cops looking for you?' he asked.

'Probably not. Probably no one is.' Saying those words, even though she had created them to appease him, was surprisingly painful.

The woman returned from the kitchen. 'Please leave,' she said. 'Both of you.'

'Juanita.' The guy sat down on a stool. 'Ten more minutes.'

'Not ten more seconds.' She lifted a phone from the counter as if it were a gun. 'Don't make me use this.'

He stood and gave Kit a lopsided smile. 'Nice to meet you, mystery girl. I'll be back tomorrow night. What about you?'

'I'll think about it,' she said. 'Good luck finding Angel.'

As soon as she heard the rattle of the shades as the door closed behind him, the woman drew closer to the counter. 'Wait for a moment. Let him leave first.' Kit wasn't sure if her eyes held anger, fear, or both.

'What can you tell me about him?' she asked.

'Big Ike?' The woman shrugged, and her expression went as blank as the plaster wall behind her. 'He tips well. That's all I know.'

'You must have known he was coming tonight.'

'He comes most nights, even when it's not to . . . He just likes the food.'

'Yet you tried to close early and get me to leave before he showed up.'

'Like I said, I worry about you kids too much.'

Yellow headlights shone through the drawn blinds. Kit walked over to the door and peeked through. The outdoor lights, watery in the fog, shone on what she hoped was Richard's car.

'I've got to go now,' Kit said. 'Thank you for the coffee. And the chips.'

The woman took the cup and rinsed it. 'Be careful,' she said. 'Remember what I told you about the shelter.'

'I can't.' Kit pulled her scarf so tightly that it scratched her neck. 'Not until I find Jessica.'

Then she got up and hoped Richard would be in the parking lot. When she stepped outside and saw the car, she ran for it.

'What did you find out?' he asked her.

'I'll tell you once we're home,' she said, and looked around to be sure no one was watching them.

'Home.' Richard's expression reminded her of how he had looked at her years before when they had fallen in love. 'I like that word.'

TEN

Angel hadn't shown up the night before, and Ike went back for her as much to see the girl with the curly hair and curious eyes. He'd been surprised when she had glared right back at him as if to say nothing about him, including his size, scared her. The minute he spotted her that night, he realized that she had too much hair and too much confidence to be Angel. Kind of pretty, though. 'The sign of a strong man is a strong woman,' his dad used to say back before everything at home went to hell. But his dad used to go on, 'And what's wrong with a little argument now and then? It makes the sex better.'

Sex was the last thing Ike should be thinking about right now. What he needed to do was pick up Angel if she was there, and only maybe flirt with the mystery girl if she showed up again. If she did, it might mean she liked him.

Ike always looked inside a place before he got out of his truck. Funny that most people didn't. Why would you want to go in somewhere when you had no idea what waited for you? He and

Lucas had figured that out a long time ago. They had figured out a lot of things. If Lucas wanted to bring in Jessica, Ike could live with that. No way was she going to bitch-slap him with words, though, even if she had been a First Year.

As far as Ike could tell through the slanted light of the window, only the Mexican woman and the curly-haired girl sat at the counter. So she did come back, and he'd bet it sure wasn't for the free chips and salsa. The woman served the girl something in a cup. Hot chocolate. The girl lifted the cup to her lips and then turned around as if she could see him.

He could recite chapter and verse every warning Lucas issued, but he took most of the cash out of the glove box. Nothing out here but vineyards and farms, but he'd still rather keep the money with him. *Take no chances.* That was the first rule. Besides, if anyone even thought about stealing from him, the truck couldn't fight back the way he could. He opened the door and realized that the red plaid jacket over his T-shirt made him look like a lumberjack, but hey, some girls liked that type. Anyway, he shouldn't be worrying about girls right now.

The restaurant smelled and felt warm. Juanita, sad-faced as always, glanced up from behind the counter. In the moment she looked from her tired hands to his face, she reminded him of his mother.

'Good to see you again.' She left the mystery girl and came around to where he stood. 'Hot tea?'

'*Gracias.* That would be nice.' Then a thought came to him. 'Oh, wait. You wouldn't have any hot chocolate, would you?'

'Mexican hot chocolate with cayenne pepper and nutmeg? Coming right up.'

'That'll do.' He had actually wanted it the way his granny fixed it – thick and creamy with melted marshmallows on top – but at the moment, he was more interested in the girl. She pretended she wasn't listening to the conversation.

'And some tamales?' the woman asked. Hot chocolate or not, she was starting to get on his nerves.

He settled on one of the stools at the counter, and the girl turned her head.

'Hi,' he said. 'You again?'

'As promised. Did you find your friend?'

He ignored the question. 'You like tamales?' Just friendly conversation. Nothing wrong with that.

'I love them. Tamales and cheese enchiladas.' She glanced down at the counter.

The cheese enchiladas could be a coincidence. Lucas should have come up with a better code – sardine sandwiches or something.

'On me.' He glanced over at one of three corner booths. He had some money. Why not? Jessica wasn't the only one who could throw it around.

'I can't do that.'

'Oh, come on. It's just a tamale.'

She shook her head, and he liked the way the dim light got tangled in her curls. 'It's never just a tamale.'

'Well, it is this time.' She shook her head again, and he thought about how that couldn't be easy, as hungry as she must be. 'I've been where you are,' he said, lowering his voice.

'I don't think so.' She took in the jacket Lucas had teased him about for washing after each use and then glanced down at his polished boots. It wasn't the first time he was glad for what old Weaver called 'the gift' of OCPD.

'I know I don't look like it now, but I have been, and believe me, when someone offers you a no-strings meal, you should take it.'

'Are you sure it's no strings?'

'Promise. You've got free will, haven't you?' *Free will*? Where the fuck had that come from?

She seemed to think about it, but then the woman came back from the kitchen carrying a tray full of dishes that smelled so good he knew the girl would have followed him to hell for just one bite. If only he had known it could be this easy. Not that he would do anything. She was company, that's all. Just company while he ate.

The tamales were so velvety hot that Ike placed an order for the next day. That made the Mexican woman smile, and maybe that was his job right now – to bring happiness. Lucas would be cool with it. He liked it when Ike went out on his own and suggested changes.

Once Juanita went back to the kitchen, Ike checked out the girl at close range this time. He'd thought about her all night, but her face seemed more ordinary now, and she was too clean to have done this runaway thing for long. From the looks of her, she had been on the street a few days, a week at the most.

She placed her fork on the plate. 'Thanks for the tamale. It's been awhile.'

'Have another one.' He pointed his fork at the plate between them.

'It's more than enough. I couldn't eat another bite.'

'How'd you end up here?' Lucas would have wanted him to speak in a demanding voice and to ask for her ID, but Ike asked the question slowly while pretending to be more interested in his food.

'A shelter in Sacramento.' She glanced down, as if embarrassed. Then she lifted her eyes which he still couldn't label with just one color.

His mind spun into them and out. 'Are you all right?' he asked.

'I'm fine. Some bitch attacked me at that shelter. Took my money. One of the guys mentioned this place.' She seemed ready to disappear into the cheap worn leather of the booth. 'I didn't know why, but it's not like I had anywhere else to go.'

'And where will you head from here?' he asked.

She pushed away her now-clean plate. 'Where do you think I should go?'

He didn't dare think about that question. 'Somewhere safe. I'm not sure if there are any shelters in the area. There's one for homeless families about ten miles away in the next town. Juanita, the lady who runs this place, gives out cards for it. She'll have the address. That might be your best bet.'

'Where are you going from here?' Her expression stayed the same, just a curve of something that might be a smile.

'I'm waiting for someone.'

'Is she your girlfriend?'

'How'd you know it's a girl?' he asked.

'Her name is Angel, right?'

'That doesn't matter. And she isn't my girlfriend. I haven't seen her in a long time.'

She looked into his eyes again, as if asking a question only he could answer. 'I don't have any place to sleep tonight.'

The freezing, screeching storm in his brain had to be a warning from Lucas.

'Juanita, the lady who runs this place. She's pretty nice. Maybe she can help you.'

'It's a restaurant, not a homeless shelter. I can't ask her.'

'And I can't help you.' Ike stood and stretched his legs. 'I'm going out to my vehicle now.'

'It's pretty cold out there,' she said.

'My friend will show up soon enough.'

'Why not wait in here? With me.'

Good question, but he knew what was behind it, and it wasn't because he had turned into God's gift to homeless girls all of a sudden. 'I can give you some ideas about where to go, but I can't take you with me.'

She gazed down, nodded, and then looked up into his eyes with the first actual smile he'd seen from her.

'Why not?

'Told you. I'm meeting someone.'

'You also said she's not your girlfriend.'

'Where I live, I can't just walk in with a strange girl.'

She stretched back in the booth and gave him just a bit more of the smile. 'Why not?'

'Because I have rules,' he said. 'You seem all right. That's why I bought you dinner. But I can't take you back with me.'

'Because of the other girl?'

Her soft-spoken words stirred him. Of course it was because of Angel. She would tell Lucas and the others if he tried to smuggle in some girl. But that didn't mean he had to give up on this one forever.

He reached across the table and squeezed her hand the way Lucas had squeezed Jessica's that night. 'I would like to see you again. I would like to help you. But for tonight, you need to find your own place to sleep.'

She released his grip, glanced away from him, and he caught something that looked like fear in her eyes. 'The street, then.'

'It's better here than where you came from.'

'Is this new girl so important to you?'

'She's important to the group I belong to,' he said. 'We're all important, all the same.'

'I'd sure like a group like yours.'

'I didn't say that right. You need to leave now.' He dug in his pocket for the money Lucas didn't know he'd held back from their fund the week before.

A few twenties. That wouldn't change anyone's life. 'Here.'

She glanced down at the bills, and for a moment he thought she was going to cry.

Her hand trembled in the air like the hummingbirds that used to gather at his granny's feeder. All wings, no substance. 'I'm sure you need this money,' she said.

'I'm sure you need it more.'

He got up out of the booth, knowing that if he didn't, he would take her back with him right then.

'But I don't know how to thank you,' she said.

'You could go out in the truck with me for a while.'

She slammed the bills on the table and shoved them toward him. 'You see? It's never just a tamale.'

That made him laugh. She had no idea that if he wanted sex that much, he wouldn't need her permission.

'Can you blame me for trying?' He sounded like his father, but sometimes the old man had made sense.

She shoved her fingers into her hair and pulled it down over her shoulders. Finally, he saw how tired she was and how many miles she must have traveled. 'You said you've been in my situation. You ought to know how many offers like yours I have to deal with in a day.'

He thought of Jessica and felt more like the way he was dressed than the way he was inside. 'I do know.' Ike tried to keep the shame from his voice. He made himself talk the way normal people did when they discussed normal fucking things. 'And I shouldn't have said that. If you don't ask, you don't get, a friend of mine says. It's not the way I am, though. If you give me a chance, you'll find that out for yourself.'

'If I did decide to give you a chance, how might I do that?'

He walked around to the other side of the booth and leaned over her the way Lucas might. 'Find a place to stay tonight, little girl. The next time we meet, it might be different.'

'That's what you told me last night.'

'Because I thought Angel would be here by then.'

She reached into her bag and pulled out a phone. 'How can I get in touch with you?'

Once she got there, if he could get her there, she would understand about phones and other so-called conveniences that the cops could use to track you in a heartbeat.

'Just be here tomorrow. Same time. Maybe I can help. Maybe I can't.'

She shook her head. 'I'm going to have to move on tomorrow. Can we get together early?'

'Meet me outside here, six-thirty in the morning. That work for you?'

Finally, she seemed to relax into the booth. 'I'm still not sure.' She looked up into his eyes. 'I don't even know your name.'

'Ike.' He reached down and shook her hand. 'I don't know your name either, mystery girl.'

'Katherine.' She kind of snapped it out, and he wondered if it was her real name or something she'd made up.

'Katherine,' he said. 'That's pretty.'

'But not pretty enough for you to help me tonight?'

He wanted to. He really did.

'I gave you enough for a place to stay. That's the best I can do.'

She stared openly at him, not afraid, not trying to hide whatever kind of bargain she was trying to make with him. 'But what if I never see you again?'

'You will.' At that moment, he wanted to hug her. Instead, he just tapped her hand with his heavy gloves as if trying to find a pulse. Not that he would try to harm her. 'I promise.'

ELEVEN

The previous night, when Kit had told Richard they should go home, they had driven to her place and not his. That made sense as it had once been theirs. Now that she may have found a link to Jessica, they took a room at a motel that promised 'clean sheets, free coffee'. That way, she could meet Ike the next morning and still get back to the station in time for work.

Kit hadn't been able to trust more than thirty minutes of sleep since that night in the homeless shelter. As soon as she drifted off, she felt pinned to the bed by invisible hands. She woke around midnight, imagining the tip of a kitchen knife in her throat. She tried to scream and felt Richard's arms around her. She sank against him, and he held her tightly.

'Bad dream,' she said, and pushed her hair out of her eyes.

'You've been having a lot of those lately.'

'It's the strange bed.' She propped herself up on a pillow. In the dim light, she could see only the outline of his face.

'Right,' he said. 'That and the fact that you put yourself in danger to help me.'

'We can't turn back now,' she said. 'I can't.'

'There has to be a better way. Maybe we could hire a professional to look for Jessica.'

'And waste how much more time?'

'You don't have to remind me.' His voice was tight, and she could feel him tense beside her.

'I simply meant that I have no options at this point, Richard.'

'And, as usual, you're the one making all of the decisions.'

Kit started to snap back that he was the one who had gotten her involved in this, but they were both under pressure, and reverting back to their old patterns wouldn't help.

'Richard, please.' She reached out for him, but he was already turning away from her on to his side.

'We need sleep,' he said. 'Let's talk tomorrow.'

Kit turned away and lay on the too-firm pillow, staring at the ceiling. They had reverted to those patterns anyway. She pushed. He retreated. And now they lay close enough to touch but not to communicate. She felt stuck. If she stopped her search, and Jessica were harmed or killed, she couldn't live with the guilt. If she continued, Richard would blame himself if anything happened to his niece or her. She had no choice but to meet Ike and hope he revealed where the runaways were staying.

Kit didn't sleep for the rest of the night. She dressed, got a cup of coffee, and waited on the bed until Richard woke. The tension in his face made it clear that the argument they had barely avoided last night still sat between them.

'Where shall I drop you?' he asked.

'Near the restaurant.'

'Fine.'

They didn't speak again, until he pulled over.

'I won't be far away,' he said. 'Be careful.'

Then he gave her a brief kiss, and she got out of the car. Richard drove slowly down the street, and she felt like crying. Finding Jessica was all that mattered now. She couldn't think about anything else.

As she approached the restaurant on foot, she spotted an old truck. Ike stood in front of it like an awkward cartoon character. In his thick, dark scarf, black leather gloves, and matching boots, he looked overdressed for the weather.

She walked up to him and hoped the sun didn't give away her age. Ten years sat between the lie and the truth. If he spotted anything different, he didn't comment. In fact, he seemed even more intrigued by her.

'Hey, mystery girl.'

'I told you my name.'

'You're still a mystery to me, though.'

'There's no mystery about what I'm looking for.' His truck vibrated warmth. Kit leaned against it.

She could tell he had shaved and drenched himself in a fragrance that, however expensive, only accentuated the fact that his face didn't look anything like an ad for men's cologne.

'I wasn't sure you'd show up,' he said in a voice too flirtatious for their current situation.

'Where else would I go?'

'It's a big valley. A big state.' He extended his right arm as if to indicate her many options.

In the bright morning light, Kit could see not only what this rock-bottom part of the San Joaquin Valley had become, but what it might have been. As she looked out into the sunrise, she caught Ike studying her.

'Let's not pretend,' she said. 'You were on to my situation from the beginning.'

'Maybe.' He took off his gloves, shoved them into his pockets, and squinted at her. 'But just to be clear, who do you think I am exactly?'

'A guy who knows about somewhere safe, something better than a shelter.'

'Safety comes with its own rules.'

She faked a disgusted sigh. 'I'm not going to have sex with

you or anyone else in return for a place to sleep. If I wanted that, I could have stayed where I was.'

He nodded, and she could tell he had made some kind of decision. 'Who was it? Your father?'

She couldn't lie that fast or that horribly. 'No. Not a relative.'

'Usually is. Those bastards who mess with young kids ought to lose their balls.'

'Agree,' she said.

'Guys like that – they don't deserve to live.' He went around and opened the truck door. 'Get in.'

'I'm not finished talking,' she said.

'Neither am I. I just don't like standing in one place too long.'

'I get that.' Kit glanced around. No sign of Richard. 'But I barely know you.'

'It's your choice, but I'm not staying here.' He got behind the wheel. 'Our first rule is *take no chances*.'

Kit had known it would come to this, which was another reason she had insisted on a morning meeting. It was what she wanted, only not this fast. 'The first rule?' she said. 'Whose first rule?'

'Mine and Lucas's.' He started the truck. 'He's my partner. And I'm leaving with or without you.'

Lucas. It couldn't be a coincidence. She had found them. At least, they had to be nearby, because if Lucas and Ike were hiding out together, so was Jessica. Kit climbed in and closed the door.

She could barely keep from hammering Ike with questions. All she could think was *Lucas. Lucas Tibbs.*

The town appeared to have slept in that day. He drove slowly through it, apparently rousing no one with the noisy beater truck. Good. Richard wouldn't have any trouble following them. They approached a four-way stop sign. Ike seemed to think about where he wanted to head next, and Kit reached for the door handle.

'I trusted you enough to get in here with you,' she said. 'Please stick to the main streets.'

He chuckled and pulled in front of a school. 'Is this main enough for you?'

In spite of the weather and the fact that it was Tuesday, only a few kids were playing on the basketball court. Kit tried to relax and didn't dare glance around for Richard. Ike drove well below the speed limit.

'How many of you are there?' she asked. 'At that place of yours.'

'Not so fast. First I need to ask you some questions.'

'Fine,' she said. 'And then I'll ask you some.'

'I'm the one offering shelter, so I'll ask first if that's all right with you. Lucas will have my ass if I show up with some chick I don't know anything about.'

That name again. She remembered the innocent-looking little boy in the photographs and wondered how this guy would be worried about him. 'I thought you were partners.'

'We are. But remember our first rule.'

'And your second rule?'

'*Live your truth.* The third is *never go back.*'

'Never go back,' Kit said. 'That's my first rule.'

He nodded. 'All right, then. Tell me why you showed up at the restaurant for two nights in a row.'

'To see you?'

'Don't try to mess with my mind, girl. Too many already tried to do that. Just tell me the truth, or let's go our separate ways right now.'

'You were looking for a girl,' she said. 'And you mentioned the code about cheese enchiladas.'

'What makes you think it's a code?'

'I'm not stupid, Ike. I heard about the restaurant in a shelter for runaways.'

'I'm not stupid either,' he said.

'I didn't say you were.'

'Some do. I just want you to know that.' He tapped his head. 'But I tested higher than anyone in that camp, except Lucas. And I may have even tested better than him.'

'Stop accusing me of an opinion I don't have,' she said. 'I was almost knifed in a Sacramento shelter. I sure as hell don't want to go to another one.'

'Sacramento.' He nodded. 'Makes sense. One of ours is from there.'

'How do you select which ones are yours?'

'Depends.' He flashed her a lazy grin that failed to hide the scrutiny in his gaze.

'Now, can I ask you some questions?'

'From what I can tell, that's what you're doing.' He continued to drive through the main part of town – churches, simple homes with flat green yards, and that same school again. Doesn't mean I'll answer.'

Kit didn't dare look around for Richard. 'How safe is this place of yours?' she asked.

'I'm in charge of security.' His arms seemed to flex as he gripped the wheel. 'What do you think?'

'Do you have weapons?'

'Enough.'

'This is really important.' She twisted on the seat to face him. 'How do people – girls – pay their way there? Because if it's sex . . .'

'Nothing's against your will. I told you that.' He approached a stoplight and glanced toward the freeway.

She reached for the door handle again. 'Please don't make me jump out.'

'Sooner or later, we have to leave town if you want to stay with us,' he said. 'As for paying your way, we figured that out a long time ago.'

'You and Lucas?'

'Don't keep giving me the third degree.' He slammed his hands on the wheel and turned toward town. 'No one's going to rape you, mystery girl, OK? No one's going to hurt you as long as you follow the rules and don't lie. Do either of those, and I can't be responsible for what happens to you.'

'So how do I pay my way?' she asked again.

'Chores around the place. Getting things we need from town.'

'Stealing?'

'Lucas likes to call it liberating items that need to be freed. You'll understand once you meet him.'

'How can you possibly survive by stealing?' she asked. 'Surely you'll get caught.'

'We have money. Most of it is Lucas's.'

'Why risk being thieves, then?'

'For the extras, and because it's fun. What we have there is a good life.' When he turned to her, she saw that his eyes were bright with emotion. 'We were almost denied that life, and now we have it.'

'Denied?' she asked.

'I might tell you about it sometime. Not now.' He pulled to the side of the road. 'Are you with me or not?'

'How many people?' she asked. 'In your group, I mean.'

'A dozen, give or take.'

'What are their names?'

'What do you care?'

'Ike,' she said. 'I asked you for help, and I'm more grateful for it than I can ever tell you. But I need to know what to expect.'

He began driving again, cocking his head, thinking about it.

'We're still just getting settled,' he said. 'More guys than girls at this point, but I can get you in. Lucas got in a girl he likes, and if he can bring in Jessica, I can bring you in.'

Kit fought to keep her expression neutral. 'Jessica?'

'Just an old friend of his Lucas likes to keep around. They helped each other out when they were real young. Lucas and me – we're partners, though. If he wants her with us, I'm all right with it.'

'Where'd you find her?' She looked out the window into a frost-bitten orchard so that he couldn't see her face.

'We knew her when we were kids. Lucas first, but only by a year.'

'Where?'

'Don't push me, Katherine. First I have to figure out a way to hide you until Lucas is OK with it.'

He pulled off on a narrow road.

'What do you mean, *hide me*?' She fought to keep the panic from her voice. 'And where are we?'

'Don't jump out of the truck.' He gave her that crooked grin once more. 'I have my own quarters. Not a suite at the Ritz Carlton, but you can stay there while I convince Lucas to let you in.'

This kid didn't look as if he'd ever been near the Ritz Carlton. 'Where are you from?'

'We'll talk soon,' he said. 'If you want to continue, that is. If you don't, I'll take you back where I found you, and no one will know you were here.'

Kit's head churned with every possible scenario. Go back to where they met and hope John Paul and his cop buddies could find a link to the homeless kids? Do what Richard suggested and hire a private investigator? Stay in this guy's so-called quarters and text Richard. The girl at this place had to be the right Jessica, and Lucas had to be that same little boy. If Richard's niece was this close, going there with Ike would be worth the risk.

'I want to continue,' she said, in a voice she knew sounded as beaten as she felt.

'Don't sound so glum. I help run the compound, and you'll be fine, Katherine.'

His voice seemed to drop and fade into doubt.

'Except for what?' she asked.

'Except, like I said, I need to get Lucas on board.'

They drove farther in silence. Richard would be frantic, and so was she. She needed to figure out a way to text him.

Ike seemed to be studying her, and Kit tried to distract him. 'Tell me about Jessica. Is she nice?'

'Not to me. And don't get any idea about you two being friends. She's going to hate you too.'

'Why?' Kit asked. 'I don't even know her.'

'She just likes acting like she's better than she is.'

'What makes her any better?' Kit asked. 'She's a runaway too, isn't she?'

'Yeah. But she's Lucas's runaway, and that makes her better, in her eyes – and his maybe.'

'So what will I be?' she asked. 'If I really go to this place with you, I mean.'

'Lucas says we need someone who doesn't share our past, and I just think you'll be good for us, that's all.'

'Ike.' He stopped at a dented stop sign and glanced over at her. 'There's one thing we'd better get straight. I want to go wherever this is with you. But I do not want a relationship with you or anyone right now. I can't handle it.'

He scoffed. 'No one said you were God's gift to anyone. Besides, we need to get this straight too. Harming a girl against her will, the way you were harmed, being a predator – that's the worst thing a man can do. It's the worst kind of crime because the victim carries it the rest of her life.'

'So? I already told you I agree with that.'

'Coming on to a guy, though, pretending you want him and then saying no – that's a different story.' His hands on the wheel looked as though he were strangling it.

'I hope you don't think I've been coming on to you,' Kit said.
'I'm just warning you.' He loosened his grip on the wheel, yet his thick knuckles remained white. 'That's all.'

TWELVE

This guy was dangerous. Not to Kit, at least not yet. But he had been one of Weaver's child patients, and he had just made it pretty clear that he had no problem raping or otherwise harming a girl he perceived as coming on to him. Kit needed to look around this place, make sure she had found the right Jessica, and then get out. As soon as Ike left her alone long enough, she would text Richard.

The road went from paved to rocky to dirt. Ike started to pull into a deserted parking lot and then said, 'Screw it. No one's back at the compound right now. Might as well save ourselves the walk.'

'I don't mind walking,' she said.

'No reason to. Besides, we've seen things out here.'

'Things?'

'Snakes. Stuff like that. One time, a bear. What a big mother that was.'

Kit huddled down in the seat. 'Are you sure no one will be there?'

'Not if we hurry. They don't usually get back from church until noon.'

'Your friends went to church on a Tuesday?' she asked.

'It's a good time to get the things we need. Good time for me to show you around too.'

Uncertain as she was, Kit couldn't resist taking a look at where he and maybe Jessica lived.

'They steal from church?' she asked in a calm voice, free, she hoped, of judgment.

'A couple of them do.' He spoke as if it were commonplace. 'You have a problem with that? It's not a religious thing. Just an opportunity.'

'No, I don't have a problem. At least, not until I hear more about it.'

'Well, you won't hear more about it today because we will be the only ones there.'

'Then let's get in and out in a hurry.'

'As big a hurry as we can,' he said. 'I do want to show you everything. Then you'll know if you want to stay.'

All she wanted was to see it and get out. 'I'll know pretty fast, I'm sure,' she told him.

'I will too.' He glanced at her out of the corner of his eye and slowed the truck. 'No reason for us to race. Like I said, noon's the earliest they ever come back on Tuesdays.'

But there might always be an exception, and Kit didn't want this to be it.

'Here we are.' He pulled the truck into a small driveway in front of scattered shelters. Clapboard farmhouses sat back from a larger home in front. The tiny community was so well hidden behind the vineyards that no one who didn't know how would be able to find it.

'How did you discover this?' she asked.

'What is this, the grand inquisition? You keep forgetting that I ask the questions.' He got out of the truck. 'Come on, now. We have a couple of hours.'

'I have a right to know where we're heading.' She jumped out before he could get around to open her door. 'I need to know what I'm getting into.'

'That's why we're here.' As she started to move toward the main house, he blocked her way with his massive body. 'Katherine, no outsider has seen this place until now. Don't make me sorry I brought you here.'

'And don't you make me sorry I came.' She glared back at him.

'What are you complaining about? You have no place else to go.'

'Sometimes the streets are fine,' she said.

'You won't last another day.' He drew away from her and stopped in front of the house. 'I always had this option. Now I'm offering it to you.'

But he was from Oregon, she thought. This couldn't be his.

'You own this place?' she asked, hoping she sounded sufficiently impressed.

'Nope, but from a young age, I always knew I had somewhere

to go when the time came. So knock that chip on your shoulder and check it out.'

He gestured toward an elaborate manufactured treehouse set back from the main road and higher than anything else on the property. Two of the four sides she could see were painted in dull earth tones that looked like chipped slabs of fading olive green and rust.

'What's that?' Kit asked.

'I warned you it wasn't the Ritz Carlton.'

'You live up there? In that tree?'

'Someone has to keep watch.' His voice went sing-song, and she realized she should leave sooner than she had planned.

'Is that where you expected to hide me from Lucas?'

He squinted at it as if seeing his home with her eyes. 'You'll have it all to yourself,' he said. 'I'll stay down here in my sleeping bag.'

'While I'm up there?'

'Don't judge it until you see it. We put wall-to-wall carpet in that thing – the plushy kind your feet sink into. It even has a heater.' He crossed his arms with more conviction than he must have felt staring at his pitiful excuse for a home. 'How's that compared with the streets?'

'If it's my only choice, I guess I can't complain.' She moved closer to the house. 'But I'll need some time to think about it.'

As they headed for the front porch, her tennis shoe tripped over something, and she almost went down. Ike grabbed her arm. She stepped back and looked at the blistered gray paint of a wooden trap door. The padlock appeared new.

'What's that?' she asked.

'Just our basement. Don't worry about it.'

A suffocating feeling came over Kit again. She felt trapped, smothered.

'I'm not going down there,' she said.

'You couldn't if you wanted to.' He glanced back up at his treehouse. 'Wouldn't you rather be up there?'

'No way. I could fall and break my neck.'

'I sleep there every night, and my neck is just fine.'

'Maybe you're just lucky. The thing's a death trap. There's not even a whole roof over it.'

'There's a second one under what you can see from here.' He took a step toward it. 'Want to go up?'

'I most definitely do not.' He stopped, and she could tell from his grim expression that she had gone too far. 'I mean, I appreciate the offer, but I would like to see the house,' she told him.

'The main house.' Ike opened the wooden front door and waited for her to go in. Kit reached into her pocket, found the pepper spray, and stepped inside.

The house smelled like vanilla. In that first glance, it reminded her of her mom's old home in Buckeye, Arizona, with its faux cozy living room, overstuffed chairs, and kitchen lit by the flickering fire of a squat wood stove in the far corner of the room. Except her mom's former home, even after the tragedy that had reunited them, never felt as cold and disturbing as this house did. The cheeriness of this room went no deeper than the surface.

Then she saw the plastic mannequin on top of a short curio cabinet. Bald and eyeless, it wore a red flame-shaped mask decorated with silver metal studs. In its lips, the mannequin held a candy cigarette. Two posters were tacked on either side of it. One was a peace sign embossed into the head of an African singer. The other was a side view of Frank Zappa poised on a toilet and tagged 'Phi Zappa Krappa'. These kids must have created their decor from whatever had been left here over the years.

'Where'd you find those?' she asked.

'In a box of stuff in the basement.' He stood rigid as if trying to evaluate her.

To the side of the wood stove, a fake green Christmas tree flooded its corner of the room with the twinkle of artificial light, blinking frenetically. Crowding the branches were religious symbols, beaded Victorian ornaments, a tiny stuffed Elmo, and little sequined frames holding photographs too small to see. At the top, a red felt-covered Popsicle stick wore a matching Santa hat above two tiny plastic eyes.

She nodded at the Popsicle Santa. 'Martha Stewart must have beaten me to this place.'

'Who?'

'I just meant it looks like you got a head start on Christmas.'

'That's from last year. Seasons don't matter around here.' He moved closer to her, clearly proud of who he was now and this life he apparently controlled.

'So nobody plays by the rules?'

'Only the compound rules. That's the point.' His grin seemed less pathetic in the light of the tree and the room. 'Come on. I'll show you the quarters now.'

'I'm not sure I want to go up there, Ike.'

'If you're worried about the stairs, I can help you. One of the guys who lived here when this place was a hippie commune taught industrial arts. Those slats he built along the side of that treehouse are so strong that they could hold you and me both.'

'In a minute, then. I'd just like to see what else you have here.'

'Katherine.' He leaned against a weathered wood Adirondack chair. 'How many times do I have to tell you? You're safe with me.'

'I'll feel safer once I see the rest of the place. She glanced over at a hall that must lead to bedrooms. Right before the hall, just inside the kitchen, a trap door similar to the one outside was partially hidden by a braided rag rug.

'Basement?' she asked.

'It has two entrances,' he said. 'Want to see the movie room?'

She looked around and grew more nervous. Somehow, she had to contact Richard, and right now.

'Where is it?'

'Right here.' He walked past the decorated tree to some weather-beaten French doors and opened them. Cool air rushed in. Kit stepped past Ike into the room, which was full of mismatched chairs facing a large-screen TV that dominated most of the wall. It had once been a screened-in porch, its wood-plank floor covered by woven rugs larger than the one over the trap door. Kit breathed in the smell of stale popcorn.

'So you have your own theater,' she said.

'And we have movie nights. It's fun.'

'Looks like it.' She walked back into the kitchen and the heat of the wood stove.

Warmth. That was the currency of this place. But the moment she found even a little, it was snatched away.

Beside her, on the tiles of the counter, sat little towers of stacked shotgun shells.

'You don't seem very impressed,' Ike said. 'What did you expect?'

'Oh, no. I'm very impressed.' She rubbed her hands together inches from the stove. 'After where I've been, it looks like paradise. I just can't figure out how you can afford a compound like this.'

'I'll tell you more later, once we decide if you're a good fit.' Ike went to the sink, turned on the water, and squeezed some dish soap on to his hands. 'Want some?' he asked, as if offering her a drink.

As Kit stood beside Ike, she saw something she had missed before: a photo pasted on to one of the cabinet walls. Dr Weaver's halfhearted smile hadn't changed. Except now, someone had slammed a dart through his forehead.

Her hunch had been right. She had better be very careful about whatever she said or did next.

'Who's that?' she asked in a bored tone.

'Just a weasel,' Ike said. 'He feeds on children.'

She stood next to him, both of them looking out the shuttered window as they washed their hands free of whatever Ike believed had infested them.

Kit glanced at the dartboard that Weaver had become.

'I probably ought to be going soon.'

'You have to stay.' Ike reached up to the old-fashioned paper-towel rack, ripped one off, and began drying his hands. 'If Lucas finds you before we discuss it, you don't want to know what's going to happen.'

'So why don't you talk to him when they get back?' she said. 'I'll take the path we drove out here on, and you catch up with me in the truck when you can.'

'No.' His tight lips and narrowed eyes reminded her of the way he'd looked when he had practically strangled the steering wheel while warning her about what happened to girls who led guys on. 'You do have to stay here, at least for tonight.'

'I don't have to do anything I don't want to do.'

She weighed her options. Leave against his will and hope they could get Jessica out of there, or stay and contact Richard as soon as possible? She might be able do that if she pretended to go along with Ike.

'You don't want to join the compound?' Ike's face lost expression, as if he had forgotten who she was.

'I didn't say that.' She forced him to meet her gaze. 'I want to think about it.'

'Where are you going to stay?' He crossed his arms and faced her, leaning back against the sink.

'In your truck, maybe.'

'Someone might find you there. An animal even. Not a good idea.'

'Maybe just another shelter, then,' she said. 'It's only one night. You talk to Lucas. I'll find a place to stay. You text me when it's all right to come back.'

'I don't know.' He looked down at his tennis shoes. In spite of the weather, they were pristine. 'Maybe you'll decide not to come back. Maybe you'll turn us in.'

'Why would I do that, Ike? You're my only hope.'

'You're right about that.' He turned around and did a few self-conscious pushups off the tile of the sink. He didn't have to say a word. The bulging muscles beneath the jacket spoke for him. Then he stopped and yanked open a wooden shutter over the kitchen window. 'Holy shit.'

'What?'

'Jessica!' He slammed his finger against the partially closed shutter. 'She's walking up the front path.'

Kit leaned forward and nearly collapsed against the sink. There, in jeans, a bulky jacket, and with that unmistakable burgundy-streaked hair partially covered by a wool cap, was the girl she had been seeking. A few feet behind her, a short boy in a cowboy hat yelled something to her. Jessica stopped and turned back toward him.

'You've got to hide.' Ike scanned the room. 'The treehouse. You can go out the back.'

'By the time we get there, they'll see me.'

'Here.' Ike kicked aside the braided rug and lifted the trap door. Kit stared down into musty darkness. 'No.'

'We don't have a choice. It's OK. I'll be here.'

'No, Ike,' she said. 'I'd rather stay up here and face them.'

'You can't. You have no idea of what he'll do.'

'But you don't understand. There's no way I can handle this. I can't stand to be locked up.'

Before she could protest further, Ike grabbed her as if she were weightless. Then he shoved her into a sitting position, pushed her down on to a cold concrete step, and shut the door over her.

'Let me out, please.' She beat her fists on the door, in spite of the splinters that rammed into her flesh.

'Keep it down,' Ike called back. 'I'll come for you when I can. It won't take long. Just stay quiet until I get rid of them.'

From behind her, Kit could still feel the warmth of the kitchen. From beneath, she could feel the darkness and the cold creep up. Something scuttled below, a critter of some type.

Laughter erupted in the room above. Music. Kit lowered her head and, as the dizziness crashed through her, fought for breath.

THIRTEEN

Ike continued leaning against the sink as he watched Jessica and Lucas laughing about what they had liberated that day. From below, he heard a thump and something that sounded like a muffled voice. Shit. He needed to get rid of Jessica for a while so he and Lucas could talk about Katherine. The look on her face as Ike had closed the door over her had been pure terror. Poor girl had been through enough already. Ike would do right by her, though, and she'd be out of there before she knew it.

Lucas put the long white box on the counter and opened it. The smell of sugar rushed into Ike's nostrils, straight to his brain. His mouth watered.

'You know how I love cake,' he said.

Most of all, he loved the frosting, but he had to be polite. His granny had taught him that.

'What do you think?' Lucas asked.

'Chocolate fudge?' Ike knew that's what it must be.

'Boston cream. Vanilla pudding in the middle.'

'Where'd you liberate it?'

'Some poor guy's funeral. He'll never miss it.'

'And two fat pink roses.' Ike reached out for them.

'Roses belong to Jessica,' Lucas said. 'The rest looks pretty good, though. Shall we dig in?'

'Maybe later.' Ike used to always get the roses. He stood up to his full height and stared down at Lucas. 'Could we go outside for a moment?'

'And freeze our butts off? Anything we need to talk about, we can discuss right here.'

Ike's dad, Mr Cop Man, would have described Lucas as a bandy rooster, the way he strutted in front of the wood stove with his gelled hair and his puffy little jacket, neither of which made him look bigger than he was.

'I was hoping we could speak alone.' Ike glanced over at Jessica.

'I've got a new logic puzzle for you,' Lucas told him. 'This is like a Rubik's Cube on speed.'

Friendship involved knowing each other's weaknesses as well as strengths. Ike didn't fall for it, though.

'There's something we need to talk about first.'

'I can take a hint.' Jessica plucked one of the roses off the top of the cake, took a big bite out of it, and gave Ike a smile full of frosting.

Lucas settled into the beat-up deck chair and watched her leave. Then he looked up at Ike. 'She's perfect, isn't she?'

'To you, I guess.'

'She's one of us.' Lucas turned around and gave Ike a grin as artificial as the frosting flower Jessica had just taken. 'Don't fight it so hard, and we'll all have a better life here.'

'That's what I wanted to ask you about,' Ike said. 'Having a better life here.'

Lucas reached in front of him and patted the big stuffed pillow he called a hassock. 'Come over here so I can see you, friend.'

Ike went but wasn't sure. The hassock always sank down heavily with his weight, and if he wasn't careful, a spring would poke him in the ass. Ike managed to avoid it.

Lucas leaned forward and widened those clear blue eyes. 'What's on your mind, Ike?'

'Well.' Ike got tongue-tied.

'It's OK, friend. Just spit it out.'

But he couldn't. All he could think about was Jessica and the frosting, Katherine down below them, and those blue eyes that seemed to mock him before he as much as spoke. He looked at the cowboy hat Lucas had placed on the table, and that made him a little brave. Lucas wasn't a god. In his own way, in spite of being a genius, he was as screwed-up as the rest of them.

'Lucas,' Ike managed to say. 'Do you know anything about the Beatles?'

'How many times have I said I have no interest in old rock and roll?'

'I don't mean the music. I mean the band. They were tight, dude, and then John Lennon hooked up with Yoko, and it all went to hell.'

'Thank you for sharing,' Lucas said in a voice so bland that he could have passed for the Weasel. And that was the point, wasn't it? To make Ike feel like an idiot.

'I'm saying that Jessica is our Yoko.'

That took Mr Smart Ass by surprise. His eyes darted for a moment, but then the smile returned. 'Nice metaphor, but incorrect. Jessica doesn't want to break up anything.'

'Then why did you give her the rose?'

'She's new, scared. And she had a hell of a time getting here. I didn't mean to hurt your feelings, Ike.'

'My feelings are fine.' He shifted his weight on the hassock and hoped the spring wouldn't get him. 'But since she's been here, you've changed. All you want to do is hang out with her.'

'Do I detect a little jealousy there? You're not interested in her, are you?'

'God, no,' Ike said too fast. 'But I do . . . I'd really like to bring in someone new. A girl.'

Lucas's eyes narrowed to slits. 'Where did you find a girl?'

'Someone I've known. She needs a place to stay, and I figure if you can invite Jessica, why can't I invite her?'

Lucas folded his hands together. He looked hurt. 'Why didn't you tell me you have a girlfriend?'

'Not that kind of girlfriend,' he said. 'She has some issues because of her childhood. Bastards ought to have their balls ripped out.'

'Does she know about our place?'

Ike stared at the basement door and prayed she didn't start making noise. 'No.'

'You sure?'

'You think I'm stupid, Lucas? Oh, that's right. Of course you do.'

'Strength isn't only mental.' Lucas got up and started for the table. Then he stopped, one foot on the trap door. 'There are many types. Strength of fairness, strength of hope, kindness . . .'

'Spare me. You're channeling the Weasel again.'

'The man's not entirely devoid of brains. In a way, we owe him.'

Ike fumbled to his feet and walked toward the sink, hoping Lucas would follow. Katherine would be able to hear their conversation if she had stayed on the stairs. Worse, Lucas could hear her if she screamed.

'Owe the Weasel? How?'

'If not for him, none of us would know each other.' Lucas frowned and then leaned down and replaced the crumpled rug over the door. Ike panicked. He needed to distract him. Then he remembered how Lucas had tried to bait him with the new logic puzzle. Yes, friendship involved knowing each other's weaknesses as well as strengths.

The red-and-black fire starter lay on the kitchen counter. Ike pointed it like a gun, pushed the release forward, and pulled the trigger. A click and then a slender flame slid out the end.

'So about this girl,' Ike said.

Lucas left the rug where it was, stood, and drifted over to the sink like a sleepwalker.

'What are you doing with that?'

'I thought we could use a couple more logs on the wood stove.' Ike extended the flame closer to Lucas. 'What do you think?'

A thud came from the basement.

Lucas jerked his head away from the flame. 'Did you hear that?'

'Didn't hear anything,' Ike said. 'Storm's kicking up tonight. Hey, I'll get the logs. Why don't you light them?'

Lucas passed Ike the potholder and followed him to the stove. Ike opened the hot door with the thin potholder and rubbed his hands together.

'How about it, Lucas? This girl Katherine's hurting as bad as we were one time. Can't you let her stay?'

'How can you be sure she'll keep this place secret?' Lucas glanced up from the fire, still holding the flame he had used to start it. In the light from their blaze, his eyes took on the same intensity.

'She's like us just as much as Jessica is.'

'But Jessica was a First Year. She remembers what we went through in order to protect who we are. She knows what that bastard put us through.'

'Katherine's torture was different from ours, but in the end it's all the same. Besides, she needs us.'

'And Ike Boy needs to be needed.' Lucas flashed that smile that made Ike feel small.

'What of it?'

'As I recall, I'm the one who selects the new people.'

'Then can't you select her?'

Lucas glanced back at the flames the way he would an old friend that he was reluctant to leave. 'I'd have to talk to her,' he told Ike. You can't just bring in any runaway off the street and expect them to fit with the dynamics of this group.'

'You told me yourself we need fresh blood – someone who doesn't share our history and dysfunction.'

'I only meant we need a variety of skills here,' he said. 'More drones. And our dysfunction, both as a group and individually, is what makes us strong. No one will ever break our bond.'

'Not even Jessica?'

'As I said, she's one of us. Besides, it's pretty clear that she likes Wyatt.'

'She always has,' Ike said. 'That's why she put that whole rescue thing in motion that night. What are you going to do about it?'

'Not a thing.' Lucas pulled his down jacket closer and stood up as straight and tall as a guy his size could. 'This compound is about being who we want to and were meant to be. It's about celebrating what the Weasel tried to take from us. If Jessica wants Wyatt, that's what I want.'

'And if I want you to let Katherine stay here?'

'Then that's what I want.'

Ike almost gasped. Dealing with Lucas was usually a bigger challenge than Killer Sudoku.

'Thanks, man.' He leaned down and closed the door to the wood stove. The room grew dimmer even though it was early afternoon.

'Except.' Lucas's voice deepened.

'Except what?'

'She'll have to do something to prove herself.'

'No sex,' Ike said. 'I told you what she's been through.'

'I get that, but she still needs a test. Something that will prove we can trust her, and something that will bind her to us in case she changes her mind later.'

Ike remembered the test at the Weasel's camp, and what had almost happened to Wyatt. He pulled his gloves over his scarred hands.

'Nothing like that,' he said. 'Don't make her hurt anybody.'

'I can't make her do anything. Let's put our heads together.' He almost bounced to the front door on the balls of his feet. If you didn't know better, you'd think he was a happy little boy, which in a way he was. 'I'm sure we'll figure it out.'

'We always do,' Ike said.

Then, as if he had forgotten something, Lucas walked back, and Ike hoped it wasn't to check out the basement.

He marched up to Ike and put out his hand. 'Still friends?'

'Always.' They shook the way they had that first day.

'No woman is going to come between us.'

'If you say so,' Ike said.

Lucas pretended not to hear. He headed to the table. When he turned, his eyes gleamed the way they had the day they met.

In his extended hand sat the remaining rose. Ike reached out for it, and Lucas shook his head.

'I'm taking this to Jessica,' he said, his tone apologetic. 'Got to keep my word. You understand.'

FOURTEEN

Kit sat on the cold step and held on to it as if she were steering a vehicle and would crash the moment she let go. She was huddled like a child, unable to speak or scream. Clammy air touched her face and slid along her neckline, making her think of those creatures Ike had described to her. Kit could barely breathe, and her mind rushed back to a time so far in the past that she barely had words for it. *Locked in. Locked in forever. Cold.* No, she could not go there. Jessica might be only a wall away. Kit had to stay strong until she could talk to her.

At first, she had tried to shout. Then she realized that enduring this and dealing with only Ike later might be far better than dealing with whatever was going on above this horrible place. Unable to see, she had leaned against a loose brick and knocked it to the floor. The hopeless sound it made when it hit the floor convinced her to just sit. As the chilled air started to feel like dust in her nostrils, she shifted position again and accidently dislodged a second brick. She felt as if she were falling. She let the brick go, but her bag went with it. Both dropped into the pit below.

'Please,' she said to no one.

Ike didn't dare leave her here. He would come back. Yet Ike must be crazy or close to it. If Dr Weaver was correct, these kids had all been lost at some point, disturbed, and maybe dangerous. Now, here she crouched, in their basement, on a Tuesday afternoon that would soon ease into night. Her bag held her phone. Kit had only one choice.

Slowly, she carefully butt-walked herself down the stairs and tried to ignore the sudden activity of creatures that had been here longer than she had and were disturbed by her presence. She could do this, one cold slippery step at a time. She tried to conjure Richard's face, and hated the fact that they had argued. Once she got to the bottom, she would call him first, and he would find her. They would deal with the rest later. Right now, she just wanted out of here. Hands on each side of her, she needed to push herself down to the next step. She could see a thin rectangle of light coming from the bottom, but that door was padlocked. She had only one way out, and that was the way she had just come. First, though, her phone. As she started to shift herself to the next step, she reached out and felt a sturdy object beside her. The bag. She stifled a cry, shoved her hand into it, and felt for her phone.

Too nervous. That's all. She just needed to empty it out, but she couldn't see well. Maybe best just to scoop through it with her fingers. She touched her wallet, her makeup bag, a tampon, her credit cards, and flimsy papers that must be grocery store receipts. No phone.

She lost track of time. As before, she sat motionless, thinking nothing, being nothing, letting time pass.

A noise at the top of the stairs alerted her. But she glanced down to where the outline of the padlocked door had been and saw nothing. It must be night.

With a creaking sound, the top door opened, and Ike's heavy shoe landed on the top step.

'It's OK,' he said. 'We worked it out. Kind of. Come on up.'

'Not sure I can,' she told him. 'Can you unlock the outside door?'

'Don't have the key.' He stepped farther down and put out his hand. 'Come back up here, to me. You can do it.'

'They're too steep.' This was ridiculous. She could climb a flight of stairs in her sleep. But these stairs – too close together, too shallow, and too cold – had no rails. 'It will take me a minute.'

'I'll come get you.'

Ike skimmed the steps like a dancer. In spite of his size, he made it down in seconds. Once he landed on the step in front of her, he put out his hand again, this time close enough for her to touch. 'Grab hold of me, Katherine, and we'll get you out of here.'

'Why did you leave me?' She fought to keep the fear from her voice.

'Had to talk to Lucas. I'm sorry. I never meant to make you stay down here, but I had to wait until I was sure he wouldn't see you.'

He reached out for her hand. As he did, his features came into focus. In the darkness, he looked even scarier. In the dim light of this place, she forced herself to ignore his appearance and focus on his voice, which was kind.

'My bag.' She handed it to him.

'No problem.' He leaned over her. 'Just hang on to my hand. We'll take as long as you need.'

'Is anyone up there?' she asked.

'Not right now. They went for pizza. Usually, Lucas, Jessica, and a few others stay here, but since Wyatt arrived, Jessica has all kinds of ideas of places to go. I know you don't like the idea of staying in my quarters, but it's best for tonight.'

'You've got to drive me back to town,' she told him.

'One job at a time. And the only job I can handle right now is getting you out of here.'

'I need to leave here tonight. Maybe we can sneak out before they get back.'

He squeezed her hand. 'Just a few more steps.'

She took a breath and struggled behind him. Finally, they reached the top of the concrete stairs, and Kit tried to rush into the warmth of the room.

She missed a step and stumbled. Somehow, the next step slid from beneath her too. She screamed all the way down, feeling the sound inside her head as well as outside as she bumped uncontrollably like a child in a snowsuit down a hill. When she landed, she wanted to cave into herself, but this was the moment she had to get strong.

'Don't move, Katherine.'

Ike hurried down the stairs. Adrenaline kicked in with a jolt. She would move, all right. She would get the hell out of this place.

Kit shot up and immediately felt her ankle.

'It's OK,' Ike told her. 'Stay right there. I told you to be careful.'

If she had a remaining brick to throw at him, she would have, but the pain in her ankle was too real for her to balance on it now. She needed him to get her out of there.

'Easy does it.' He reached down and took her arm. 'Lean against me. I could carry you out of here if I had to, but it's best if we do it this way.'

She did as he asked. Every step sent fire through her foot and her leg. She could limp, but that was about it. The only way she could get out of there now was with him.

They reached the top again, slowly. Ike opened the door and half-pulled her out into the warm room.

Tears filled her eyes. 'Now,' she said, 'please help me get back to town.'

The wood stove cast fiery shadows on the wall.

His gaze landed on a white bakery box on the table. 'Do you like cake?'

'Fuck cake. Get me out of here.'

'Lucas doesn't approve of swearing.'

'I don't care what Lucas approves of. I could have died down there. I can't do this anymore.'

'You've got to care. Besides, there's a reason for it.'

She glanced around the kitchen, looking for any kind of weapon. A knife sat on an old-fashioned butcher block beside the counter.

'A reason for not swearing?' she asked.

Ike nodded, walked over, and slammed his meaty hand over the knife. 'Don't even think about it, Katherine.' She didn't bother denying her intention as Ike pulled out a battered wooden drawer and shoved the knife inside it. 'Weasel – the guy I told you about – used to cuss to make us think he was our friend. He traced us on our phones too. Lucas caught him at it.'

'What did he do to the guy?'

'Nothing. Yet.' He moved closer to the box. 'You must be hungry.'

'Food's the last thing on my mind right now,' she said.

'You'll settle down once you're comfortable.' He seemed to force himself away from the container and closer to her. 'I'll bring you some pizza later.'

She paused in front of the wood stove to warm her hands and to think. She knew enough now to lead Richard to this place. Her job was over, her promise to him fulfilled. Yet nothing about this situation felt finished. Besides, she could barely walk without her right foot exploding.

'Cake's fine,' she said. 'As long as we take it with us.'

His face lit. 'Good idea.' He grabbed the box. 'They don't need to meet you until tomorrow. My quarters aren't that bad. You'll see.'

'I'm not staying in that thing.'

He stopped in the middle of the room, the cake box flimsy in his hands. 'It's the only place you *can* stay.'

'I want to go back to the shelter.' That's what she needed – a place away from there where she could call Richard.

'You can't do that tonight. Fog's already thick as pea soup.' He slowed his speech and squinted out the window as if looking for someone who would not be returning. 'We need to talk more.'

'Ike,' she said. 'I do not want to spend the night in that tree-house. Can't I just crash on that chair over there?'

'That'd be great, except Lucas will see you if he happens to come in, and we don't have permission for that yet.' He set the cake on the kitchen counter. 'We can meet with him tomorrow. He'll have a test for you. Once you pass it, you'll have your own bed – a nice one too. Not like the cots in the shelters.'

'What kind of test?' Kit played for time as she tried to figure the fastest way out of there. The angrier she got, the more her courage grew. 'I'm not jumping through hoops for him or anyone else, and that includes you.'

'You won't be jumping or anything else through hoops on that ankle. Don't worry, though. I already gave Lucas some boundaries.'

'Boundaries?'

He patted her arm, and she fought the impulse to jerk away. 'No one will hurt you or make you hurt anyone else.'

'Oh, that's comforting,' she said.

'Watch the attitude.' He let go of her, and his cheeks darkened into red. 'You were homeless like five minutes ago.'

She glanced over at the mannequin in its silver-studded mask. 'At least I wasn't trapped anywhere.'

'You're not trapped now, and you'll be even better off tomorrow.'

'Not tomorrow.' She needed to reason with him, yet nothing in this kitchen, from the out-of-season Christmas tree to the candy-cigarette-smoking mannequin, held any semblance of reason or reality. 'If I left right now, what would you do?' she asked.

'Nothing,' he said. 'You have free will, as we all do here, but it wouldn't be a wise move for you.'

'Why not?' She started toward the door and tried to ignore the pain shooting into her foot. 'Would you send the others after me?'

'Nothing of the kind. I'm not an animal.' He walked over to the door, opened it, and let the winter wind rush in. 'You really want to go out into that in the middle of the night?'

His voice sounded deceptively kind, and she wondered whom he was trying to imitate.

'I don't want to stay in your treehouse either.'

He nodded and didn't change his expression. 'At least it has a heater.'

'I've been cold before. I've been cold all day, Ike, while you kept me prisoner down there.'

'What don't you understand about security in this place?' he said. 'It was for your own protection.'

'Protection from what?'

'From whatever Lucas might have done if he'd found you before I talked to him.'

'That just proves my point. I'm better off away from here.' She limped back to the counter, picked up the cake, and handed it to him.'

He threw it against the wall. The smells of chocolate and vanilla filled the room. 'So you really won't stay here after all I did for you?'

'After that?' She gestured at the mess dripping to the floor.

'So I lost my temper. I threw it at the wall, not at you. Come on.'

'No, thanks,' she said. 'I'll try it on my own.'

'With a bum ankle? You know there are snakes out there.'

'Yeah, a few of them were in the basement too,' she said. Then she glanced at the cupboard where Weaver's photo had been. The dart had moved to his throat. She moved closer and saw tiny pricks all over the paper.

'That's Doctor Weasel. The dart was in his head earlier.'

'We move it around,' he said. 'Come on. Take your best shot.'

She turned her back on Weaver's passive smile.

'Was he horrible to you?'

'The worst. He put some of the kids on drugs.'

She backed up to the counter, and her hands collided with the stacks of shotgun shells. Some of them clattered to the sink.

'No problem,' he said, and started scooping them up. 'We play a game with them sometimes.'

Kit wasn't even going to ask. She tried to think of some way to strike a bargain with him.

'This Weasel guy.' She turned and gestured at the photo again. 'If he did bad things, we should report him.' She was careful not to sound like a responsible adult.

'He has our records,' Ike said. 'They'd look for us, and if they look hard enough, they'd figure out we all left our homes. Lucas's grandfather owned this place. They'd find us.'

'But if the Weasel broke the law, he's the one who'd be in trouble.'

He stacked the shells carefully on the counter. 'Want to learn a new way to play Jenga?'

'You know what I want, Ike.' Her heart still beat in bursts. She didn't intend to stay here another minute.

He glanced down at the shells. 'OK, then. I'll walk you to the road.'

They stepped outside, and Kit caught her breath against the cold. Floodlights cast a metallic hue to the front yard.

'You serious about this?' Ike asked.

'I am.' Kit reached into her bag again.

His eyes shone silver in the moonlight. 'It's not there.'

'What?' She whirled around and caught his smile. 'You didn't take my phone. Please tell me you didn't take my phone.'

Ike looked down at his spotless shoes and then up at her, the light hitting his uneven features.

'I couldn't risk anyone tracing you here,' he said. 'It's better for all of us this way.'

'You stole my phone?' The fear and claustrophobia took hold of her again. She felt helpless, lost, unable to speak.

'I did what I had to do. You'll have it soon enough.'

'Now,' she cried. 'Give it back, Ike. Now.'

'Can't take the chance.' He pointed at the fog, which moved like a living disembodied thing toward them. 'You can't possibly go out in that.'

'You said you'd walk me to the road.'

'And then what?' He stood next to her, and the heat from his body felt as falsely protective as the wood stove. 'I don't want you to get hurt, Katherine. Stay tonight, and tomorrow I'll try to help you.'

The fog looked dense, and the longer she stared into it, the more rational he sounded.

'But you stole my phone.' She felt the power drain from her voice.

'Only temporarily.' He glared at the white mist so thick she could not see where the front entrance started. 'Believe me, we reject technology for a reason here.'

She thought about the hours trapped in the basement, her sprained ankle. She couldn't go through that again. She turned and stared up at the treehouse as she had earlier that day. Like the trees in the back, it was hidden within a haze.

'If I did agree to stay there,' she said, 'would you give me my phone?'

'I'll do everything I can,' he said. Then he flashed her that crazy grin again. 'Katherine, you'll die if you try to find your way back to town tonight with one bum ankle. You'll get run over, raped, or attacked by an animal, and I can't let you do that.'

'Give me my phone, and I'll stay,' she said.

'You know very well what would happen if I did that. You're

upset, and this place would be crawling with cops as soon as I left you alone.' He spoke slowly as if explaining something to a child. 'You forget that *I'm* in charge, not you.'

'Not as long as I can walk.' She looked at the impenetrable path and back at the relative safety of Ike's tree.

'Spend the night, and I'll consider returning your property tomorrow.'

'Shit,' she whispered.

'I told you, Lucas prefers we don't use that kind of language. At the place we met, it was encouraged only to make us feel part of the pack.'

Tears filled her eyes. 'I can't do this, Ike. I'll feel like I'm still locked up in that basement.' She shuddered.

'I told you I'm sorry. I know it's creepy down there.'

'You don't understand. I was locked up as a child. I can't handle it.'

His head jerked toward her. 'Where were you locked up?'

She dug for the memory and failed. 'I don't know.'

But she had been alone and terrified, hidden away from everyone and everything. Kit knew that now. Something had happened to her. She couldn't remember what, but she knew it was connected to her fear of being locked in.

'We all have demons in our past.'

She gestured back at the house. 'You ought to know. Do you make a habit out of throwing cake at the wall?'

'So I got carried away. I don't do that often. Come on. It's crazy to keep standing out here when you can be safe.'

'That is such a joke.' She wiped her eyes. 'Nothing about this is safe for either one of us, but you don't get it.'

'Don't act like I'm stupid,' he said. 'We'll talk later, I promise. Tonight, though, you just get some rest. I'll look out for you.'

He turned toward the path leading to his tree, and the thought of it softened Kit's anger and fear. No. She couldn't trust him.

'You swear you won't come up there while I'm asleep?'

'I won't allow anyone else to come up either.'

She wanted to bolt, and she almost did. But the night around them seemed to grow darker and colder by the moment.

'You're basically keeping me captive here. And yet you claim that you're protecting me?'

'Because I am,' he said. 'The bad stuff, I can't help. Security measures. But the rest is me, and I won't let you down.'

She almost believed him. Yet she was terrified. She couldn't walk. She had no way to contact Richard. If she hid up in that house of Ike's, when the sun rose and cleaned the sky, she would have a chance to get out of there.

Richard would have called the police. People had to be looking for her. That's what she had to think about. Not what might happen if Lucas found her there. Not how frightened her mom must be. They had both spent more than twenty years without knowing the other's identity, and now her mother worried if they spent more than a couple of days without speaking.

Although Kit had feared the claustrophobia that had terrified her most of the day, the little man-made treehouse was as comfortable as a structure built for children to play in could be. Although the space was tiny, it was as obsessively clean and neat as Ike.

A large sleeping bag covered the beige plush carpet, and a quiet heater glowed red in the small space. He actually had electricity up here. Kit looked around for anything she could use as a weapon. On one wall hung a web like a cargo net used on a sailboat. She dug into it and took out clean, perfectly folded socks, a bottle of men's cologne, and some bamboo oil hairspray. Another net hung on the opposite wall. She pulled off the towels covering it, and yanked out a cellphone. Not hers. She hit the emergency button. Nothing. The phone was as dead as the night around her. Kit considered tossing it and then shoved in her bag anyway.

Other than revealing how meticulous Ike was, the treehouse offered her little more than a place to sleep. As if she could. She looked at the plushy sleeping bag and thought about it. Although Ike had taken her phone, he hadn't found the pepper spray. She reached deep into her jacket. Maybe she could get some rest if she held on to it all night.

'Katherine?' Ike whispered. He must be on the ladder.

'I thought you were going to leave me alone.'

'I brought you something.'

'Then put it inside,' she said.

'Goodnight.'

In through the front came a paper plate with a folded napkin and two pieces of pizza on it. Kit reached for it and saw that next to them lay a neatly cut piece of chocolate cake.

She waited until the creaks on the ladder steps disappeared, and then put her head down on the floor and sobbed.

FIFTEEN

K it Doyle had crossed him, and John Paul was pissed, not at her, but at himself for expecting anything better than that from her. So she and Richard McCarthy, her ex or whatever he was, thought they could find where the runaway kids met up in Fowler. John Paul guessed McCarthy was behind that, in a hurry to find his niece even if it put Doyle in danger. She should have known better, and she owed him more than just a recorded message on his phone.

On Tuesday after work, he helped Jasper knock down the last of the pistachios from the trees in Jasper's orchard, completing the harvest that had begun the month before. They'd have to hull the nuts tonight before the moisture trapped inside stained the shells.

John Paul felt more like his old self when there was even the slightest physical challenge involved. Not to mention a bottle of scotch as payment. Besides, he liked helping Jasper work alongside the laborers he hired to pick from the remaining trees on his ranch.

'Don't beat my daddy's trees to death,' Jasper shouted from the ladder that made him look like a man on stilts.

'Sorry,' John Paul yelled back up at him. 'I was thinking of my ex-old lady.'

A lie, and they both laughed harder than they needed to, the way they used to when they were younger, and the laughter came from inside.

Jasper whistled and ran a hand through his thinning hair, mostly gray now, just a few blond tufts remaining. Apart from his appearance, he was the blackest white man John Paul had ever known. This was what John Paul had needed to clear all of the static out of his brain: just Jasper, him, the sweet, moist fall air, and the towel-covered brooms above their heads. Every time John Paul struck the limbs and let the nuts rain down on the tarp beneath him, he felt a little better.

'I think that's good enough,' Jasper said. 'What do you say we go to your place and get better acquainted with Mr Ballantine?'

'Not yet.' John Paul slammed his broom into the branches again.

'Oh, come on, man. The trees will be here tomorrow.'

'First, I want to ask you something.'

'About that woman?' Jasper never called Kit Doyle by name.

'About the missing kids.'

'Same thing.' Jasper came down the ladder and faced him.

'No big deal,' John Paul told him. 'I just wondered if you heard anything new about those runaways.'

'Imagine that,' Jasper said. 'I was just about to ask you if there's anything new on our old case.'

'Doyle's right about one thing,' John Paul said. 'We need to find the kids before we worry about anything else.'

Jasper wiped the sweat from his wide forehead and sighed as if to indicate he wanted to say much more. 'What's this *we* shit?'

'All right, then. *I* want to find the missing kids.'

'Because that Doyle woman does, and because she's pulled you into this.' Jasper looked up at the trees again, as if measuring how much work remained. 'You already know what a troublemaker this chick is. And she's media.'

'These days,' John Paul told him, 'you could say the same about me.'

'No, man. She's media in the worst way. You didn't choose the career. She did, and she lives for it. She's not always too kind to law enforcement either, in case you haven't noticed.'

'She pissed me off too at first,' John Paul told him. 'But she needs help. Those kids, if they're still alive, they need help too.'

'I don't even know what to say to that.' Jasper glanced toward the truck and then glared at John Paul 'You're walking a dangerous line, my friend. This chick is not reliable, and in case you forgot, when the dust settles, the black man is always the one left holding the bag.'

'No shit?' John Paul shot the look back at him. 'You're telling *me* how it is for the black man?'

'Ironic, ain't it?' Jasper ran his hand through his pale hair, turned his back, and headed for the truck.

They didn't say much as they drove back to John Paul's place. Finally, Jasper shrugged as he did when he wanted to apologize for something.

'It's OK,' John Paul told him.

'I only said what I did because I know those media types.'

'So do I,' John Paul shot back. 'Doyle's not like that. She cares. Besides, she's already following up that Fowler lead.'

'Alone?' Jasper's voice dropped, barely audible among the sound of traffic.

'With her ex.' They pulled into John Paul's driveway, beneath the overhanging branches he didn't have the heart to cut back. 'Come on,' he told Jasper. 'Let's talk about anything else.'

'You're on.'

On the way into the house, John Paul took out his phone and glanced at it. The number of the missed call wasn't familiar, but the name on the voicemail was. 'John Paul. This is Richard McCarthy, Kit Doyle's husband. Call me as soon as you get this. I've already notified the police, but I need to talk to you too, because . . . well, because Kit has disappeared.'

All the way down Highway 99, John Paul tried to shut off his thoughts the way he'd been taught when a personal situation became a professional one. Only this wasn't professional. It was someone else's case.

When he pulled up in front of the Mexican restaurant, a pale, turned-off sign and the dim lights from the freeway lit the shape of Richard McCarthy pacing in front of the tiny building.

Doyle's little red Prius was in the lot. John Paul parked his truck. *Make it professional, not personal.* That was his goal. Find out what the fuck this guy knew.

Richard walked up to his truck. John Paul got out and, for a moment, considered whether or not they should shake hands. Then his cop brain kicked in, and he studied Richard McCarthy. Six foot one, maybe two, dark hair covered by a baseball cap. Bloodshot, hyper-focused eyes. Something was off in his expression. Guilt. Yeah, that was an easy one to call.

McCarthy looked numb, and not just from the weather. 'The woman who owns this place closed early,' he said. 'I asked her to keep it open, but she said it was too cold.'

'Tell me what happened.'

'I let Kit out of the car this morning.' McCarthy motioned vaguely toward town. 'And when I came back around the block, she was gone.'

'You what?' John Paul pulled his jacket closer. For a moment, he caught Kit Doyle's scent. 'I was supposed to drive her here. We agreed. Why'd she change her mind?'

'I wanted to do it,' McCarthy said, 'but then she met one of the kids – a guy named Ike – and she insisted that she had to talk to him again this morning.'

'And then?' John Paul felt his scalp burn. He could barely control his voice. 'You let her go with this guy?'

McCarthy glared at him. 'You ever try to tell Kit she can't do something? As I said, I drove around the block, and when I got back, she was gone. I already called the police, and I've driven every one of these country roads looking for her.'

'Then you've done all you can, Doctor McCarthy,' he said in what he hoped was a professional tone.

'You're not telling me to go home?'

'That's exactly what I'm suggesting. I'm sorry, but there's nothing else you can do here.'

'What about you?' McCarthy demanded. 'What are you going to do?'

'I'm going to call my former partner and ask if there's been any word.' John Paul stared into the darkness wondering how much more he should say. 'Then I might drive around a little myself.'

'Let me go with you,' McCarthy said. 'I can describe the truck to you.'

Anything to keep from feeling useless. John Paul knew the feeling.

'That won't be necessary. I'm really not sure why you called me anyway since it's a police matter now.'

'Because you care about Kit. Whatever your official designation, it doesn't matter to me. I think you can help.' McCarthy shoved his cap back from his head, and John Paul could see how tortured he was. Yet he was the reason that Doyle was missing right now.

'I'll look into it.' John Paul stared at him as if to make him realize that there was much more he'd like to say. 'Good night, Doctor McCarthy.'

'Wait.' McCarthy came close to him, and John Paul realized they were about the same height, and that, eye-to-eye, Doyle's ex or whatever he was could hold his gaze.

'All I'm asking is for you to keep me informed about what you find out.'

'That depends on what law enforcement wants to share. As you must know, she's probably in danger now.'

'I get that,' McCarthy said.

'And you're the one who drove her here without protection. You're the one who let her get into a vehicle with a stranger. Forgive me if I don't have a lot of patience with you right now.'

Fuck. He had done what he'd promised himself he wouldn't. He had baited Richard McCarthy, made himself come off as less than professional.

'She's my wife.' Under the light of the dim sky, McCarthy's dark hair seemed to glow. 'Where were you last year when she was nearly killed trying to find her mother? Where were you any day of any week when Kit couldn't think about anything else?'

'This isn't about you and me,' John Paul shot back.

Then, for the first time that evening, Richard McCarthy paused and seemed to consider this conversation of theirs.

'Isn't it?' he asked.

John Paul felt the anger ease out of him. Without it, he felt exposed, beaten.

'My friend Jasper will let me know what's going on,' he said. 'I'll keep you up to date on everything I hear. And that's a promise.'

SIXTEEN

Kit couldn't remember how long she had sobbed on the floor of that treehouse. The cold pizza and stale cake pretty much summed up her day and night. One way or another, she would be out of here by sunrise. She had to be, before Richard and her mom had to worry another moment. She had to admit that the pizza – with pineapple and some kind of red hot sauce – wasn't bad. Four pillows stacked behind the sleeping bag formed a kind of headboard. Kit propped herself up on them and huddled in her jacket. Although she would be warmer inside the covers, she already felt creepy enough lying on top of Ike's bed. She wasn't about to venture inside it.

Up here, at least, she could think, and she could let go of the darkness that had engulfed her when Ike had deserted her in the basement. Pictures flashed in her mind. Ike's crazy smile. Richard's arms around her, John Paul and Farley. Her mom. They would do everything they could to find her. She had to try to keep herself safe until they could, and that included pretending to herself that it was perfectly normal to be up in this insane imitation of a home.

Tomorrow. Hours away. She had felt this way at the runaway shelter, just trying to pass time until morning. As she drifted off, she thought about Virgie, the girl who had rescued her when the blonde and her buddies had been willing to kill Kit for her boots. John Paul always said you can't help them all. Kit hoped Virgie could be helped.

She blinked back into the sunlight slanting through the upper window and reached for her phone to check the time. Then she remembered that she didn't have a phone. The sooner she got out of this place, the better.

Slowly, she crept down the steps. On each new rung, pressure and pain shot through her foot. That was OK. She could live with pain and move as slowly as she must to survive.

A small camouflage dome tent she hadn't noticed before sat

just a few feet from the treehouse. A couple of immaculate tennis shoes partially covered by a blanket, extended from it. Ike.

She tiptoed past the tent and looked out. The fog had lifted a little. She could see the road. If she followed it toward those shadows of cars along the freeway a few miles away, she could find the Mexican restaurant again. The woman who ran it seemed like a nice person. She would let Kit use her phone.

'Hey.'

Kit jerked around and came face to face with a tall, slender girl who appeared from behind the treehouse. She looked cold, as if she had been standing there for some time, and what Kit could see of her short fringe of burgundy hair under her fleece beanie looked damp and frizzed by the weather. Kit looked into the unsmiling face she had seen in numerous photos. This girl she had seen with Lucas yesterday was the one she had risked every-thing to find. Richard's niece.

'Jessica?'

'How do you know my name?'

'I saw you earlier,' Kit said. 'And Ike mentioned you to me.'

'Are you with him?'

'He's a friend. That's all. What are you doing out here so early? You look cold.'

'I was meeting someone, but you've screwed that up. Come on inside.' The sun filled the sky like a light switching on. Jessica squinted at Kit. 'Does Lucas know you're here?'

'I think Ike talked to him.'

'What are you staring at?' Jessica demanded.

'Nothing. I mean, I was just leaving.'

'Hold on, both of you.' Ike stepped out of the tent and loomed over them. 'What's going on out here, Jessica?'

'You tell me.'

'Does Lucas know you're prowling around out here this early?'

'I'm not prowling. And you can't tell me what to do. I live my truth.'

'Until when?' he asked. 'I'm impressed that someone as intel-ligent as you can remember the second rule, though.'

'I remember all of them.' She shot Ike a nasty look. 'And you should have followed them. Take no chances. Remember?'

'She's OK,' he said.

'What do you think Lucas would say about that?'

'I've already talked to him about her,' Ike said. 'Come on, Katherine.'

Jessica didn't budge. 'As if you and Lucas are the two great leaders.'

'Wait.' Kit pulled her jacket closer with numb fingers. 'I can fix this right now. By leaving.'

'How're you going to do that when you're the problem?' Jessica asked.

Kit glanced back at Ike, so close to her now, so protective, that she could feel his body heat. 'As I said, by leaving. I'm out of here.'

'That works for me,' Jessica said. She stepped on to the wooden porch. 'Thanks for screwing up my morning. I'm going to go thaw out.' The door slammed behind her.

'I'll be going too,' Kit told Ike. 'I'd sure appreciate it if you'd give me my phone back. I'll feel a lot safer with it.'

'You'll get it.' His expression hadn't changed. 'But Lucas won't let you leave without his permission.'

'He doesn't even have to know until I'm gone.'

'Lucas has to know everything,' Ike said. 'He's inside. Let's go.'

'No.' She turned toward the path and knew she could not make the walk to the freeway. She would have to hitchhike, try to get someone to stop and help her – assuming Ike or one of the others didn't follow her.

Along the path, facing them, a boy almost as tall as Ike walked up. With black curly hair to his shoulders and a guarded smile, he seemed almost an illusion, a trick of the light. Only the anger in his eyes made him human.

'Where's Jessica?' he asked Ike. 'And who's that?'

'Inside,' Ike replied. 'Katherine, this is Wyatt.'

Wyatt nodded a greeting but didn't address her directly. 'Does Lucas know about her?'

'We're handling it,' Ike said.

'See you in there.' He stomped his feet on the wooden steps as if shaking loose invisible snow.

When the door closed behind him, Kit turned to Ike. 'Does he think women don't know how to speak?'

'He's not like that,' Ike said. 'We just distracted him from what he hoped to find here.'

'Jessica?'

'That's not important right now,' Ike told her, and nodded toward the house, 'We need to go in there too. It's the only way.'

'I said no.'

The door opened again, and Kit looked up, expecting Wyatt to reappear. Instead, Lucas stepped outside. Without the cowboy hat, he looked shorter, and his gelled hair did little to compensate. His wide blue eyes looked unnaturally innocent.

'Welcome.' He spoke in a clear, clipped voice that was larger than he in every way. 'Are you the new friend who is causing all of the commotion around here?'

'I don't mean to cause anything,' Kit said. 'All I want to do is leave.'

'She doesn't really want to leave,' Ike said. 'She doesn't have any place to go.'

'Then why the sudden change of heart?' Lucas walked up to her, and even though she had to gaze down to meet his eyes, she felt his power. It wasn't like a charge of electricity. More like a gentle warmth pressing against her resistance.

'Because I thought this would be a good place to stay,' she said. 'But then Ike took my phone, and he said some things that concern me. I just don't think it's going to work out.'

'Oh, Ike.' Lucas grinned at him and looked ready to give him a playful punch on the shoulder.

Ike's body stiffened.

'She begged me to bring her here, Lucas. You know I've never done anything like this before. I'm just trying to help.'

'But you took her phone away from her?'

'He did,' Kit said.

'I was just following the first rule,' Ike said. 'Take no chances.'

'If we return it, could we have a less tense discussion?' Lucas asked. 'Inside, perhaps?'

His words came too easily to trust.

'What's wrong with right here?' Kit asked.

'Nothing,' he said, 'if you like freezing. Come on. Let's go inside and talk. Sissy's making tea.'

'Come on, Katherine,' Ike said.

She shook her head.

'Do come in,' Lucas told her in that same clipped voice. 'Even if you decide to leave us, we need at least to give you a decent meal and reunite you with your phone.'

'Give it to me first.'

'Ike?' Lucas spoke with a smile in his voice, but Kit could hear the echo of much more there.

'Are you serious?' Ike dug into his jacket pocket.

'Please retrieve what you took from her.'

'Fine.' Ike yanked it out and handed it to her.

She gripped it and went straight for Richard's number. The screen looked as blank and dead as the sky.

Lucas watched her efforts to revive it and finally said, 'We can charge it inside.'

The phone was her lifeline, the only one she had left. As Kit followed Lucas up the stairs, her chest tightened, and she could barely breathe.

He stepped ahead of them, went into the kitchen, and plugged the phone into a waiting charger.

'While we wait, would you like some pizza?'

'No, thank you,' Kit said, keeping her gaze on the counter.

'It may take some time. You might as well make yourself comfortable.'

'I'm fine,' she said.

'You don't look fine.' Lucas strode up next to her, his voice as gentle as a concerned parent's. 'I'd say you look worried. Where will you go when you leave?'

'I don't know.'

'Why not hang out for a while?'

'Ike said I'd have to go through some kind of test to stay, and I'm not into hazing.'

'This is not a fraternity,' Lucas said. 'It's a compound of like-minded individuals – a family, as it were. And whether you stay with us or not, you need to prove that you are who you say you are.'

'I don't have to prove anything to you.' Kit moved closer to the counter.

'You stayed at our compound, spent the night here. You know how to find us, and we need to know that we can trust you.'

'I stayed against my will, and I'm leaving. No test.' She reached out for the phone, and Lucas tried to grab it from her. It fell to the floor. Lucas picked it up and handed it to her.

'Clumsy of me.' He looked down at the phone with remorse so well replicated that she would have believed it if she didn't know better. 'We're lucky it didn't break.'

Kit checked it. No signal.

'What have you done to it?'

'Kept it from smashing into pieces,' Lucas said proudly.

'But it's not charging.'

'Apparently not.'

'You don't have reception here?' she asked.

He shrugged. 'We are careful about any of the electronic devices our generation was brainwashed into thinking we couldn't live without.'

His naïve way of speaking covered something much more arrogant – maybe more than arrogant. Kit reminded herself that he was the youngest person in this so-called compound.

'Do you really expect me to believe that you don't have a working phone in this place?' she asked.

'Of course we do,' he replied in his clipped, friendly way. 'If we were to experience an emergency, we would need contact with the outside world. But' – he gazed at the others, even Ike, all of whom nodded – 'we know where to find them. We don't want them to be able to find us.'

'How do you maintain that contact?' she asked.

'I'll share that information with you once you agree to the rest of it.'

'The rest of what? And if I don't, what are you going to do to me?'

'In our compound, we have no violent punishments.' He glanced over at the basement door and the braided rug still bunched over it. 'We have only one, actually. An opportunity to chill. A time out.'

'I'm not going back down there.'

Lucas glanced at Ike. 'So that's where you hid her. That's strike two.'

'Don't push it.' Ike's voice dropped. 'And let's not start counting strikes.'

'You're right, friend.' Lucas frowned down at the counter and lifted Kit's dead phone. 'No worries. If we can't revive this one, we'll get you another one.'

'When?' she asked.

'Once you do this one thing to prove we can all trust each other.'

Kit glanced at Ike, who shrugged.

She looked back at Lucas. 'What is that?' she asked.

'You'll find out. Come with me.' He glanced back at Ike. 'It involves a building.'

'What kind of building?'

'An old farmhouse – an eyesore, really.'

'Why?'

'It's way too soon for you to ask questions. If you're with us, prove it. If not . . .' He glanced over at Ike.

'She's with us,' he said. 'Aren't you, Katherine?'

'What choice do I have?'

Lucas glanced toward the basement, his stance that of a child assuming the role of an adult. 'I can't take the responsibility for letting you leave in this condition.'

'You could drive me to town,' she said. 'That would be pretty responsible.'

'I will. Ike will, I mean. Once we know we can trust you.'

'And I already told you, no fraternity hazing.'

'Absolutely not,' he said. 'You clearly don't understand our values. It's a minor chore. Something you wouldn't necessarily do, but once you do it for us, in front of us, we'll know we can trust you.'

'That sounds great in theory,' she told him, 'but what are you talking about specifically?'

'Let's take a ride.' Lucas nodded toward the door. 'You'll learn the rest once we get there. Fair enough?'

'Nothing about this is fair.'

'I'll take that as a yes.' Lucas seemed pleased. 'We'll need to hurry, though. It's movie night.'

She started to tell him that she wouldn't do anything she didn't want to, but that would be prolonging the inevitable. Maybe Richard was nearby, or John Paul and his cop friends. Perhaps one of them could follow these kids wherever they were taking her, but she was no longer sure anyone could follow them out here in this forgotten vineyard.

The other kids rode in the pickup bed. Kit was wedged between Ike and Lucas in the front seat.

Kit pressed closer to Ike to distance herself from Lucas as much as possible. Yet Ike was crazy too. This is what happened in Stockholm syndrome situations, she knew. Ike and Lucas could play good cop, bad cop with her until she believed Ike was on her side. Soon she would identify as a group member. That wasn't going to happen, though. The swelling around her ankle had already lessened. One more night, and she would be gone, with or without their permission.

SEVENTEEN

K atherine leaned closer to him as they drove, and Ike had to keep himself from putting his arm around her. He felt bad for Katherine, but he also trusted her to do the right thing. Once she proved herself, Lucas would let her stay. But what if she didn't want to? Ike remembered what Lucas had said about Jessica. The compound was about being who they were and were meant to be. If Katherine decided to stay once she calmed down, that would be cool. If she chose to go back on the streets, he could not and should not stop her. Right now, they just needed to get this over with before Lucas came up with any more crazy ideas.

Jessica always said Ike was like a big teddy bear. It was the only nice thing she ever said about him, and she probably didn't even mean it that way. She probably meant he was a brainless pussy. Still, Ike liked the idea of a woman feeling safe with him. That's what he was thinking as they drove in the dark down the dirt road.

They found the farmhouse and pulled outside it on to a skinny driveway that was actually two little strips of concrete, each about as wide as a tire. Ike kept the truck running, both to keep the heater going and to put off what they were going to have to do.

The kids jumped out of the back of the truck almost soundlessly, their shoes like leaves brushing the ground. Ike recognized the place at once: the ramshackle fruit stand run by the old Armenian lady. Shit, he hoped she wasn't in the shack. No, she was usually gone this time of year, wasn't she? Lucas would know. He was kind of obsessed by the nosy old woman. Good thing she didn't know where they lived, or she would have been snooping around for sure. It was their fault, though, for trying to steal tomatoes last summer, never expecting she would pull out a gun and chase the truck down the road.

'What are we supposed to do here?' Katherine asked in a voice that was tougher than she was. 'Because if you think I'm going to spend the night in that shack, you are out of your mind. I'd risk coyotes and any other predators.'

'Do calm down,' Lucas said, but, staring at that place with its brown wood shutters, she got even more worked up.

'If I have to go back on the streets, I will.'

'You can stay with us,' Lucas said. 'At least for now. I already told you that.'

The other kids danced around the house quietly. Too late to stop it now.

'Shall we?' Lucas opened the door and glanced back at them.

'Coming,' Ike said, feeling as if he was back at home and talking to his father. He almost added '*sir*'.

He started to open his door, but Katherine looked up at him with large, frightened eyes.

'What's he going to make me do out there?'

'Nothing we can't get through. Then it will be over, and everything will be all right. Come on. We'd better get going.'

'Not yet,' she said. 'I want you to tell me something, and I want the truth.'

'I'm not a liar, Katherine.'

'Then tell me. If it were up to you, would you make me do this? In the cold? On a dark night? In the middle of a deserted field?'

Ike flopped his arm over the back of the pickup. His hand landed on her shoulder. She looked at it but didn't flinch.

'If it was up to me,' he said, and knew he wasn't going to lie to her. 'No.'

'No what?' In the dark, her eyes gleamed like the flames on the candles his granny liked to burn when she made him hot chocolate.

'If it was up to me, I wouldn't ask you to do this.'

'Yet you introduced me to the guy who is,' she said.

'It was the best thing and still is. Besides, I've got your back. It will be over in no time.'

'I'm not going inside that thing.'

'You don't have to.' Again, he wasn't lying. 'Five minutes, ten, and we'll be back on the road, laughing about it.'

'I doubt that,' she said, and he could see the exhaustion in her eyes.

Ike made himself think only of the job ahead. He couldn't start feeling sorry for her now.

The passenger door yanked open, and cold air sneaked in with Lucas's smiling face. 'Ready, Katherine?' Lucas asked. 'Your audience is waiting.'

'I've got your back,' Ike repeated.

'You're doing a lousy of job of it so far.' She pulled the truck door shut and then slowly opened it again.

Ike imagined the cold air chilling her legs.

'Why does he want me at this particular place?'

Because he thinks the old lady spies on us. 'I don't know. Just hurry up. It's cold as hell out here.'

'You think hell is cold?' she asked.

'I don't have time for riddles, girl. Let's just get this handled.'

She started out the door and then looked up at him as if for one last time. 'If I do this and do it right, do you think Lucas will let me go?'

'Maybe.' He felt like the magician clown he used to watch on the TV back before everything went to hell. 'Lucas doesn't lie,' he said. 'Remember what I said.'

The kids piled their bundles around the front of the structure. Fire starters. Now she understood. Kit wanted to run. Instead, she had to burn down a deserted shack. Her hands trembled, and she felt a wave of nausea.

I can't. That's what she wanted to say, what she should have said the moment she considered taking one step from her relatively safe life into this one.

Instead, she said, 'What do you want me to do?'

The shack was one of those that farmers built for their laborers. The once-white wood had gone dingy, and as Kit looked at it from across the safety of the field, she tried to imagine its insides. No entry hall from the front door, just a square room. To the left, a kitchen with a wood stove. To the right, a hall with one bedroom and, not much farther down, one bath. Windows, what there were of them, would look out on wet grass and black earth. It didn't deserve to be burned.

Kit glanced back at Ike. He responded with a quick shake of his head, as if to say this was the only way she could get out of here.

She looked into the field behind her again and saw only Ike in his thick camouflage-print gloves and matching jacket.

Do it. Ike mouthed the words. *Now.*

The other kids continued piling kindling, gleeful but silent, as if holding in their laugher only excited them more.

Kit walked up to the front door of the house and almost told it she was sorry. Her nostrils burned with a sharp chemical smell. All right, then. For a moment, as she reached for the fire starter and aimed it, she thought of her mother. After the treacherous journeys that both of them had taken to find each other, her mother would not approve of this detour. 'Just tell the truth,' she would say. 'Tell those people what you need.'

But her mother was probably with Richard, trying to be strong while she imagined the worst. She didn't need to know what her daughter was about to do.

One more glance back at Ike. One more approving nod, and she reached down, squeezed the trigger of her fire gun, and watched the logs outside the front door of the house turn blue and orange. Heat drove her back before she could light more, but the fire and the flames reminded her that whatever happened was out of her control now.

The moment before she turned away, Kit looked into that blaze and thought of her mother again. How could she ever explain that she had burned down a perfectly non-threatening farm shack for no reason other than to appease some crazy kid who had put himself in charge of other kids' lives?

The intensity of the flames shoved up hot gray billows of smoke into the air.

'Come on,' Ike shouted. 'We're done.'

Kit needed to turn away. She had to. Her feet made the decision before she did.

In a few steps, she would sit with Ike, proudly arriving at the compound. Having proven herself, she would be accepted by Lucas long enough to get out of there and tell Richard where his niece was.

'Help. Fire.'

Kit stopped. The voice sounded like the whine of the trees.

'Come on.' Ike seemed nervous. 'We've got to get out of here. Fire trucks will be here before you know it. Cops too maybe.'

'Help me,' she heard again. *Oh my god, someone is in there.*

Ike didn't have to say he heard it. Kit could see it in his face.

'There's someone in there, Ike.'

'We need to run.'

'Are you kidding me?' She started for the house. 'You go, then. You coward.'

She went around the back, hoping that part was still intact. It was. An old woman stumbled toward the back door. 'Help, someone.' Her high-pitched voice sounded like everyone in Kit's life she hadn't been able to save. The woman moved in a disoriented dance.

'I'm here,' Kit said. 'I'm here now.' She might have shouted or whispered the words; she no longer knew.

The woman fell. For a moment, she looked dead. Then she stirred.

Kit ran on to the smoke-filled back porch and grabbed her.

Lighter than she looked in her heavy tapestry-printed robe, she let Kit lift and carry her from the burning house.

Once outside, Kit helped her sit on a tree stump. Only then did Kit realize that the woman could barely breathe. On her knees, she gulped in air and realized she had almost committed murder.

'I'm so sorry.'

'You saved my life.' The woman spoke in a heavy accent.

Kit heard the sound of a fire truck. 'You're safe now.' *I'm so sorry.*

'My house.'

'The firefighters are on the way. They'll be able to save it.'

The woman put her face in her hands and sobbed.

Kit ran to the front. She had done this and would have to pay for it, but at least the firefighters could help this poor woman. Once she told them the truth, she would be free of Lucas and the others.

'Not so fast.' Ike grabbed her into his powerful arms and carried her to the truck.

'No!' she shouted.

'You're just upset, Katherine,' he said. 'We've got to get out of here before she sees us. You could be arrested.'

'I don't care,' she cried. 'I don't care.' Kit shouted it over and over until she realized there was no hope, no hope at all, and they pulled into the compound.

EIGHTEEN

'Impressive.' Lucas strolled around the kitchen, his back so stiff and stance so rigid that he must be imagining himself in a military uniform. 'Everyone has a strength. Yours might be your bravado, Katherine. That's different from bravery, of course, but it's still admirable, considering.'

'Do you realize what almost happened?' she demanded, beyond outrage, but trying to express it the way Katherine would. 'That woman could be dead.'

'So could you. It's nice how it worked out, isn't it?'

Kit started for the front door and had to grab for the frame to steady herself. She needed to find a working phone, but no one was going to hand one over. Maybe just try to get close to Jessica, then. If Kit could gain her trust, she might be able to get out of here.

'You made it worse with your heroics back there, didn't you?' Lucas walked over to where she stood trying to hide her pain. 'It was worth it, though. You saved a life. We all have talents here. Everyone contributes something. After what I just saw, you might be exactly what we need.'

'That's what I've been trying to tell you,' Ike said.

'Your message, friend, has been far from clear – to me and I'm guessing to yourself.'

'I can do whatever Katherine can,' Sissy put in.

'You'll get your chance.' Lucas glanced toward the wood stove. 'Got any coffee over there?' Sissy glared at him, and then hurried to the cast-iron coffee pot, lifted it, and shook her head. 'Tea will be fine,' he told her, and then turned his attention to them. 'Remember how the Weasel used to say we needed a new challenge?' he asked.

The others responded with groans and grunts.

'He called them growing opportunities,' Ike said. 'So we could discover all we were capable of. I can still see the Weasel in my nightmares.'

'We all can,' Lucas said. 'That's why we're here. One of the reasons, at least. And he had a point. Katherine just proved she's not afraid of fire.' He smiled at her. Kit looked away and limped to the table. 'What else can we work on?' Lucas asked.

'Strength,' Ike said.

'Loyalty.' Wyatt turned toward Jessica, who returned his look so briefly that Kit thought she might have imagined it. But then she saw the cold freeze of Lucas's gaze and knew better.

'What do you think our next challenge should be, Katherine?' he asked her.

'You're the so-called leader,' she said, 'and I'm not going to be here that long.'

He walked around the group, checking out each one of them. Finally, he stopped in front of Sissy, who stood beside nerdy dark-haired Theo.

Sissy turned, wide-eyed, from the wood stove. With their blond hair, slight build, and façade of innocence, she and Lucas might have been brother and sister.

'What quality of life and survival would you like to see tested here?' he asked her.

Sissy pouted and looked at Jessica. 'Trust maybe. Yes, trust.'

'That's pretty nice.' Lucas returned to his natural understated voice and turned his approving smile on Sissy, who blushed. 'If we don't have trust, I guess we don't have anything, do we?'

'We don't have anything,' Sissy echoed, and stroked her fingers over her arms. The rest of the kids mumbled to themselves and each other.

'Would you not agree, Katherine?' All of a sudden, Lucas

glided as if on skates, and faced Kit with that contrived smile of his.

'That depends.' She rose from the table. 'I don't know about the rest of you, but I'm not setting any more buildings on fire.'

They responded with chuckles.

'Is that so?' Lucas produced another feigned smile. 'But are you willing to play a little game of trust?'

'I don't know.' She glanced at Jessica, who shook her head. Then she met Lucas's gaze. 'Probably not.'

'Sissy,' Lucas said. 'If I were to ask you to prove your trust for me right now, what would you do?'

'Anything.' She shrugged and looked down at her hands.

'Would you walk through fire if I told you I'd be on the other side and guide you through it?'

'Fire's out,' Kit said.

'It was an example.' In a response to the force in her voice, Lucas lightened his even more. 'If not fire . . . would you walk through ice if I waited on the other end of it?'

Sissy nodded. 'I would. What about you, Jessica?'

'I would,' she shot right back at Sissy. 'If Wyatt waited for me.'

They were playing into Lucas's hands, Kit realized, but she could not figure out what the game was, or what he wanted from it.

'And you, Ike?' he asked, his clipped voice forced and polite. 'Would you walk through ice blindfolded?'

Ike chewed on his bottom lip, and Kit knew he was trying to figure out the game as well. 'I would,' he answered slowly. 'If Katherine was waiting.'

'Perfect.' Lucas took the mug from Sissy, sipped, and then grinned at them over the top of it. 'I think I've figured out our next challenge.'

'Not tonight, I hope,' Ike said. 'I don't want to walk through ice blindfolded.'

The others chuckled softly – all but Sissy, who shoved her hands to her hips and glared at all of them as if she wished they would leave.

'Not walking, friend.' Lucas moved slowly around the inside of the circle that had closed around him. 'Not *walking* blindfolded.'

His easy, almost sweet voice sent a chill through Kit.

'What, then?' she asked.

'What about this?' He stepped closer to the wood stove, and they all turned to face him. 'I know it's been difficult with many of you arriving at the same time.' He smiled at her. 'And Katherine kind of arriving out of nowhere.'

Everyone turned to look at her and seemed to draw nearer each other.

'As my guest,' Ike said, and stepped beside her.

'But not mine, friend. Not ours.'

'He's right,' Sissy said.

'Considering these developments, it might be time – if you all agree, of course – for a kind of Weaselized test for trust.'

'Walking through the ice?' Sissy asked. Then her eyes widened. 'You mean the fog, don't you?'

'Weasel would come up with something better than that.' Lucas lifted his arms as if hoping to make himself appear taller and stronger. 'Everyone, right now, pick a partner you can trust.'

Kit reached out for Ike the same moment his arm shot out for her.

Jessica and Wyatt held hands. Other couples grabbed each other, and Kit wondered if they did so as rapidly as they did so that they could avoid being paired with Lucas.

'Looks as if that leaves you and me, Sissy,' Lucas said.

'Sounds good.' She gave him an adoring look.

So that's what was going on. Luke played the two girls against each other, even though he made it clear that he preferred Jessica.

'Ike, let's start with you and Katherine,' he said.

Ike groaned. 'In this weather?'

'No worries about the weather.' Lucas grinned as if they were sharing a joke. 'You have a heater in that truck, remember?'

'In the truck?' Ike asked and clutched Kit's hand. 'I thought we were supposed to walk blindfolded.'

'Not walk,' Lucas said.

'Oh, come on, man. You don't expect me to drive blindfolded, do you?'

Lucas smiled. 'You won't be alone, friend.'

'What are you talking about?'

'You trust Katherine, don't you? Isn't that what you just said?'

'Don't answer him,' Kit told Ike. 'He's trying to set you up.'

'Katherine.' Lucas chirped out her name. 'You appear less and less grateful for the fellowship we've offered. Why wouldn't Ike want to prove that he can trust you?'

'Because of what I just told him.' She glared from Lucas to Ike and back again. 'You are setting him up for some reason. Ike, why would he be trying to harm you?'

'I don't know.' Ike squinted at Lucas. 'You aren't trying to pull something funny here, are you?'

'Katherine proved herself by setting that fire,' Lucas said. 'She's one of us now, and if you don't believe it, we have it in our movie-night archives. But you've all agreed we now need to feel trust, and I'm willing to take this test if you are.' He walked over to the bald mannequin, took off her red satin Mardi Gras mask, and held it out.

'Don't,' Kit said just as Ike grabbed it.

'Want me to go first?' he taunted Lucas. 'Want me to go before you?'

'I'm more than willing if you're having second thoughts.' Lucas put down his mug and looked up at Sissy. 'Apparently, our friend here doesn't have the necessary courage to go first. Shall we take the first drive to town?'

Town.

Kit realized this might be her only chance.

As Sissy grinned and hurried to refill the cup Lucas had offered her, Kit reached out and took the mask from his hands.

'Fine. Then Ike and I will go first.' She squeezed Ike's hand and flashed Lucas what she hoped was as ice-cold a gaze as he given her. 'And, yes, we have the necessary equipment, don't we, Ike?'

'We sure do,' he said. 'Come on, Katherine.'

They hurried outside as fast as Kit's aching ankle would allow. To her surprise, the battered truck waited just down the drive.

'When did that get here?' she asked.

'More important . . .' Lucas walked up to her. 'Can Ike trust you enough to direct him down the road to the highway?'

He had said *town* earlier. He was already changing the rules. Still, if she and Ike could get to the highway, she could find her way from there.

'I don't want to die in the fog any more than he does,' she said. 'Is that reason enough for him to trust me?'

The others laughed again, but it was nervous laughter this time.

Ike grinned and opened the truck door. 'Come on, Katherine. Let's show him.'

She looked at Jessica, who gripped Wyatt's hand and leaned against him as if only he could save her from what was happening.

'We're doing this,' Kit told Lucas.

'That's nice,' Lucas chirped like a child. 'I like that.'

As they climbed into the truck, Kit knew the little bastard already thought he had won this game of his, whatever it was.

'I like it too,' she said. 'When we get back, it will be your turn.' She slammed the truck door and added, 'You sociopath.'

Through the window, she caught the frozen expression on his face, followed by clenched fists, which he shoved into the pockets of his down jacket. He had heard her. Good. With luck, she would never see him again.

NINETEEN

'You shouldn't have called Lucas that name,' Ike said, and squinted at her.

'Called him what?'

'A sociopath. We're running from labels, all of us. We're rejecting them as definitions of ourselves.'

'Well, Lucas is living up to his,' she told him. Then she remembered why she had agreed to this – not to argue with Ike, but to get where she needed to go. 'Don't make me guide you through this. Pull over as soon as we're out of here, take off your blindfold, and let's talk about it. Lucas is exactly what I called him. He tried to make me leave that old woman for dead.'

'He didn't know she was in there.' The blindfold tied around his head, Ike pulled out on the dirt drive. 'We'll get through this and be back in the compound in no time.'

He went slowly, but Kit realized that he would barely be able to see through the fog even without a blindfold. 'Pull over now,' she said. 'You need to realize that Lucas is trying to destroy you. He's afraid of your strength.'

'That's crazy.' The truck lurched forward. 'We're best friends.'

'He only says that.' Kit raised her voice. 'You scare him in some way. And slow down, please.'

Instead, Ike hit the gas. 'You watch for traffic,' he said. 'Stop talking about my friend.'

'Maybe you were friends once, but you've got to know that Lucas is threatened by you.'

Just then, a semi pulled through the four-way stop.

'Stop,' she shouted, and grabbed the sides of her seat as her own foot hit the floorboard.

Ike slammed on the brake, and the rattling vehicle came to a halt. 'What happened?'

'You almost hit a fucking semi.'

'Please.' He didn't finish what he was about to say, and perspiration glistened above his lips. The mask covering the scarf over his eyes was as strange in its own way as his features were. He turned to Kit. 'You don't understand. Lucas is the mental strength in the compound. I'm the brute strength. Together, we can do anything.'

He started the truck once more.

'Talk about labels,' she said. 'Anyway, maybe that was true when you met, but it's not now. Maybe that's why he's sending you out here. Maybe he thinks you're too smart, and he wants to get rid of you.'

'He knows he needs me.'

'Maybe he thinks Wyatt or one of the others can take your place.'

'Wyatt?' He hit the accelerator, and Kit gripped her seat again. 'Wyatt's a loose cannon. Besides, he's the one Jessica wants.'

The battered red of an illuminated stop sign came into view. Kit let out her breath and whispered, 'You need to stop now.'

'You sure?'

'Stop, damn it, Ike, and then make a right when I tell you.'

Maybe she should jump out at the stop sign. Maybe she should just rip the blindfold off his eyes and force him to see. But Ike was too big, too volatile for Kit to second-guess. Thanks to Lucas, her safety depended on Ike now, and his safety depended on her.

'How do I know you're leading me the right way?' he asked.

'It's about trust, remember? Besides, you're doing fine,' she lied. 'We'll get there and back, and then if you won't drive me away from the crazy camp of yours, I am going out on my own.'

'Lucas will calm down after this.' Ike slammed on the brake. 'He always does.'

He started to step on the gas again, but Kit already felt queasy.

'So, Lucas does these little tests frequently?'

'Not like this.' Ike nodded behind his mask. 'But sometimes.'

'How are we going to ever get out of here?' she asked.

'I'll go slowly. You'll direct me. Got to say, though, this is the creepiest thing Lucas ever asked me to do. I wonder . . .'

'Wonder what?' she asked. 'Slow down more.'

He did as she asked, yet Kit couldn't control her heartbeat. 'Nothing really. I just can't figure out why he came up with this so quickly.'

The fog seemed to grow thicker. 'Slower,' she whispered. 'And you do know why, don't you? I just told you.'

'If I knew, I wouldn't be wondering,' he said.

'He's mad because you overrode his authority and let me in.'

'That's crazy, Katherine. We're partners, Lucas and me.'

'Until you decide to let a girl in without permission.' The truck drifted to the right side of the road. Good. Slow and to the right.

'But he let Jessica in.'

'My point exactly, Ike.' She kept her voice low, gentle. 'I have an idea. Why don't you take off that blindfold? He won't know.'

'He will. Lucas knows everything. He's probably listening to our conversation right now.'

She couldn't fake calmness much longer, but she needed to try. 'What do you mean? Does he have you under some kind of electronic surveillance?'

'I don't know. That's what a monster did to us at a camp one time. Fucker Weaselized us. That's why we allow no technology.'

'None at all?' she asked. 'How do you play your logic games?'

'Not very often, and I'm OK with it now. Technology is the fastest way to get tracked, caught even.'

'Which is why Lucas destroyed my phone?'

'He didn't destroy it.'

'It's dead, Ike.'

'Because we have no way to fix it.' He nodded as if she could see the sorrowful tone of his voice reflected in his eyes. 'We'll get you another one.'

'Pull over and tell me what that means.'

'I can't,' he said.

'You've got to. Ike, I can't think. Please, just for a minute.'

'Against my better judgment.' He pulled the truck to the side of the road too far, and they bumped into a dirt path. 'Oh, great,' he said.

'It's OK,' she told him. 'We can't keep doing this. Tell me how you can get me another phone if you can't even charge mine?'

He turned his head as if they were having a confidential chat. 'Don't tell anyone. We've got a few on ice.'

'What's that supposed to mean?'

'On ice in headquarters. It's a code word for where we keep them.'

On ice. Only one place in the main house was that cold, and Kit didn't dare go near it again.

'When we get back, will you help me get a phone?' Not that she had any intention of going back.

'Depends on what Lucas says.' He revved the engine again. 'I know he's timing us. Tell me where to go next.'

The fog huddled over the road, yet Kit knew that if they went straight, she should be able to find the restaurant. At that point, she would jump out of the car, in spite of her raw ankle, and beg Juanita to help her.

'Lucas says to the freeway and back,' she said. 'That would be straight ahead, but go even more slowly, will you? I can't see a thing.'

'I don't think we're heading for the freeway.' He jerked around and seemed to glare at her though his creepy mask. 'I've got a weird feeling about sense of direction.'

'Keep your eyes on the road,' she demanded, and then realized how ridiculous that sounded. 'I mean, please don't distract me, Ike.' A noise rumbled loudly through the dark. 'And stop right here. Now!'

They barely avoided a truck lumbering through the fog as if it were the only vehicle on the road.

'What was that?' Ike asked, his voice a little thinner and less certain.

'Not sure,' she said. 'An unmarked truck, going way beyond the speed limit.'

'Could be anything out here,' he told her. 'Drugs. Guns.'

'I think there was some kind of printing on the side,' she said. 'It looked legitimate.'

'That's the point.' He turned his head toward her again. 'It wouldn't be hauling ass through here in this weather if it was doing something legal.'

'Just so you understand,' she said, her entire body numb with fear, 'another second or two, and it would have hit us.'

He sighed and lowered his head over the steering wheel. 'Lucas didn't have any way of knowing that truck would be out here at this hour.'

'Didn't he? Wouldn't he know that only crazy people drive in weather like this?'

'I'm not crazy.'

She didn't like the way his voice tightened.

'That truck could have killed us,' she said.

'I get it.' His face, even hidden by the mask, seemed contorted. 'We need to get moving, though. Don't lie to me, Katherine. You're my navigator, but Lucas is probably tracking us. Where's the freeway for real?'

'To the left,' she said. He started to move forward, and she touched his arm. 'Ike, can we just talk about this for a moment?'

'Lucas won't like it.'

'He won't know,' she said.

'OK. But not for long.' He lifted his mask, looked out at the white-on-white that had closed in on them, and shook his head in disbelief. 'Holy shit.'

She didn't bother to remind him that Lucas didn't like swearing. 'We can't do this,' she told him. 'Lucas is trying to get us killed.'

'I told you, he wouldn't do that.' Ike seemed blinded by the haze surrounding them, almost in a trance.

Another truck blustered past.

'Don't you think we've proven our trust?' Kit asked him.

'I don't know what to say. We've had tests before, but nothing like this. How did Lucas think . . .'

'My point exactly.' He looked at her with as much sorrow as confusion. 'I realize how much this sucks,' she told him, 'but you have to know Lucas is not your friend. He wouldn't ask you to take this kind of chance if he cared about you.'

'I don't know.' He spoke slowly as he peered at the fog. 'How did we get this far?'

'By sheer luck,' she said. 'Now, I'm going to ask you to help me with something.'

'I'm not taking you anywhere,' he said. 'As you said, we're lucky we got this far.'

'What about the Mexican restaurant, then?'

'On a night like this, Juanita will have closed.'

'She didn't the night I met you, and the weather was every bit as awful as it is tonight.'

'But she recognized the pickup and let me in.'

Kit tried to hide her surprise. 'So Juanita is part of what you do?'

'Of course not. She just tries to help by giving us food when she can. For a while, she was cool having me pick up kids there. She's too curious now, though. I don't know how long we can keep using her place.'

'How many more are coming?' Kit asked.

'Just Angel for now. Something must have happened to keep her from showing up on time.' He glanced over at her again and gave her an awkward grin. 'Just think. If Angel had showed up when she was supposed to that night, I never would have met you.'

'And maybe we wouldn't be stuck at a four-way intersection looking into a wall of fog,' she said.

'I'm glad we are, Katherine. Not the fog, but us knowing each other.'

She looked away, unable to lie to him more than she already had. 'I'll be a lot more grateful if you get me out of this place without smashing into a truck.'

'I'm not trying to hit on you,' he said. 'It's just good to have a friend.'

'You're right.' She gave him what she hoped was an older-sister look. 'Let's be here for each other, OK? We don't need to rely on blindfolds anymore.'

'I don't know,' he said. 'If Lucas says it, we have to do it.'

'I already proved myself by setting fire to that building.' She trembled as she thought about how wrong it could have gone. 'It's time for you to help me get out of here.'

'I don't want you to go.' He looked down at his huge hands. 'I'm starting to think you're my only friend.'

She wanted to tell him she wasn't, but she couldn't seem to come up with a lie.

'If you want to come with me,' she said, 'I'll try to help you.'

'How?' he asked.

'Never mind. Maybe you should just let me out on one of the highway off-ramps. Once I get settled – and you know I will – I'll come back for you.'

He shook his head. 'That's what they all say. Besides, I couldn't just leave you at some gas station or coffee shop. That's how girls like you get killed.'

'I could call someone to come meet me,' she said. 'A friend from before.'

'Don't lie to me.' His headshake was more vehement than before. 'If you knew someone who cared enough, you wouldn't have ended up here in the first place.'

No way could she tell him that she had a mother, a husband, a radio talk show partner, and a former cop who were probably crazy to find her by now.

'What if we headed somewhere far away from here?' Kit asked. Like Sacramento, where she could jump out of the truck and find her way home.

He tapped the gas gauge. 'Ain't gonna happen. At least not tonight.'

She sank back against the seat. 'So you're telling me I have no choice.'

'I'm telling you neither one of us does. Not right now.'

'Will you at least go by the restaurant?'

'I can't, Katherine.'

Once they neared the compound, Ike replaced his blindfold.

'This is tough,' he said. 'I never lied to Lucas before.'

'You aren't lying now,' she said. 'You just aren't telling everything.'

'That's still a lie.'

Lucas's test had almost killed them in the fog, but Ike couldn't tell a lie. Yet they hadn't died. Kit's breath began to even out. 'How do you know these things?' she asked. 'Right and wrong, I mean.'

'My dad's a cop. My granny's a lay minister. That means—'

'I know what that means. How did you ever make friends with Lucas?'

'Long story,' he said. 'Another time. Hey, I have a riddle for you. This dude lives on the tenth floor of a New York apartment building, see?'

'I don't see, and I don't want to hear this,' she said, 'especially after almost getting killed out here.'

'Too bad. You have to. I've been listening to you. Now you listen to me. The dude takes the elevator every morning to the first floor. When he comes back on a rainy day or with other people in the elevator, he goes to his floor. If not, he goes to the seventh floor and walks up to his apartment. Tell me why?'

Ike's maniacal voice matched his grin.

'I've heard that one,' she said. 'I just can't remember it right now. Not to insult you or anything, but I have more important things on my mind.'

He chuckled as if he hadn't heard her.

'It's a classic,' he said. 'Turns out the guy is even shorter than Lucas. Only way he can push the elevator button is with his umbrella or if someone else pushes it for him.'

'So why would he carry his umbrella only in the rain? Or if he's self-conscious about that, why wouldn't he bring something else to push the elevator button?'

He scrunched up his face as if sorting out her words from his story. 'You can be a real ass, you know that?'

'I'm sorry,' she told him. 'But I don't want to stay here one more minute, OK?'

'You have to. I want to talk to you more, though. Some of the stuff you're saying – well, I don't like it. If Lucas knew you were talking that way, you'd be in trouble, maybe even—'

'A time out? That's why you need to help me get out of this place, Ike.'

'You can do that yourself, once your ankle is better,' he said. 'Another day, I'll bet.'

'Do you really think Lucas will help me do that?'

He sighed. 'I don't know. I'm not going to lie to you.'

It's what she had suspected from the start. At least now, she could trust Ike to tell her the truth. 'Oh, that's encouraging. Can you see why I need to leave?'

'Can you see why I can help you only so much?' He gestured toward the house. 'He'll be standing out there waiting for us, probably figuring out how many miles we drove and if we stopped anywhere.'

'He can't wait that long,' she said. 'He and Sissy are the next ones to drive blindfolded. I'll bet they cheat too.'

'What about Jessica and Wyatt?' He grinned.

'They'll probably follow next,' she said.

'Fuck them.' He paused, seemed to swallow his words, and said, 'I don't care what they do.'

'You like her, don't you?' Kit reached over and pulled down his mask.

'Who?' he asked. 'Jessica? She's the most arrogant bitch – I mean, girl – I've ever known.'

His face blazed.

Kit nodded. 'I'm guessing she likes you too, Ike, and she probably knows she can trust you. Jessica and you are two of the most decent people here.'

TWENTY

Jessica liked him? That was nuts. Him liking her was crazy too. In spite of her smart mouth, Jessica had never been like the rest of them. Her nasty attitude had put a distance between her and them, but only because she was so scared. Ike knew that because, to tell the truth, he had been scared too.

If Ike allowed himself to think about what Katherine had said, it might lead him right off the nearest cliff without the truck. He kind of trusted Katherine, even though he knew Lucas would say he shouldn't. She had tried to tell him things that stirred around in his own head. When she left, he would lose maybe his only truth-telling friend in this place. For one crazy moment, Ike wondered if he could leave with her. No, he needed to stay here so he could take care of Jessica if she needed him. That settled it, then. Katherine would have to stay longer.

His eyes were used to the fog now, and he could make out the shapes of the broken fences leading to the compound. He looked at Katherine the same way he looked at the weather, not just the way he would check out a cute girl. Something about her was different from Sissy and the others. He wondered if she really had a home she could go back to. That would explain why she didn't care about the rules of the compound.

'What are you thinking?' she asked.

'That you aren't like Sissy.'

'Not crazy, you mean?'

'Watch that word,' he said.

'You're right. I apologize.' She glanced away from him, even though he knew she couldn't see any better than he could.

'Why'd you run away?'

She looked down at her hands in her laps. 'Everyone has a reason. I knew mine was going to get worse and not better.' She glanced up at him. 'What about you? Family problems?'

'Too many rules, I guess.' He pulled into the drive. 'We're here.'

She didn't move. 'Rules aren't always bad.'

'When your dad's a cop, they are. He and my granny raised me – she mostly.'

'And your mother?'

'She took off.' His head felt as if it would explode. 'But please don't play shrink, Katherine. I've already been through that shit.'

'I thought you didn't swear. Anyway, I didn't mean to play shrink, as you call it.' She reached for the door handle. 'Why did they put you in that place where you met the others?'

'That's none of your business, friend.' He tried to sound the way Lucas would. He couldn't tell her that it was because of the night his mom came home drunk and beat him awake. Yes, he had hit his own mother, and when they asked him why, he couldn't say that it was because she had beaten him. It would have been worse for her, so he had taken the charges, protected her from the law, and done time in the Weasel's camp.

'Don't call me friend if you're not going to trust me,' Katherine said.

'I just don't remember it all,' he said.

'Try harder.' He did. 'What about Lucas?'

'He was a First Year.'

'That's not what I'm asking, Ike.'

'He came in young. Had some problems adjusting in school.'

'Why?' she asked.

'I don't remember.'

'Of course you do.'

'I don't, Katherine.' He gripped the steering wheel until he felt he could rip it out by the roots. 'I don't remember any of that.'

'Why did Lucas come in at such a young age?'

He met her searchlight eyes, looked away, and then back at her. 'Some issues after his father died.'

The encouraging smile on her face seemed to freeze. 'How did his father die?'

'Fire.' He said it before he realized how that word sounded and what it meant. 'Not sure, actually.'

'I think you're sure, Ike.'

She climbed out of the truck before he could stop her.

'I don't know much about any of this. You have to realize that.'

'Oh, you know, all right.' She glanced at him over the shoulder of her blue down jacket. 'You just don't want me to know.'

Now he had done it. Lucas had his demons like the rest of them, and they never let those demons loose in front of strangers. Besides, the Weasel had said one thing that did make sense. No one could blame Lucas. No one could blame a child. He was so young when it happened that it must have been an accident. But Ike had let a demon out, one that wasn't his, and Katherine knew more than she should.

They walked inside, and Jessica grabbed Wyatt's hand. Then she leaned up to whisper something in his ear. Her hair had seemed to grow overnight, almost black to her ears, the red streaks like wine-colored spikes highlighting her head.

'What's going on?' Ike asked her.

'Come on, Jess.' Wyatt attempted to ease her out the door. 'It's our turn.'

'No, it's not,' Ike said. He always remembered the order of things. 'It's Sissy's turn. Sissy and Lucas.'

'Not tonight.' Jessica pressed her finger to her lips and hurried out behind Wyatt.

Ike started to follow. The two of them didn't look matched. Jessica was too tall, slender, and frightened, Wyatt too angry.

'No.' A hand touched his arm, and then he remembered Katherine. But Katherine wasn't Jessica, and Jessica was about to drive with a blindfolded Wyatt through the fog Ike had just barely survived.

'I've got to help her,' Ike told Katherine.

'She has Wyatt,' Katherine said.

'He can't drive worth a shit *without* a blindfold. What do you think he's going to do *with* one?' Ike looked down at the planks of the floor and felt shame. His granny always said when you say one bad thing, you have to say three good ones you really mean. But he couldn't do that right now. He was too worried about Jessica. 'You're the one who said Lucas wanted us to die out there. What if that really is what he wants for them?'

'You're right.' Katherine turned around. 'We have to stop them.'

They ran back outside, but the truck was gone.

'What about the golf cart?' Katherine seemed to be in panic mode. Ike didn't want Jessica hurt either, but the golf cart was as old as this place was.

'Not in this weather. Besides, I owe it to Lucas to stay here.'

'Why do you owe that little creep anything?'

'I told you before. You don't get it.'

'I get that we're finally not being watched. Let's go while we can, Ike. I'll help you, I promise.'

Something in his head didn't feel right all of a sudden. 'Where is everyone?' he asked her.

'Who cares?' Katherine started for the door. 'We've got to find Jessica.'

'There's something wrong, and it's my job to care. A couple more minutes isn't going to change anything.'

A burst of laugher came from the back end of the house.

'Are they outside?' she asked.

More laughter, a loud excitement that was more roar than words. 'Come on.' Ike said it politely enough but took her arm so firmly that she must have known she had no choice. Together, they made their way through the living room to the kitchen, and then to the hall that led to the back door.

The door stood open, and several kids crowded the hall the way they did when they watched Wyatt and his fucking knives, except Wyatt and his fucking knives weren't here. At least Wyatt wasn't.

The door at the end of the hall stood open, and Ike started to shut it. Then he saw what was going on in the open shower outside.

'What are they doing?' Katherine asked.

'Go back inside.'

'My god.' Katherine gasped. 'They're naked.'

'Showering.' That's the best reply he could offer, for there, in front of the spray of shower, stood a shining wet Sissy. She giggled and dug her fingers into the long, dark hair of the guy beside her. Theo. Still wearing his thick glasses, he smeared chocolate cake over her shoulders, her breasts. Even with the others crowded around, the two of them seemed not to care or even remember why they were there. Ike knew why.

He grabbed Katherine's hand and pulled her back inside. She leaned against the narrow plaster of the hall and almost knocked down the mounted sword above her head.

'What's wrong with them?' she demanded.

'It's not Sissy's fault. Not Theo's either.' He pulled her down the hall beside him. 'The Weasel treated us with different shit. I got the good. Sissy got the bad.'

'Which is?' Katherine pulled away from him and refused to move. Ike hoped she didn't look up at that bouquet of dried yellow sunflowers circling the ripped-off porcelain head of an antique doll.

'Today you'd call it ecstasy. Come on. I don't want you to see what's going on out there.'

'We've got to help Sissy,' Katherine said. 'Then we need to find Jessica and Wyatt.'

'We can't. Sissy won't listen. She's done this before.' He stopped speaking before more words escaped.

'With you?' Katherine's expression begged him to tell her the truth, and Ike could not turn away from it.

'Almost.'

'Lucas?'

'Another attempt, but Lucas would never do anything like that. If he finds her like this, he'll punish her.'

'Do excuse me.' Just then Lucas appeared from the front of the house and blocked their exit from the hall. 'We're going to need some assistance here, Ike.'

He wanted to say he couldn't. He wanted to say he was tired, but he stepped aside and let Lucas pass.

'I have to help Lucas,' he told Katherine. 'You do whatever you want.' He knew she wouldn't get far, and right now he needed to follow Lucas to whatever had gone wrong outside. And something had gone wrong. Ike could tell that by the mounting energy of the voices out there.

On his way to settle the problem, Lucas plucked a blue towel from the pile on the laundry table. Then the others parted, and he and Ike stepped into the overhead light of the patio. Ike felt Katherine beside him and was glad she hadn't tried to run off.

'Sissy,' Lucas said. 'We've discussed this before. You must stop it now.'

She moaned and ran her fingers over her cake-covered body. It looked disgusting even to Ike.

'Sissy,' Lucas said again. 'This is unattractive behavior.'

Still she didn't respond. Theo seemed to blank out, as if not remembering why he stood there or what he was supposed to be doing with this naked girl.

'Ike.' Lucas motioned to him. 'Take care of this.'

'I don't know what to do, man.'

'She needs to learn her lesson.' He moved closer to her. 'Sissy, you're getting a time out. Don't worry. We're going to offer you some help.'

Ike glanced at Katherine. She shook her head quickly. For that moment, as short as a breath, he glanced between Lucas and her. He had a choice. He could grab Sissy out of the shower and give her a time out, or he needed to leave with Katherine, to find Jessica and maybe plan an escape away from here.

'Ike?' Lucas softened his voice. 'Perhaps you didn't hear me.'

'I did.' Ike felt clumsy and stupid.

'Our Sissy needs your help.' Lucas reached for her naked arm as if handing her to Ike. 'You're out of control, Sissy. You're going to have a Bleeds.'

She screamed, and Ike wished Lucas hadn't called it that. When the Weasel gave them a Bleeds, it meant the worst punishment for the smallest infraction.

'That's not helping your case,' Lucas said.

'No,' she shrieked back at him. 'No more Bleeds.'

Theo scrambled out of the shower, shook his head as if waking up, and stumbled out toward the planted-over swimming pool, where he appeared to pass out.

Ike tossed Sissy a towel.

'Leave me alone.' She rubbed the towel along the contours of her body as if getting off on the smell, taste, and texture of it. 'Go away, asshat.'

Where was Jessica now that he needed her? Oh, that's right. With Wyatt, driving through the fog or doing whatever they did when no one was looking.

'Come on, Sissy.' He put out his hands.

'No, you creep. Don't touch me.'

Lucas stepped forward.

'Would the rest of you please leave the area?' he asked. 'Ike and I need to help this poor girl.'

'No,' Sissy shouted.

The others left. Ike nodded. 'I'll take care of them,' Lucas said. 'You take care of her.'

For the first time, Ike realized Katherine had disappeared as well. Only naked Sissy, defiant now, stared back at him.

'How would you like me?' She licked her lips.

'Come on, Sissy.'

He reached in, lifted her, and placed her towel-wrapped body over his shoulder.

'Put me down.' She beat on his back. 'You ugly son of a bitch. Let go of me.'

'I wish you wouldn't swear,' he said. One way or the other, Sissy needed that time out tonight.

'The basement?' he asked Lucas.

He shook his head, and Sissy sobbed louder.

'Where?' Then he realized that Lucas was walking through the back, past the pool, to the cooler. 'You can't,' he said. 'She'll die in there.'

'Not if we use a chain lock on it.' Lucas seemed sad and concerned, and Ike felt Sissy's body grow heavier in his arms.

'No,' she moaned. 'Bastard, fucking bastard. He's going to kill me.'

After Ike got her in there and locked the door, he felt a tightness in his chest. This reminded him of the Bleeds the Weasel used to give them, when he punished the whole camp for something one person did.

'I don't know,' he told Lucas.

'I have an idea,' Lucas said. 'Everybody is pretty hungry, and we haven't even had dinner. What if you go pick up pizza? Bring extras too. Everyone can eat as much as they want tonight.'

Ike did what he said, but for once he had lost his appetite. All night long, even after Jessica and Wyatt got back safe, while Ike scrunched up on the ground in his tent and made sure no one bothered Katherine up in his quarters, he heard or maybe imagined Sissy's screams in his head. *Bastard. Fucking bastard. He's going to kill me.*

Ike could not sleep that night, even though he had left her room to breathe in the cooler. Something had changed, something that could not be undone. They – he and Lucas – had damaged one of their own members.

'Ike. Are you down there?'

He jumped up so fast that he stumbled up the stairs.

'You need anything, Katherine?'

She poked her head out of the door of his quarters. Her hair was down and curly, and she looked afraid. 'Why is she screaming, Ike?'

'She hates being locked in. That's what the Weasel did to her.'

'Let her out.'

'I can't.'

'Of course you can,' she said. 'You put her in.'

Her voice had that tone of reason his granny's always had.

'I'm not sure.'

'You have to, Ike. It's not her fault she's going through this. Think how you'd feel if someone did that to you.'

'If he found out, it would be the end of our friendship. The end of everything.'

'You're stronger than he is,' Katherine said. 'Don't be afraid of him.'

'I'm not afraid.' But he felt his voice tremble. 'Get some sleep, Katherine.' He went back to his tent.

TWENTY-ONE

They gathered the next morning in the kitchen, and the rumors buzzed through the room. Sissy was gone. She had escaped, run away. The coffee brewed, the eggs and bacon solidified on the cast-iron pans, and Sissy's disappearance was all they could discuss.

As Kit had listened to her muffled shrieks all night, she had fought with herself about whether or not she should risk trying to rescue the girl. Twice, she had stepped outside and put a foot on the ladder. Both times, she glimpsed Ike standing outside his tent. Now, they couldn't just sit around and discuss Sissy over breakfast. They had to start looking.

In his down jacket, with his hair perfectly gelled and his posture both casual and erect, Lucas looked so innocent that Kit felt a chill. He cleared his throat, stood in front of the wood stove, and faced them. In that moment, Kit glimpsed the blank slate of his face before he selected the appropriate emotion.

'She will find her way back here.' He spoke slowly, his eyes wide. 'She loves us.'

They sat on stools, benches, and rugs in the kitchen, the only light coming from the stove fire Lucas and Ike had built. Ike sat on the hassock, Kit on the floor beside him. At the stove, her hand clutching the battered coffee pot, Jessica sobbed quietly. Kit wanted to go to her, but she didn't dare show any emotion for the girl.

'It's not as if Sissy's dead or anything,' Lucas said in the voice of a child.

Wyatt got up from the floor and joined Jessica. 'She screamed most of the night.' He grimaced. 'I can still hear her.'

'So can I.' Jessica wiped her eyes. 'Like an animal. I'll never forget it.'

'We shouldn't have asked her to join us here,' Lucas said. 'We knew how damaged she was even back then. It's the Weasel's fault.'

'Damned Weasel.' Wyatt crossed the room and tossed the dart at the photo. It landed between Weaver's eyes.

The others broke into applause.

'Doctor Weasel's the one who drugged her,' Lucas said softly. 'He needs to pay for that and everything else he's done to us.'

'Wait.' Kit finally found her voice. 'Sissy probably hasn't gotten that far. We need to look for her.'

'No one can find anything in the fog,' Lucas said. 'Isn't that right, Ike?'

Kit nudged Ike. 'What would it hurt?'

'We couldn't find her,' Lucas said. 'I just tried to explain that.'

'I don't know.' Ike's expression was tormented, and he struggled to speak. 'A lot of things out there.'

'Just one more reason to go looking for her.' Kit got up and went to where Lucas stood before the stove. 'If we go together, we'll be safe.'

'No one's safe out here,' Lucas said. 'We can't risk everyone's wellbeing because of one person's mistake.'

'Mistake?' Kit faced his bland expression and realized she hadn't been wrong. She really was dealing with a sociopath, one who might have already harmed Sissy. 'You knew she was terrified of that cooler, and yet you locked her in there.'

'Actually, it was your friend Ike who did that.'

'At your direction.' She turned to the others. 'Sissy could die out there. Do you really want to be responsible for that?'

'She could die if we don't risk our lives,' Lucas said. 'She's the one who chose to defy us. I say she's on her own. Once she finds out what that's like, she'll come back.'

'Katherine's right.' Jessica pulled her cap down over her hair. 'I vote that we go looking for her.'

'Me too,' Wyatt said.

'I didn't realize we were taking a vote.' Lucas stroked his chin in the same way Kit had seen Weaver do. 'I thought we agreed that the risk is too great to attempt it.'

'The risk is too great if we don't,' Kit said. 'If Sissy dies or is killed, even injured, do you want the attention it's going to bring to this compound?'

'I see your point.' He walked across the room toward the dartboard. 'If it hadn't been for him, we wouldn't have to deal with this.'

'This isn't about him right now,' Kit said, unable to control her voice. 'It's about trying to save that girl.'

'In that case, how about this?' He rubbed his hands together as if he had come up with the perfect solution. 'Let those of you who feel compelled to do so go looking for Sissy. Those who agree with me that the risk is too great, you stay here with me and the rest of us.'

'Jessica,' Kit said. 'Are you with me?'

She nodded. 'I'm sorry, Lucas, but I can't just leave Sissy out there.'

'Who else?' Kit asked. No one moved. Wyatt stared at the ground. Ike and Lucas exchanged glances. 'No one?' Kit asked. 'Fine. Let's go, Jessica.'

'Wait.' Ike rose to his feet. 'Your ankle.'

'No,' Lucas said. 'She has free will. They both do.'

Kit left before they could discuss it. Jessica sprinted ahead of her. The air outside felt frozen, the way the basement had. Kit limped to the cooler. The door stood open. Sissy hadn't made the escape on her own. Straight behind them was fallow land. No sign of anyone. Kit wanted to head there anyway but then turned to her right, toward the road that led to the farm of the woman Lucas had tried to make Kit kill. She choked back tears. That was what he had hoped would result from the fire. He wanted Sissy dead too. At the very least, he wanted to punish her because, in spite of his words, it wasn't the group she was defying. It was Lucas himself.

'Where would you go if you were trying to get out of this place?' Kit asked Jessica.

'That way.' She pointed in the direction of the freeway several miles away. 'That's where Sissy would head. I can't believe Wyatt and Theo didn't have the balls to stand up to Lucas.'

With Jessica's help, she might find Sissy and make it to the Mexican restaurant. After that, she would call for help, and that would be the end of Lucas's compound.

'I'm sure Ike will come,' Kit said. 'Do you mind if I hang on to you? My ankle is killing me.'

Jessica offered her arm. 'He won't come. None of them will.'

They made it to the road, and Kit tried to ignore the shooting pain that now traveled up her leg. She could take care of that once she was out of here. 'What are they afraid of?'

'It's not fear,' Jessica said. 'And don't kid yourself. Ike isn't going to help us.'

'I think he will.'

She shook her head. 'He's not very bright. At the camp where we met, Lucas was the smart one, and Ike was the strong one. Brute strength. That's the only reason he's here.'

'But it's not all he is,' Kit said. 'People aren't just one thing. Ike's smart. He just doesn't know it. His mother beat and abandoned him. That's why he ended up at the camp.'

Jessica stopped. 'Ike never talks about his mother.'

'What about you?' Kit asked as they made their way along the edge of the single-lane road. 'How did you end up there?'

'Kind of similar to Ike.' Her voice trailed off. Jessica stopped and covered her face with her hands as if trying to drive away an image in her brain.

'What do you mean?' Kit was stunned. If this were true, Richard had no idea. It might even explain why Sarah had kept Jessica away from him. 'Your mom harmed you?'

'Doesn't matter now.' She pointed toward a haze of lights. 'Freeway's not that far from here. I'll bet Sissy got picked up by a motorist.'

'No, please,' Kit said. 'Tell me what happened to you.'

'You've heard the story a hundred times.'

'I haven't heard *your* story, Jessica.' She glanced toward the lights. 'Tell me while we walk.'

'I don't know. Lucas is going to be pissed.' She already looked defeated.

'You're not changing your mind, are you?' Kit asked.

'It's just that the farther away we get away from the compound, I start to remember what it was like before, back in one freaking apartment and one freaking boyfriend after another.'

'Your mother?' This was the last thing Kit would have guessed. But kids didn't run away without a reason. 'Oh, Jessica,' she said. 'I'm sorry.'

'No need for that.' She turned and faced Kit. 'And no matter what happens, I am not going back where I came from.'

'No one's trying to make you,' Kit said, hoping she didn't sound as shocked and sad and angry as she did. 'As Lucas always says, you have free will.'

'That's what he says, but I've never crossed him before. He knew Sissy was afraid of the cooler, and that's where he put her. He knows I'd rather die than go back to my selfish bitch of a mother.'

Kit still couldn't believe what she was hearing, but she didn't doubt Jessica.

'Lucas is not going to send you back,' Kit said. 'You could tell people where he is and destroy the whole operation.'

'The video he has of me would get me arrested,' Jessica told her. 'I stole from the church. It's like you setting that fire. You do anything that threatens the compound, and Lucas makes sure you're too busy defending yourself to the law to go tattling on him.'

'Why would you even want to stay here?' Kit asked.

She lifted her head and met Kit's eyes. 'Because it's better than where I was.'

'But maybe there are places better than this. Safer places.'

'How would we know where to find them?'

'Let's try. The Mexican restaurant can't be far away. That's probably where Sissy would stop.'

'You're trying to leave, aren't you?' Jessica's eyes widened, and she stepped back. 'You're trying to make me leave with you.'

'I just want you to think about your options. That's all.'

'Why do you care about my options?' she demanded. 'You'd better give me a good answer, or I'm heading back right now, and you can rot out here.'

'Because that's what you want to do anyway,' Kit said. 'You're afraid of Lucas and what you think he can do to you.'

'Believe what you want.' Jessica lifted the hood of her jacket higher and pulled it down over her cap.

'Fine,' Kit said. 'You go running back, but the next time you misbehave, ask yourself who will stand up for you.'

'Lucas will.' She turned in the direction they had come from, and Kit knew she had lost her. 'He was my first friend. The first friend in my life.'

'And you met him at the Weasel's camp?' Kit asked.

'Lucas knew I didn't belong there, but he protected me. He didn't bother me, and he didn't let anyone else come near me. One night, when I was in a terrible place, freezing and maybe even dying, he brought me a blanket.' She bit her lip, and Kit fought every impulse to tell her who she really was. But she couldn't. Jessica was too fragile.

'Back up for a minute,' Kit said. 'If you didn't belong, why were you sent there?'

'Doesn't matter now. I'm heading back to the house.'

'It does matter,' Kit told her. 'I'm not going back with you, but before you leave, please tell me the truth.'

'Tell you the truth about what?' She took on the tough persona again, and now Kit understood why. 'In a way, what we share in the group is functional insanity. I'm aware of that. It might even be what binds us. And we are bound, you know. When one of the others is hurt, I feel it. It started in the camp. When the Weasel gave one of us a Bleeds – that's a punishment – he gave the same to everyone.'

'I understand your connections,' Kit said. 'But don't you see? If you get out of here, you can help the others.'

'You're the one who doesn't see.' Jessica turned. 'Come with me or don't. I don't care either way. Free will and all.'

From not far away, Kit heard a moan as soft as the wind.

'What's that?' she asked.

'What's what?' Jessica said.

Kit heard it again, louder, and ran in the direction from where it had come. Before her, on a tree stump, partially clothed in a long gray sweatshirt and not much else, sat Sissy, her blond hair like pale feathers around her face.

'She's here,' Kit shouted to Jessica, and they both ran up to the girl. 'Come on,' Kit said. 'Get up, Sissy. We'll get you out of here.'

Sissy looked up at her, and her eyes rolled back into her head.

'Get up,' Kit said.

No response.

'Get up,' Jessica echoed, and struck Sissy across the face.

'Bitch.' Finally, she seemed to jerk to life. 'Leave me alone. Let me die.'

'You're not dying, Sissy.' Kit put out her hand. 'It's going to be OK now. We're going to leave the compound.'

She moaned. 'I want my people.'

'We'll find them,' Jessica said. 'Sissy, we're going back.'

'You can't return her to that monster,' Kit told Jessica.

'She's too sick to risk it.' Jessica held out her arm, and Sissy grabbed it.

'I want Theo,' she said.

'He's back at the compound,' Jessica said in a gentle voice. 'Let's go back. We can talk about this later.' She glanced over at Kit. 'It's the only way.'

'Good luck, then.' Kit turned and started in the other direction.

A few steps, and her ankle turned. Pain shot through her, and she almost went down.

Jessica stopped and looked back at her, and for a moment Kit thought she was going to leave her there. 'Come on,' Jessica finally said. 'There's only one place we're going this morning, and that's the closest one.'

They walked slowly, Sissy without a word, Jessica humming as if as much for her own comfort as theirs.

Most of the compound members had stepped outside for their arrival.

Ike ran forward.

'I'm so sorry, Sissy. I was going to come looking for you if you didn't get back this morning.'

Sissy looked back at Kit and pleaded with her eyes.

'She needs some time alone,' Kit said.

'Sissy.' Lucas headed from the front door, an expression of joy pasted to his face. 'She was lost and has been found. All has been forgiven.'

Sissy walked past him, into the living room. They all followed. Then they watched as she dug into the broken cake box and scraped a few remaining pieces into her mouth.

Lucas tried to approach her again, but she pulled away.

'Tell us,' he asked her. 'What happened to you?'

She shook her head and white-blond curls fell over her eyes.

'Please speak to us.' His voice held that little-boy appeal Kit was sure Sissy heard.

But no. The girl didn't even look up. It was as if she could no longer hear, no longer speak. Maybe both.

TWENTY-TWO

That night, after watching Sissy act so strangely, Ike couldn't settle down. They had come here so they wouldn't be hurt any longer, yet Sissy had been harmed and could have been killed. Lucas seemed to have forgotten about it as he moved around the kitchen. He had sent Wyatt, Theo, and a couple of the other guys out for more pizza because it was clear Sissy wouldn't be able to cook for them. For the first time since they had lived here together, everyone would have enough to eat.

Theo acted as if he didn't even remember what he had done in the shower with Sissy, but that was his way. Ike knew better.

At the counter, Lucas removed a shotgun shell from the bottom of the stack and put it on top.

'Come on, Ike,' he said. 'Play Jenga with me.'

Ike's stomach rumbled. He didn't have the coordination for it tonight. Not the mental strength either. 'I heard that some guy built one more than forty levels.'

'I'm not asking about history, friend,' Lucas said. 'I asked if you wanted to play.'

He was wearing a new jacket, a bulky khaki that seemed to pull him closer to the ground.

Ike stared at the shells and their uncertain structure. It said so much about this place, more than he wanted to deal with right now. 'That guy was playing the real game,' he said. 'He wasn't using shotgun shells.'

'It appears you're avoiding my invitation.' Lucas turned away from the counter and went to his favorite lawn chair by the stove. 'Come sit, Ike. We need to talk.' He patted the hassock.

'What's up?' Ike settled on the floor beside the broken-down hassock the way he had earlier when they were trying to figure out what to do about Sissy.

He still felt bad that he had let the two girls go out there alone. That's not the way a man was supposed to act, not what his dad would have done.

'What happened today divided our group in a way I thought nothing ever could,' Lucas said. 'That's what the Weasel tried to do.'

'I know.' Ike looked toward the wood stove and tried to shut the Weasel's face out of his mind.

'Remember the Bleeds he gave us? You were late one day, and we all had to decide how the group would be punished.'

Ike stared down at his shoes. One of the laces looked loose. He tightened it until he could feel the stretch across his foot, and then he re-tied the other one for good measure.

'You guys decided that we'd all have to get up at four thirty the next morning,' he told Lucas. 'Weasel thought the only way he could make us feel anything or force us to care about each other was through pain.'

'That's quite perceptive, Ike. And you know it's why we had to get away from him. He tried to kill Wyatt.'

'No, Lucas. *We* tried to kill Wyatt.' Ike closed his mind and saw the fire in the cage that left those burns Wyatt – and he – still had today.

'We were children – innocents.' Lucas leaned forward. 'The Weasel let it be known that the only way the camp would be shut down was if someone died. Wyatt was the smallest.'

'The weakest,' Ike corrected him. 'You were the smallest.'

'I was also younger than the rest of you.' Lucas shot up from the chair. 'What I know now, though, is that the Weasel can't just run free while we're all still cowering here.'

'How can we stop him?' Ike asked. 'He's the one with our records, the one who can tell all the things we did before and during that camp.'

'He'd go to jail for what he did to us.' Lucas marched back to the counter and struggled with a few shell casings. Then he walked back and stood above Ike. 'You opened the door to the cooler for Sissy to escape last night, didn't you?'

Ike felt sweat break out along his forehead. 'What makes you think that?'

'Don't lie to me, Ike. I'm not judging, just pointing out what I know. You let her out the same way you broke Wyatt out of the Weasel's cage that night after Jessica screamed and got all of the kids out there.' He dropped his gaze to Ike's gloves.

'I'm glad they both got a second chance.' Ike's jumpy nerves kept him from saying more.

Just then, Katherine and Jessica came into the kitchen with Sissy between them. One of them had smoothed down Sissy's hair and tucked it behind her ears, yet she still looked blank-faced and terrified. Katherine had pulled up her own frizzy curls into a ponytail. Jessica, as usual, had hidden most of her face with a knit cap.

'Sissy needs a place to sleep tonight,' Katherine told Lucas.

'She has to bunk with the others,' he said in a voice too sweet for Ike to believe. 'I'll make sure they look out for her.'

'You're not hearing what I'm trying to tell you.' Katherine's voice broke. 'Sissy needs to be with us, Jessica and me. We need to be together.'

'So you're saying you'd like the same quarters?' Lucas asked. 'There's the shed in back, but we can't start repairs on it until next spring.'

'We need a place where she'll be safe,' Katherine told him. 'She isn't herself, and once she wakes up, we've got to be there for her.'

'Only one place I can think of that will meet that many demands.' Lucas glanced over at the rug covering the basement door. 'It's pretty cold, but I'll make sure you have quilts.'

'No way.'

'If it gets too bad, you can take breaks up here,' he said.

'I'm not going down there.' Katherine seemed to shudder.

'Sorry, then.' Lucas shrugged. 'I thought you wanted a place where you three women could spend the night. This isn't a resort hotel, and as much as I'd like to help you . . .' His voice trailed off.

Sissy swallowed hard, but she didn't make a sound.

'They can stay in my quarters,' Ike blurted out.

'Great idea,' Jessica said. 'I'll get some quilts.'

She headed down the hall, and Lucas stepped back as if as much in shock as Sissy. Then, as if he had instantly recovered, he said, 'Ah, yes, the noble treehouse. Are you girls up for that?'

'It's our best shot for tonight.' Jessica stopped in the hall and looked back at Katherine. They both glanced at Sissy, who stared straight ahead without speaking.

'You're right,' Katherine told Jessica. 'Ike, can we really stay there?'

'We'll need to help Sissy up the ladder,' he said.

'Do you think that's a good idea?' Lucas asked. 'Katherine's limp seems to be getting worse.'

'It will be fine,' she said. 'I just put too much pressure on it when we were looking for Sissy this morning.'

'And if this one should walk in her sleep or even attempt to jump . . .'

Sissy jerked around and glared at him. Katherine put her arm through Sissy's and squeezed her hand.

'She wouldn't do that,' Katherine said. 'Besides, she's exhausted, and the sooner we get her up there, the better. Jessica and I already decided to take turns sleeping.'

'Is that all right with you, Sissy?' Lucas moved closer and lowered his voice. 'Will you feel safe enough to spend the night in Ike's quarters with these two girls?'

She drew back against Katherine.

'Considering where she spent last night, I'm sure she's just fine with this arrangement,' Katherine snapped back.

That wasn't smart. Ike would have to look out for Katherine now too. Lucas never forgot an insult.

'Thanks for supporting Sissy,' Lucas told her in that voice he must have pulled up from his childhood. 'If you'll take responsibility for her tonight, I'll be comfortable putting her in your care.'

'I took responsibility once I left your kitchen and went looking for her,' Katherine said. 'That's not going to change.'

His cheeks grew rosy, and Ike guessed it wasn't from the heat of the fire this time.

'I'm going to take the girls up now,' he said.

'I'll wait for you here,' Lucas told him. 'Oh, Katherine.' He nodded toward the stacked towers of shells. 'Do you like to play Jenga?'

'Not really. Besides, I need to get Sissy out of here and to bed.'

Ike stared at her and thought, *Shut up, Katherine.*

Lucas turned to study her as well. 'Just out of curiosity, what do you have against the game?'

'It's all right for kids,' she said, 'but before you make the first move, you know you'll destroy whatever you build. How stupid is that?'

'As stupid as life, maybe?' He walked over and extracted a shell from near the bottom. 'You can also look at it as extending life.'

'Or playing God.' She shot Ike a look that said they needed to get going. 'Come on, Sissy,' she said.

Ike felt bad for Sissy. More than cold, more than tired, she looked as if she were disappearing little by little, as if she needed to distance herself from them, from life, any way she could.

Ike knew that feeling. He had left it behind at the Weasel's camp. He hated that it had followed them here and tried to take Sissy. He wouldn't let it, though. He and Katherine – Jessica too – they would help bring Sissy back to them.

Just to give Lucas a little reminder that he shouldn't push Katherine around, Ike walked up to him at the counter, pulled himself into his tallest self, and looked down. 'I'll be back as soon as they're settled,' he said.

Lucas glanced up at Ike and then down at his own boots. 'Do that,' he said. 'I think we have some cookies around here somewhere.'

Helping Katherine and Sissy up the ladder was a slow process. Ike went first with the two girls, and Jessica followed behind in case anyone slipped. He couldn't help thinking about how his granny would be praying for him if he told her he had three women in his bed. Only his bed was a sleeping-bag-covered floor in a carpeted treehouse. And not one of these women belonged to him. He could protect them, though. And he would.

He made sure they were as safe as they could be. If Sissy didn't get better by tomorrow, they would have to consider other options. Ike was the only one who knew that Lucas hid the one working phone in the foil-covered box in the basement. If worse came to worst, he'd liberate that phone and get help for Sissy.

He set up his tent below again and made it ready for another night in the uncertain weather. In spite of the dropping temperature, Ike felt he had given these women their best chances, if only for one night.

Katherine sat on his sleeping bag next to Jessica, both of them with blankets covering their laps, both of them wide awake. Actually, the thing was big enough for an elephant or two. Ike had always liked plenty of room. Sissy curled up on the smaller bag beside them, two quilts over her, sleeping soundly, as she had the moment she had settled into the nest of covers.

'Please don't go far,' Katherine said, as if sensing what he was about to do.

'I'll be back as soon as I can.'

'Please,' she said. 'You know what he did to Sissy last night. I don't want to be up here alone with no way of getting help.'

'I understand, but I have to go talk to him now. I promised I'd be back.'

He left them, hurried down the ladder, and went into the house. Lucas would try to distract him with a cookie, maybe part of a leftover enchilada that he'd hidden from them somewhere, but, regardless of how hungry he was, Ike wasn't about to act like some slobbering idiot. Once he realized Lucas was giving the stolen roses off that cake to Jessica, he didn't care if he ever again ate the sweets they brought into this place.

When he walked into the house, he smelled the sugary scent of coconut. His favorite. He wondered if Lucas, in all of his spying ways, had somehow found out about the coconut cream pies Ike's granny made every summer. No, that was impossible even for Lucas, wasn't it? Still, Ike wasn't going to touch whatever treat had filled the room with its scent.

Lucas had set an open box on the tile counter beside his Jenga game.

He turned when Ike walked in. 'You must be feeling pretty good about yourself,' he said. 'About those girls, I mean.'

'It's the best I could offer them, and I need to get back.'

'I'm sure they're sleeping safely.' He grinned. 'It's kind of you, although we all know Sissy needs more help than anyone can give her.'

'She might be OK,' Ike said.

'Time will tell. Want a cookie? Wyatt liberated them from an elementary school in town.'

Wyatt hated liberating things, so that was probably another test, another video for the files. Still, Ike's mouth watered. 'Maybe later,' he said.

'That makes more for me.' Lucas took one from the box and bit into it. 'Almond Joy bars. They're good.'

'I need to go now.' Ike reminded himself that they were only cookies, as meaningless as the Jenga game.

'You'll feel better now that you've helped Sissy – knowing it was your fault she escaped and lost her mind, I mean.'

'Don't, Lucas,' he said. 'I'm tired, and I'm not looking forward to sleeping in that fucking tent again.'

Lucas flinched at the word. 'Your choice. Sit down, please.' He patted the battered hassock. 'We need to figure out how we're going to get the Weasel.'

'Let's discuss it tomorrow,' Ike said.

'I asked you to sit down.' Ike nodded toward the hassock. 'We need to make some decisions now that Sissy is in such a bad place. The Weasel needs to be punished, and you and I need to figure out how right now.'

'We can figure out anything you like,' Ike said, 'after I'm sure the girls are safe.'

'Got it.' Lucas headed to the kitchen sink and the bullet game again. Ike followed.

'Glad to hear that,' he said, 'because this is how it is, Lucas.'

'I'm impressed.' He glanced over his shoulder with that smile that seemed both innocent and sneaky. 'And do tell me how it is, Ike.'

'Let's start with this.' Ike walked up to him and stepped about a foot away. 'That ragged piece of shit you call a hassock is too small for someone my size.'

'Indeed?' Lucas frowned at the threadbare thing.

'Try it sometime,' Ike said. 'I'll never sit on it again. I'm never driving blindfolded again either, and I'm never going to help burn up some poor old lady's house just because you don't like her.'

'Got it.' Lucas lapsed into Weasel speak once more. 'We do need to make a plan, friend. When might that happen?'

'I'm not sure.' Ike breathed in the freshest air he could remember. 'Right now, I need to check on the girls, and you need to stop talking to me like I'm an idiot.'

'Whatever floats your boat, my friend.' He said it in the same tone the Weasel had, the same way, word for word, with the same bland smile. His idea of a joke.

Ike didn't bother responding.

TWENTY-THREE

K it woke up terrified. She had to get out of here. Ike's quiet, glowing heater had warmed their small space. For a moment, she was grateful for that alone. Heat. She glanced over at Jessica, still asleep, her hair smashed to her head. At that angle, she resembled Richard. Kit turned toward Sissy, who seemed too tiny and too vulnerable on her sleeping bag.

She had almost gotten Jessica to leave with her yesterday, but the girl was still too tied to this place or just too afraid to return home. Once she and Jessica had talked out there on the road, Kit realized that John Paul was right. Kit had come here to try to reunite Jessica with her mother and with Richard. If Jessica had told her the truth, Sarah didn't deserve her. That would mean all this was for nothing. But maybe not. Richard did want Jessica; he wanted a family as much as – maybe more than – he wanted Kit.

And she cared about these kids now – Jessica and Ike especially. Whatever they did after here was up to them. But one way or another, she had to help them break free of Lucas.

She tried to sit up quietly, but Jessica stirred and sat as well. Heads propped against the back wall, they said nothing for a moment.

Finally, Kit whispered, 'She looks better.'

'She couldn't have looked any worse,' Jessica whispered back, 'unless she was dead.'

'We've got to get her out of here, to a hospital.'

'How?' Jessica asked. She reached around beside her, found her cap, and pulled it over her head. 'Lucas has videos of all of us breaking the law. I told you that.'

'Don't you have any of him?' Kit asked.

She shook her head on the pillows she had propped against the wall. 'Lucas never breaks the law. He doesn't smoke, drink, or swear.'

'Yet he did that.' Kit nodded toward Sissy's twisted body. 'She can't stay conscious. If we get her out of here, we might save her life, and we can expose Lucas.'

'We can't prove he had anything to do with it. Besides, we'd expose ourselves too.'

'Are the lives we left behind worse than what's going on right here?' Kit asked. 'Because maybe there's someone – an old friend or family member – who can help us.'

'Not my family member.' Jessica pulled the fake patchwork quilt up to her chin. 'The woman wanted me dead.'

'Your mother?' Again, Kit tried to remember Sarah at the farmers' market and the way she had seemed to care about her daughter. It had all been a lie.

Jessica nodded. 'She sent me to that camp knowing I didn't need to be there. And only so she could get the money and keep her new boyfriend from hitting on me any time he felt like it.'

'That can't be right,' Kit said. 'The doctor would have screened you out at some point when he found that you weren't like the others.'

'He was happy to have me.' She sank down into the sleeping bag. 'That was the big secret. I wasn't emotionally disturbed, or whatever they called it, like the rest of them. I was just screwed-up because my mother wanted to get rid of me. Remember, the shrink had gotten a grant for this study. He had no time to decide how crazy I was.'

'Weaver let you in that camp without any medical records?'

Jessica pulled back as if she had been struck. 'What did you just call him?'

Heat flooded Kit's face, and she realized this was the first time she had spoken his name.

'Isn't he the guy on the dartboard?' she asked.

Jessica squinted at Kit in the early light as if trying to see what she was hiding.

'You know he is.'

Kit scrambled for an answer. 'Well, his name is right there. Doctor Weaver. Can't remember the first name.'

'Yes, his name is there.' Jessica didn't seem convinced. 'In very small type. We always call him the Weasel.'

'I can see why you named him that. He does have that ferret vibe going on.'

Jessica's smile was guarded.

'And he let you in without seeing your records?'

'I didn't have records,' she said. 'I had nothing but a dead father, an uncle who wanted nothing to do with me, and that woman I refuse to call my mother. She sent me to get rid of me and to get whatever kind of stipend she could.'

Kit wanted to tell Jessica that her uncle did want her and always had, but she couldn't, not now. 'You must have told the Weasel that you didn't belong there,' she said. 'You did, didn't you?'

She shook her head.

'But why?'

'Because, in a way, I felt that I *did* belong there. It might have been the first time I'd ever belonged anywhere.'

Kit knew she was telling the truth, and she suddenly understood the reason Sarah had been so hesitant when Richard asked Kit to find Jessica. Sarah didn't want Jessica found, and she never had.

'But Lucas can't be any better. He's a monster.'

'I hadn't counted on that.' Jessica spoke softly, even though no one but Sissy could hear them, and she still slept fitfully. 'He was so young before, so smart. He had this great idea and, after his dad died, the money to pull it off.'

'Do you have a working phone?' Kit asked.

'Not allowed. You know that.'

'Could you talk to Ike?'

She stretched her legs into the sleeping bag and smiled. 'He hates me. Besides, he's an idiot.'

'You two are like squabbling siblings,' she said. By now, you've got to know how Lucas operates. Ike might not fit your definition of smart, but he wants to do the right thing, and he cares about what happens to you. He let us stay here last night when Lucas wanted to shove us into that basement. Talk to him, please.'

Jessica seemed to think it over. 'I don't think it's a good idea for me to approach him.'

'Why not?' Kit demanded. 'It's our only chance.'

'If Ike tells Lucas, you realize we could both end up in that cooler, don't you? Worse, maybe.'

'Ike knows that too. He was shocked when he saw what happened to her.' She glanced at Sissy. 'Please talk to him, Jessica. I know he'll help us.'

'Then why don't you?' Jessica asked.

'I've tried, but I wasn't around from the beginning the way you all were. Coming from you, it will make a difference.'

Jessica rose from the sleeping bag. 'You're asking me to put everything on the line.'

'I'm putting everything on the line too.' Kit got up as well. 'It's called escalation. If we don't get away from here right now, the games are going to involve more than darts, shell casings, and a night in the cooler.'

'Escalation?' she asked. 'What are you really doing here, Katherine?'

'Trying to stay alive. The same as you are. Come on. Let's hurry before Sissy wakes up.'

'There's only one way I'll talk to Ike,' Jessica said, 'and that's for you to come with me when I do it. That way, you're risking as much as I am.'

'I'm fine with that.' She wasn't fine with it, though. Jessica would stand a better chance alone, but she still seemed suspicious of Kit. 'Let's go.'

Although she was able to make her way down the ladder, she knew the constant use of her ankle had made it worse. Only a sprain. She needed to hope it was only a sprain, nothing worse.

Jessica beside her, Kit limped toward the house and stopped before they reached the porch.

'Lucas is probably in there. We've got to figure out a way to get Ike alone.'

Ike came around from behind them. 'Get me alone? Why?'

Jessica gasped, and Kit stifled a scream.

'What are you doing out here?' she demanded.

'How soon you forget. My job was to look over you all last night.' He glanced up at the treehouse. 'How's Sissy?'

'Still sleeping,' Kit said, 'but she seems worse than before. She keeps passing out. Jessica and I need to talk to you.'

'Might as well go in and discuss it with the group.'

'You know better than that,' Kit told him. 'What's going on here is wrong.'

'We'll work it out.' He squinted toward the house.

'Lucas has changed,' Jessica said, and glanced around nervously as if someone were overhearing the conversation. 'Ike, we've got to leave here.'

'Lucas has other ideas.' Ike motioned to where the truck had been parked the night before. 'Angel's finally here, but Lucas sent Wyatt to pick her up. Picking up people is my job.'

'He's trying to get rid of you,' Kit said. 'I told you that when he made us go out in the fog.'

'And I told you it was a test.'

'What about what happened to Sissy? Was that a test too?'

'Technically, she was breaking the rules,' he said.

'But she didn't know what she was doing. I thought you believed in free will.'

'We do,' he said. 'I talked to Lucas last night. That's the best I can do.'

'He's not going to listen,' Kit said. 'He thinks you crossed him, that you're getting too much power.'

He stared down at his spotless shoes, meticulous like everything else about him. 'It's not the first time I crossed him. We always work it out.'

'You want to believe that, but you know better,' she said. 'You all shared a vision of what this place would be like, and it probably got you through some hard times, but it's not what you thought it would be like because he isn't what you thought he was.'

'She's right,' Jessica said slowly. 'Lucas isn't on our side any more – if he ever was. We need to leave before he does something really crazy.'

'He already has,' Kit said. 'What are you waiting for?'

'Transportation, for one thing. We won't get far on foot.'

She looked at the pocked road leading from the place and knew they would not make it as far as the restaurant without a vehicle – any vehicle.

'What about that?' She pointed at the side yard.

'The golf cart?'

'It's better than nothing, and we don't have that far to go.'

Ike stared at the dim shape through the wisps of white. 'It's about as secure as a skateboard.'

'There are only three of us,' she said. 'We'll be OK.'

He took a step toward it. 'What about Sissy? We can't leave her like this.'

'We'll come back for her,' Kit said.

Ike looked at the empty parking place in front of the house. 'Lucas has videos,' he said. 'All of us doing something. He calls them his files.'

'The Weasel had files too,' Kit reminded him. 'But if he uses them, he exposes himself. The same is true of Lucas. Hurry, you two. We need to leave before Wyatt gets back.'

'Why not wait?' Jessica stepped away from them. 'Wyatt doesn't like it here either.'

'He'll like it better now that he's driving my truck,' Ike said. 'Let's come up with a plan. We can't just run until we know where we're going.'

'I have some friends who could help us,' Kit said. 'One of them is a former cop. Another one has a true-crime blog and radio show.'

'Why didn't these high-up friends help you before?' Ike asked.

'I don't know.' She scrambled for an answer. 'Maybe I was too ashamed to admit I needed help.'

'And now these friends will still help you? Don't believe it, and don't believe they will help *us*.'

'Trust me,' Kit said. 'I promise I won't let you down. You know you hate it here, Ike. And the next crazy scheme is going to be even worse than locking Sissy in that cooler.'

Just then, the pickup pulled into the gravel drive before the house. Wyatt drove, a woman beside him.

'It's Angel,' Ike said. 'She's here.'

The pickup door opened, and a large girl in a brown jacket a couple of sizes too small for her jumped from the truck. She had broad shoulders, thick red hair, shaved on one side, three bird tattoos on her neck, and an attitude Kit could feel from where she stood.

The redhead walked up to her, and Kit wanted only to run. But she couldn't go anywhere, could only hope the girl didn't recognize her. That was ridiculous – of course she did.

The smallest tattoo rested just beneath the redhead's earlobe. No, not birds. Bats. The girl from the shelter. The one who took her boots. Their eyes met, and Kit knew that Angel recognized her.

'What are you doing here?' she demanded.

'I don't have to answer to you,' Kit said.

Lucas and Theo drifted outside.

'Angel.' Lucas came out on the porch and put out both hands. 'Welcome. Now that you're here, we're all together again.'

'What about *her*?' Angel gave Kit the same predatory look she had in the shelter. 'She's not one of us.'

'She is now,' Lucas said sweetly. 'You two play nice.'

'That might be difficult,' Kit said. 'Considering that this girl stole the boots right off my feet at the Sacramento shelter.'

Angel laughed. 'Wish they'd fit me. Turns out I got a good price for them, though. I only wish I knew you were heading here. I would've hitched a ride.'

'Same here.' Kit backed up closer to Ike, knowing she had missed her only chance to talk him into leaving. 'When we met, I didn't know where I was going.'

'Oh, no?' The girl started for the front door. Ike opened it for her, and she turned before going in. 'All you wanted at that shelter was to find Jessica. Looks like you found her after all.'

All eyes turned on Kit.

'It wasn't this Jessica I was looking for. I never found my friend.'

Nobody spoke.

Finally, Lucas went to the top step and looked out at them as if picturing himself a rock star greeting his fans. 'Let's forget the disagreements for now,' he told them. 'That would make the Weasel too happy. Come inside, and let's plan how to finally get ourselves some good, old-fashioned vengeance.'

TWENTY-FOUR

The sign in the arch-shaped window of Richard McCarthy's animal hospital said *Closed*. John Paul knew he should have called first, but he had driven here on impulse. Part of the reason he had decided to was regret that he had ended his last meeting with Kit Doyle's ex by losing his temper. The rest of the reason was that he knew the poor bastard must be out of his mind with worry.

In the parking lot, he called the office, expecting voice mail to pick up. Instead, McCarthy answered in a harsh, scared voice. 'Hang on,' he said, and John Paul heard the front door rattle. 'I'll be right out.'

The door opened, and McCarthy stepped outside. Although he looked professional enough in his white coat over jeans, his movements were overly careful, like a man taking every precaution to keep from falling apart.

He met John Paul on the sidewalk and stopped abruptly. 'Is she OK?'

'I don't know.' John Paul headed down the walk, unable to stand in one place. At this time of day, the parking lot was full, and shoppers pushed carts in and out of the supermarket at the end of the center. 'We did find someone – a witness.'

'Someone saw Kit?' McCarthy motioned past the supermarket to a park-like area. He must need to move too. That's what not knowing could do to you. It could make doing nothing, even just standing still, feel like giving up.

'The witness who came forward saw somebody in Fowler who matches Ms Doyle's description,' John Paul said.

'God, where?'

'It's bizarre.' John Paul studied McCarthy's fixed expression, trying to guess how much he could handle. 'There was a fire.' No other way to say it.

Other than his clenched fist, McCarthy registered no emotion. 'Was Kit hurt?'

'Apparently not.' They walked past a park bench, and the smoke from a smoldering cigarette on the sidewalk burned John Paul's nostrils. 'The witness was almost killed. She ran a small produce stand that she and her late husband had operated for years. Some kids in the area were harassing her, stealing fruit, trashing her displays, that kind of thing.'

'Kids.' McCarthy managed to keep the anger from his voice, but he couldn't hide the flush that spread over his cheeks. 'Did they set the fire?'

'That's what the witness says.'

'And Kit? How was she involved? Was she hurt? Where is she?'

'Hang on,' John Paul told him. 'The witness is barely coherent. They burned her place down with her in it. Ms Doyle got her out.'

McCarthy sank down on the park bench. 'So Kit's alive? For sure?'

'As of Wednesday.' John Paul sat at the end of the bench. 'She left with the kids in an old truck. Firefighters arriving on the scene saw them.'

'But if the kids set the fire, and Kit rescued the woman, why would she leave with them?' he asked.

'I'm just telling you what happened. That's all I know.'

'And my niece?' he asked. 'Jessica?'

'The witness couldn't identify any of the others. Just a bunch of kids, she said.'

They sat there like that for a moment, McCarthy clearly trying to make sense of what he had just learned, and John Paul telling himself he had done the right thing to come here.

'What's going to happen next?' McCarthy finally asked.

'I wish I knew. Farley and I are going to do a segment on it. Maybe somebody else will come forward.'

'You can't do that.' McCarthy whirled to face him. 'You could be putting Kit and Jessica in worse danger.'

'The media has already covered their disappearance,' John Paul said. 'We want to do more, go deeper, and appeal to anyone who might have seen anything out of the ordinary.'

'I'm asking you not to. Those kids are psychopaths. We already know that.'

'Then the sooner we get Kit and your niece away from them, the better.'

'I said no. It's too risky.'

'It's worth the chance,' John Paul told him. 'We don't have anything else.'

McCarthy rose from the bench and shot John Paul a look of disgust. 'You're really going to gamble with their lives, aren't you?'

You did that the day you let you ex get in the truck with that kid. John Paul didn't say it. Instead, he reminded himself that McCarthy was expressing fear more than anything else.

'Ms Doyle . . . Kit is more than our co-worker,' he said. 'She's our friend. We're going to use everything we have at our disposal, and that includes the radio segment.'

'And that's the real reason you came here today, isn't it?' McCarthy said. 'It wasn't to tell me about the witness who saw

Kit. It was to make yourself feel better about what you've already decided to do.'

'That's ridiculous.'

'It's the truth.' McCarthy started back toward his office again. Then he stopped. 'I knew Farley Black was a media whore,' he said. 'I wouldn't have guessed it of you.'

As John Paul watched him stride down the sidewalk, he tried to tell himself McCarthy was just dealing with fear. And it was true, wasn't it? He hadn't come here today because he had doubts about doing the segment.

The stench of smoke burned his nose, his eyes. John Paul stretched out his leg and crushed the cigarette butt with the toe of his shoe. Then he took out his phone and called Farley.

TWENTY-FIVE

As the others filed into the living room like children coming into school from the playground, Kit stood outside in the cold, shivering with Jessica and Ike. Part of her shivering was fear, though. Somehow, she had to explain away what Angel had just revealed: that she had been looking for Jessica.

Jessica's brown eyes radiated suspicion. She shoved her hands into the pockets of her jacket. 'It's pretty creepy that you just happened to be looking for someone named Jessica and ended up here.'

'All you and my friend have in common is a name,' Kit lied, forcing the panic from her voice. 'She doesn't look anything like you. Besides, we have more important things to discuss. Like how to get out of here.'

'It's too soon.' Ike walked in the direction of the treehouse, and they followed. 'Lucas says I always overreact, and maybe he's right. Let's wait a day or two until Sissy is better.'

'Sissy isn't going to get better if we stay here,' Kit told him. 'If we wait, she may never get better.'

'Well, until your ankle is stronger, then.'

'Jessica,' she said. 'Tell him we need to leave now.'

'Lucas will be suspicious if we don't go in with the others.' In spite of her hesitant tone, Jessica's jaw was tight and stubborn. She looked back toward the house. 'We might as well hear what he's going to say.'

They were having second thoughts. More than that, distrust seemed to be part of their DNA. The moment Angel made her revelation, they had drawn closer together and farther away from Kit.

'You heard what he said. He wants to plan revenge on the Weasel.'

'He's been talking about that since we were kids.' Ike's rigid posture made it clear he wasn't going anywhere. 'Let's not piss him off any more than we already have.'

'You go on,' Kit said.

Bad ankle or not, the day was as clear as it was going to get, and she might be able to make it to the main road alone. In spite of the fog, the weather had warmed somewhat, and she had a good chance of making it to the restaurant or maybe hitching a ride with a nearby farmer.

Jessica and Ike exchanged glances. 'Better if you come inside with us,' he told her. 'We can't plan until we hear what Lucas wants to do.'

'I don't want to go back in there,' Kit said. 'If you won't come with me, I'm going on my own. I can make it if I take my time.'

'Not a chance.' Ike towered over her on one side, Jessica only a few steps ahead of them. 'Let's go in there unified,' Ike said. 'We don't want Lucas to sense anything else, and he probably already suspects something.'

'You really think you owe him anything after he gave your driving job to Wyatt?' she asked.

'Wyatt and I go back pretty far.' Ike looked down at his gloves.

'But he's a First Year,' Kit said. 'And so is Angel. I can already see Lucas playing divide and conquer.'

'Sounds like the game you're trying to play.'

Kit pretended not to understand. Jessica was wrong to believe that this guy wasn't bright.

'It might sound that way, but it isn't.' She met his odd, mismatched gaze. 'I'm just trying to explain how it looks to me.'

'What do you think, Jessica?' His voice dropped, and Kit sensed a tenderness Jessica didn't appear to notice.

'I don't like it,' she said, 'but we've got to look united. Lucas knows what happened when the Weasel tried to turn us against each other. We all turned against him.'

'Then it's decided,' Ike said. 'Take my arm, Katherine.'

'I can walk.'

It wasn't a lie, but the pain had grown sharper and more persistent. Kit guessed that Ike knew it. He slowed down as Jessica reached the front door ahead of them and went inside.

They walked into chaos. Voices rose as the kids helped themselves to cookies and mugs of coffee from the battered pot on the wood stove. Angel, still wearing her brown jacket, so tight Kit wondered if she had obtained it the way she had Kit's boots, picked up a dart and sailed it into Weaver's photo.

Wyatt stood in the front of the room, as dark as Lucas was blond and as exaggerated as Lucas was understated. He hadn't bothered brushing his long, curly hair from his eyes, and he wore his newfound confidence the way he wore the scars on his neck.

'I almost died in that cage,' he said to the others, shoving his fingers against the scars. 'This is what the Weasel did to me. He needs to pay.'

'I agree,' Lucas said. In the light blue of his eyes, Kit couldn't see anything close to reason. 'Tell everyone what he did to you, Ike.'

'You know.' Ike glared back, his lips tight.

'Ruined your life, didn't he? Convinced your father you we're too damaged for the future in law enforcement he'd planned for you.'

'I'm not damaged, Lucas.'

'Just your garden-variety psychopath, right?'

'Weasel said sociopath, probably because he got more money to observe me. That's what he really wanted. To observe and control. When you told us that we didn't have to be controlled, that we could fight back, everything changed.'

'Except we were kids, Ike,' he said, his voice rising. 'We couldn't really fight back, not until now.'

Kit could feel the pressure in the room swell like a balloon ready to burst. Lucas, who had orchestrated it, clearly felt it too.

'Weasel treated Sissy and some of the others with drugs,' he said, unable to hide his pleasure. 'I wonder how he'd like to be treated with drugs.'

'He chained me up for biting him,' Angel said. 'I screamed, but no one could hear me out there. I wonder how he'd feel if he had to scream all night, chained to a tree.'

'Katherine?' Lucas pointed at her, and she moved closer to Ike. 'What do you think ought to happen to him?' He picked up a dart. 'Where do you think this should go?'

'I didn't know him, but from what you said, he sounds like a monster.' That was no lie. She walked to the front of the room and stood to Lucas's right side. 'I would bury that dart, though. You are all finally free. Who cares what happens to that pathetic little man now?'

'He stole our childhood,' Wyatt said from the other side of Lucas. 'He stole something we won't ever get back, no matter how far away we run.'

'Very good, Wyatt.' Lucas beamed and handed him the dart. 'Where would you bury this?'

A grin spread across Wyatt's face. 'First, I'd want him naked, chained up to one of those fucking trees maybe. Sorry, Lucas.'

'Just tell it, Wyatt. What next?'

Then I'd want all of us to come up and tell him what he did to us, and then throw a dart where he'll feel it the most.'

Lucas was sicker than she had imagined. He had engineered this conversation as carefully as he had the stacks of shells on the counter.

'Do you have a problem with retribution, Katherine?' Lucas asked softly. She had no idea he had been studying her so carefully.

'You could get caught,' she said. 'Why don't you just try to forget about him and move ahead with your lives?'

'The way Sissy did?' Lucas shook his head, and she could see him trying to conjure sadness. Every emotion he expressed seemed like a step in a dance. 'The longer we are together here, the clearer it is to me – to all of us – that we can't leave the Weasel's camp behind us until that camp is no more.'

'Can you imagine the danger involved in what you have in mind?' Kit asked him. 'Do you really want to subject everyone you claim to care about to that?'

'We're not helpless children this time,' he told her. 'How many kids do you think he's destroyed since he practiced on us those first times? He's probably really good at it by now. Probably breaks them way faster, with much less of a struggle.'

'Do you really think destroying his camp will set you free?' Kit asked him. 'What will you do next? Spend the rest of your lives in this place?'

'That was never the intent.' Lucas munched on a cookie as if in no hurry to convince anyone. 'This was our place to help each other get over what that monster did to us, a place where we wouldn't be judged and forced to conform to what some real sicko thought we should be.'

Kit glanced at the door and saw it was cracked and that light shone on the shadow of the dark rug. A slight figure stood just outside, listening.

'Who's there?' Kit called out.

The front door swung the rest of the way open. Cold air rushed in, followed by Sissy, wide-eyed and with a disoriented smile. She ran her fingers up and down in the air as if playing an invisible musical instrument.

'Let's get him,' she said, and everyone cheered. Everyone except Ike, who glanced over at Kit. Everyone except Jessica, who ran to Sissy's side, just as she collapsed to the floor.

Lucas looked stunned, and Kit wasn't sure whether or not it was an act. 'She's just one more reason,' he said. 'Just one more reason we have to stop him. Isn't that right, Wyatt?'

'Right, Lucas. Let's stop him.'

But Ike was as stunned as the rest of them, as they all moved to where Sissy sobbed on the floor.

Jessica knelt down, saying over and over, 'It will be all right.'

Kit could tell that everyone in the room knew it would never be.

'I suggest we leave first thing in the morning,' Lucas said.

'But all you have is that truck.' Everyone, even Ike, turned to look at Kit. 'Well, isn't it?' she asked.

Lucas took another bite of his cookie. 'There's a camper shell,' he said.

'And you think that truck – camper shell or not – is going to take you all the way to the Weasel's camp?'

'Us.' Lucas gave her a smile that chilled her. 'It's going to take us. No one – including you – is staying behind on this trip.'

TWENTY-SIX

All together again. Ever since Ike heard Lucas say that yesterday morning when Angel walked into their compound, he couldn't get it out of his head. All the Originals, the First Years, he meant – Angel, Wyatt, Theo, Sissy, Jessica, and Lucas, of course. They were the first ones who agreed to keep the Weasel from breaking them the way he did the other kids at the camp. Sure, Lucas returned the next year and found others, but the Originals – the First Years – they were the ones who mattered.

When it came down to it that morning, Lucas decided they should leave everyone but the First Years behind to protect the compound while they went off to settle the score with the Weasel. For a moment, standing in the yard by the truck, Ike was afraid Lucas would ask him to stay behind as well.

Finally, Lucas said, 'It's up to the Originals to get justice for ourselves and for all the kids who followed.'

'Then let's go,' Ike replied.

Lucas hesitated for just a moment and then said, 'OK, friend. Let's go.'

The First Years and Katherine took off that day, as soon as they could get the white camper shell on and settle everyone inside. The shell was like fresh frosting on a stale cake. Newer than the battered pickup, it had a tinted window in the back and shiny black knobs that attached it to the truck.

At first, they had what Ike's dad would have called a pissing match about who was going to ride in the front seat with Lucas. Then Ike pointed out that this wasn't the easiest truck to drive, and he knew Northern California better than any of them did.

That seemed to convince Lucas, only then he turned to Wyatt and said, 'You could drive it, couldn't you?'

'Sure.' Wyatt's voice shot up an octave.

'Tell you what?' Lucas said. 'Why don't you ride up in front with us, and you can take over when Ike gets tired.'

'Shouldn't one of the girls ride in front?' Ike asked. 'Sissy, maybe?'

'She can rest better in the back,' Lucas said. 'Don't worry about the logistics, Ike. I've got that covered.'

Only Katherine resisted riding in the back, but then she had resisted making this trip in the first place.

They drove off into the fog and then, once on the freeway, into the clear darkness. In a matter of hours, they encountered air so fresh Ike felt he could drink it.

Wyatt hadn't been much of a talker, and he kept his earbuds in.

'It's a long trip,' Ike told Lucas. 'Can't be easy for those in back.'

'They'll be fine.' Lucas sipped from the latte he had picked up on the way out of town.

Easy enough to do. Sure, they had money for coffee, but it was easier to just pull up in front of a coffee shop, run inside, and pull a fresh one off the counter. Employees and customers were always so friendly in those places. No one would care who took what and why. Just make another latte and call the customers by their first names, and everyone was happy, or trying to be.

'This is going to be the test for Katherine,' Lucas said.

'Why are you so focused on her? She's done everything you want her to.'

'Her attitude, for one. She needs to be the one to finish off the Weasel.'

'I don't know,' Ike said.

'I'll do it.' Wyatt grinned and tapped his toe against the case on the floorboard. 'They're my knives. A girl won't know how to do it.'

'You ever killed anyone?' Ike asked him.

Wyatt shook his head. 'Only in my dreams. A lot of people, especially the Weasel. I've killed him a thousand times.'

Lucas chuckled, and Ike said, 'I've never killed anyone either. I've beat the crap out of plenty, though, and if it comes to that, I could run one of those knives into the Weasel for all he's done to us.'

'You'll both get your chance,' Lucas told him. 'Finally, you can do anything you want to, and he won't be able to fight back or tell lies about us.'

They drove a few more miles, all of them thinking about the Weasel. Ike could feel the bastard's smirking presence in the truck. He remembered all those group sessions when they had to spill their guts, whether they wanted to or not.

'What about you, Lucas?' Ike asked.

'What about me what, friend?'

'Have you ever killed anyone? In real life, I mean, not just in your mind.'

Wyatt's eyes widened as if Ike had done something wrong. But Lucas had just asked them. No reason Ike couldn't ask back.

Lucas sat up straighter in the seat and smiled as if reliving something in his mind. 'Yes,' he said. 'One time. Any other questions?'

'Are you sorry?' Ike asked.

'No, I'm glad. You will be too once we know for sure the Weasel will never destroy another kid.'

'Right,' Ike said, but the calm expression on Lucas's face bothered him.

It was as if he knew what they were doing. But he really didn't. Katherine might have been right about him, but it was too late to worry about that now. Besides, if anyone deserved to suffer, it was Dr Melvin Weaver.

Lucas sipped his coffee slowly. Finally, he said, 'What are you going to do if you realize Katherine isn't one of us, Ike?'

'I don't think that's going to happen,' Ike said.

Lucas nodded and got a faraway look in his eyes again. 'Well, if that's the way it turns out, I think you know what we'll have to do.'

TWENTY-SEVEN

Lucas had won. Kit had no choice but to ride with the rest of them on the hard carpet of the truck bed as they headed toward Northern California and Weaver's camp. Ike had shoved in his sleeping bags, and Kit and Jessica had gathered them around Sissy, who had fallen asleep again. The trip would take more than six hours, and they had been on the road close to three.

As the bumps and vibrations of the highway numbed her body, Kit leaned back against the wall of the camper shell and closed her eyes. For a moment, she felt more like Katherine, the runaway, than Kit, who had come in search of a missing girl. Kit, the crime blogger, would not have lasted a day in that cult-like compound. Stripped of contact with the outside world and with an injured ankle, she had become dependent on any human interaction she could make.

Living this life, connecting with Jessica, Ike, even Sissy, had pulled her so far away from who she was that she had to remind herself that she had a newly found mother, people she loved, and a job to return to. Once they got to Weaver's camp, maybe sooner, she would have her chance to escape. Right now, she had to stop these kids from committing murder. That's what they thought they wanted to do, and it was the reason Lucas forced them back to this place.

She tried to tell herself that they might back out once they arrived, but she had watched Lucas expertly stir their anger. He was also blackmailing them with his video library of each of them breaking the law. In their compound of free will, he held all the power.

Jessica curled up to her right. Angel sat directly across, closest to the cab. She had zipped up the tight brown jacket, covering two of the three bat tattoos on her neck. Kit had hoped she would stay behind, but Angel was a First Year. She was also suspicious of Kit, obviously because she had been looking for Jessica, but maybe also because she was street-smart enough to recognize an imposter. Whatever the reason, she pretended to ignore Kit but always seemed to be watching her out of the corner of her eye. Theo, the long-haired kid with glasses who had been in the shower with Sissy, played some kind of card game on the carpet, dark hair hiding his eyes. In spite of the cold, the air inside was stale and Kit already felt claustrophobic.

'You asleep?' Jessica nudged her. Bundled up in one of the sleeping bags, she looked like a little girl, which in a way she was. Her eyeliner had worn off and, without it, her eyes seemed even larger.

'Not really.'

Jessica yawned. 'I'm hungry.'

Angel opened the cookie box, and the smell of coconut filled their tiny space. 'Have one,' she said. 'They aren't bad.'

'I'd rather have a hamburger.'

'I'm sure we'll stop soon,' Kit told her. 'It's going to be three or four more hours.'

'How would you know how far it is?' Angel leaned toward her. 'You were never part of our camp.'

'You think that's the only way I would know how to get to Northern California?' she asked.

'Come on, you two.' Jessica rubbed her forehead as if trying to erase their voices. 'Lucas told you to play nice.'

'She wasn't playing nice when she stole my boots,' Kit said above the noise of the truck.

'For all I know, you stole them in the first place. Where would you get the kind of money to buy something that nice?'

'Why don't you leave me alone?' Kit said. 'I haven't done anything to you.'

The truck hit a rough place, and they all scrambled to hold on.

When the road smoothed out, Angel said, 'Guess I don't like people who aren't part of the group trying to crash the party.'

'Some party.' Kit gestured around them. 'I asked Lucas to let me leave, but he wouldn't. Now, I'm stuck with you guys.'

'I asked you two to cut it out.' Jessica took a cookie, frowned at it, and offered the box to Kit, who shook her head. 'That means you too, Angel. Lucas said he wanted to bring in other kids, and Katherine's OK.'

The truck began to slow, and Kit grabbed on to the side of the camper shell. After a short bathroom stop, they purchased sodas and some gross burgers from a convenience store.

Kit's body felt so tightly tangled that when she tried to stretch, pain shot though her. When she tested her ankle, though, the sprain had dulled to an ache, and she found she could put all of her weight on it without wincing. That was one more secret she would keep from the rest of them.

Honky-tonk music filled the small store. Willie Nelson or someone trying to sound like him. No other customers were in line before the cash register. Kit thought about trying to talk to the clerk, to beg him to let her use his phone. But if she failed, she couldn't predict what Lucas and the others would do. Through the window, she could see them gathered around the truck, laughing, slapping each other on the back. Lucas handed out bags of chips and then returned for more food.

Jessica came out of the bathroom with her face washed and her eyeliner in place.

'Need to hang on to me, Katherine?'

Kit started to reply that she was fine, and then remembered that she would be safer if they didn't know how much better she was.

'Thanks.' She reached out for Jessica's arm.

Just then, Angel approached Lucas while he was paying at the counter.

'She's probably complaining,' Jessica said. 'Bitch.'

'He doesn't care what she thinks.' As if to prove her point, Lucas gave Angel a distracted smile and headed outside with Ike while she was still talking.

'Was she always this bad?' Kit asked Jessica.

'I don't remember.' She looked down at the plastic bag containing her pathetic excuse for a meal. 'We were children.'

'That's my point. You were too young, too abused, to think rationally. You can't really go through with what Lucas has planned.'

'Maybe he just wants to scare the Weasel.'

'He wouldn't come all this way for that, Jessica.'

'He might.' She glanced out through the windows at the gas tank where Ike pumped and Lucas watched. 'You don't know him.'

'That's the problem. I *do* know him.'

Jessica looked down at the burger bag again. 'I have to get this to Sissy while it's still hot.'

'And why can't Sissy get her own food?' Kit said. 'Because Lucas decided to punish her. That's why. And now she's so broken she may never heal.'

'I didn't say he was perfect. But you have to understand. He was trying to protect us, including her. Tough love.'

'Then,' Kit said, 'why did he have Sissy locked in the cooler? Why not Theo? He was in the shower with her.'

'You know why,' Jessica said. 'It was all her idea.'

'Oh, so Theo didn't have free will?'

'Maybe not at that moment.'

'Sissy led him on, you mean?' Kit squeezed Jessica's arm and stared into her eyes. 'Ever have some guy say that about you?'

Jessica seemed to understand this. Then she lifted the burger sack and said a little too quickly, 'Sissy needs to eat.'

'Hurry up, everyone,' Ike announced. 'We're heading out.'

The other kids headed for the truck. In that moment, with dim sunlight bouncing off them, Kit tried to imagine how these First-Year kids had looked and felt when their parents delivered them to Weaver's camp.

She heard someone approach her from behind and looked up into Ike's mismatched eyes.

'What are you thinking?' he asked.

'That symmetry is overrated.'

'What's that supposed to mean?' He scowled. 'Some kind of dig?'

'Just looking at the way the trees overshadow this little place,' she said.

'Wait until you see the camp. It's really remote.'

He was right about that. 'I'll bet,' she said. 'Mind helping me to the camper?'

'I was just going ask.' He put out his arm, and when she touched it she could feel the tension that his voice barely hid.

'Ike,' she said, as they walked slowly toward the truck, 'you're not what Lucas says you are.'

'I'm fine.' He barely moved his lips. 'Here you go. Won't be long now.'

'You know what I'm saying,' she said. 'This is not who you are, Ike.'

'Careful.' He leaned his head down close to her ears. 'Be really careful, Katherine. He doesn't trust you. If he starts something with you when we're this far away from everyone, I might not be able to stop him.'

Kit tried to ignore his words. Then she realized this was her only chance. She headed back for the convenience store, sprinting now, no longer caring about the pressure on her ankle.

'Please help me,' she gasped to the man behind the counter. 'I need a phone, I need to call the police. My name is Kit Doyle.'

Ike thundered in the front door. 'Come on, honey.' His arm shot around her. He picked her up with one hand and tossed some bills at the guy behind the counter with the other. 'My girlfriend gets a little nutty sometimes, friend. Don't pay any attention to her.'

The moment they stepped outside, he slammed her feet to the ground.

'Kit Doyle, is it?'

'My nickname,' she said, knowing that she had run out of chances and lies. 'Kit's my nickname. What are you going to do?'

'Nothing, and neither are you.' His cheeks blazed, but his voice was calm. 'Let's get out of here before Lucas asks what's going on.'

'Are you going to tell him?' she asked.

'Not if you hurry up,' Ike said. 'As far as Lucas is concerned, you just had to take a leak. Don't pull anything like this again, though. Don't keep testing me, because I can't keep saving you every time you screw up.' He grinned, but there was no humor in it. 'Understand what I'm saying here . . . Kit?'

TWENTY-EIGHT

Once she was back in the truck, Kit remained silent as they took off. She knew the others must have seen her talking to Ike, and she couldn't try to convince them of anything at this point. Sissy propped herself up next to Jessica, her fine hair matted to her scalp, and finished her hamburger. The fresh air that had filled the camper shell was soon replaced by the smell of grease and potato chips.

'Want a cookie?' Jessica asked, and Sissy snatched it from the box.

At least she was better, but she needed real food and undisturbed rest. Kit didn't know how she could possibly arrange that, but once they were in a community with even the most basic technology, she was going to try.

Theo continued playing cards by himself. He didn't seem interested in Sissy's improving health, nor did she seem to recognize him.

They stopped again in Mendocino and let everyone out to stretch their legs. They were all exhausted, and the sight of this community of high cliffs, deep drops, and rushing blue-gray ocean revived

Kit and made her more determined than ever to stop Lucas. The others also seemed to come alive. Jessica stood alone, apart from the others and stared at the breaking waves. Kit wanted to talk to her but knew Lucas would notice, so she left Jessica alone with her thoughts.

Next, they drove to a nearby campground with coin-operated showers the kids seemed to take for granted. Ike handed out change, meeting Kit's eyes with a look of warning.

'Three minutes, max,' he said. 'You can go first. I'll help you back to the truck when you finish – if you think you need help.'

'I'd appreciate that,' she said, and stepped inside. Other than the slot for coins, the shower looked only slightly better than the one at the Fowler compound.

She removed her shoes and stepped on to the ice-cold gray floor. As she turned on the shower, a dark shape shot out from the far right corner of the cubicle. Kit screamed and then slammed her hand over her lips too late to stifle the sound. Either a huge bug or a small mouse. She didn't want to contemplate which.

'Are you OK?' Jessica called from outside.

'Just a critter,' she said. 'It's gone now.'

'I should have warned you about these places.'

Another clue that Kit had never experienced the kind of life the others had. Ike already knew her real name. She didn't have long before Lucas decided she was a danger. By then, she needed as many of the others on her side as possible – Ike especially.

The water had finally turned warm. It massaged her shoulders and shot heat into her muscles. When she got home, the first thing she wanted was a hot bath. She had forgotten how good it felt to be clean.

Just as she started to wash her hair, the shower snapped off. Three minutes gone, and she had barely started. She stepped on to the cold floor and tried to dry off with what looked like a hand towel. It smelled of bleach, but that didn't comfort her. At least she was cleaner than she had been, and for a few moments she had felt the heat of warm water against her body.

Jessica waited outside next to Sissy. Angel stood behind them, her brown jacket wrapped around her waist.

'How bad is it?' Jessica asked.

'The shortest three minutes you'll ever experience.' Kit pulled up her dripping curls and fastened the hair tie back around them. 'At least the water is warm now, so you'd better hurry. Meet you over by the picnic table.' Angel stood there as if knowing she wouldn't be acknowledged. 'You too,' Kit said to Angel, and although she nodded, she couldn't hide her surprise.

Once the girls had showered, the guys took their turn. Kit and the girls settled at a weathered redwood table overlooking the ocean.

'Beautiful,' Sissy said. 'It was the first time she had spoken. Next to her, Jessica patted the arm of her jean jacket.

'Yes, it is, Sissy.'

'Have we been here before?'

'No. Not here.'

'Good.' She stared out at the blue-white waves. 'Can I have a cookie?'

Jessica blinked hard and motioned to Angel, who got up with a heavy sigh and returned to the van. 'You can have all the cookies you want, Sissy,' Jessica said.

Just then, Ike joined them, followed by Wyatt and Theo, who squinted as he wiped his glasses dry with his jacket.

'Where's Lucas?' Kit asked.

'He wanted everyone else to have their showers first.'

Meaning he knew the water would already be heated for him. Kit bet he wouldn't shower for only three minutes.

Angel returned and slammed the tired-looking bakery box in front of Jessica. 'Anything else your majesty would like before I sit down?'

Jessica's short burgundy spikes crisscrossed her brows, and the light brown eyes beneath them grew fierce. She handed the box to Sissy and then looked up at Angel.

'If you got sent to the camp to get cured of anger management issues,' Jessica told her, 'your parents ought to ask for a refund.'

'It's none of your business what I got sent there for. At least my parents wanted me when I got out.'

'Hey,' Kit said, as if it were a joke now. 'Remember to play nice.'

'Guess I'm just tired,' Jessica said.

'At least,' Angel shot back.

They were all edgy, and after that ride, Kit didn't feel much

better than they did. This was the time to take her best shot –
before Lucas returned. She looked around the table at Jessica next
to her and then Sissy and Angel. Across from her, Ike pretended
he wasn't worried about what she was going to do. Next to him
sat Wyatt and Theo.

Kit rose and walked to the front of the redwood table. 'You –
we – we're way too young to ruin our lives this way.'

'That's enough out of you,' Ike said.

'No, it's not. You need to listen to me, all of you. I realize that
Weaver harmed you. There are better ways to get even – lawsuits,
the media. So many ways.'

Sissy finished chewing her bite of cookie and looked up at Kit.
'Why not just do what he did?'

'Who, honey?' Jessica asked.

'He tried to kill us. Lucas said so.'

'Hold on a minute,' Kit said. 'The Weasel wasn't the one who
put you in that cooler.'

Sissy pouted and glanced over at Ike. 'You did that.'

'Don't confuse her like this.' He glared at Kit. 'Sissy, I told
you I'm sorry.'

'I know.' She smiled. 'You let me out too, but I can't tell.'

For a moment, only the calling of gulls and the answering rush
of the ocean filled the air.

'That's how you got out?' Jessica finally asked. 'Does Lucas
know?'

'We talked it over.' Ike stood and walked up next to Kit. He
shoved his navy hoodie to the back of his head, and she saw
that his hair was still damp. 'Lucas would have made the same
decision if he'd been out there, but I was, so I did what I thought
was right.'

'He might have decided to do that,' she said, 'or he might have
let Sissy die. He wasn't in any hurry to go looking for her.'

Sissy whimpered, and Jessica put her arm around her, which
seemed to upset Angel even more.

'This is First-Year business,' Angel told Kit. 'Originals only.'

'Yet here I am with you.'

'You're still a no-year. No one says you have to understand
what we're doing.'

'Do *you* understand it?' Kit asked her.

'Of course I do. You weren't the one who got chained to a tree and told you were an animal.' Her face turned ruddier, and she looked away, toward the ocean, as if she could see into the past.

'But you aren't chained to a tree now,' Kit said. 'Remember the rules of the compound. *Take no chances. Live your truth. Don't ever go back.* What Lucas is planning goes against every one of them.'

Kit took a breath and waited until all of them around the table looked up into her eyes.

'Lucas is going to convince you to harm the Weasel,' she said. 'Maybe kill him. You can't do that. It will ruin your lives.'

'The Weasel already took care of that,' Sissy said. 'Didn't he, Jessica?'

'I don't know about you, honey, but I was pretty messed-up before I got there.' Jessica looked down at her long fingers and ragged cuticles. 'He just made everything worse.'

Angel stood, and for a moment Kit thought she might attack her the way she had that night in the shelter. 'I still don't get it,' Angel told Kit. 'Why are you trying to protect the Weasel? What's he to you?'

'I'm trying to protect *you*, not him,' she said. 'From what you've told me, he treated you like laboratory animals. I've heard about other so-called camps where kids were abused that way. But committing a crime is just playing into his hands.'

'Not if he's dead.' Angel smiled and glanced over at Theo, who nodded.

'Especially if he's dead,' Kit said. 'Then you live up to the crazy label, and you just get put back in the system, for good this time.'

'Not necessarily.' Angel paused, as if making sure the others were all paying attention. 'Not if we get away.'

'You won't. Lucas has convinced you that you can get away with anything.'

'So far, we have,' Angel said.

'At what cost? His compound is no better than the Weasel's.' Kit looked around the table into their eyes. Beside her, Ike squinted and shook his head. Angel jutted out her chin and pretended to be bored. Wyatt and Theo both seemed curious. Jessica looked down. 'It's not too late. We can all walk out of there together the minute we're in town. Tell them, Ike.'

'I don't know.' He took a step back as if to distance himself from her statement. 'We just have to see how it plays out. Shit, here comes Lucas.'

He hurried over to Lucas, and Kit hoped he wasn't sharing the conversation they had just had. She walked back to her place beside Jessica but did not sit down.

Lucas hadn't bothered to dry his hair. It looked as if he had squeezed out the water in front. Under his jacket, he wore a blue T-shirt the color of his eyes. It looked new, and Kit wondered where he had gotten it.

'That sure felt good,' he said as he approached the end of the table where Kit stood. 'Did you have a nice shower, everyone?'

No one answered. Theo seemed distracted by polishing his glasses with a paper napkin. Jessica picked at her nails. Even Angel appeared distracted by a gust of sea air. Although the weather was warmer now, she pulled her too-small jacket closer.

Lucas's eyes were so startling in their color and depth that, at first glance, they would be considered beautiful if only because they were his only noticeable feature. But his blue irises and large dark pupils held no depth, no life.

'You're awfully quiet.' He maintained eye contact with Kit as easily as if he were staring at a wall. 'Did you enjoy your shower, Katherine?'

'I don't enjoy any of this,' she said, and saw Ike shake his head as if in pain. 'I thought you cared about these kids.'

'Oh, I do, Katherine. The challenge will be to see how much you care about them.' He looked at the others. 'You certainly got quiet when I approached. What were you talking about? Anything I should be aware of?'

No one answered.

'Ike?' he asked.

'Nothing much.'

'Angel?'

She glared at Kit and then said, 'Jessica was ordering me around, as usual. We kind of got into it, and this one tried to break it up.'

Thank you, Angel. Kit met her gaze but didn't dare smile.

'Sissy?' Lucas asked.

She stood beside the picnic table looking like a waif in the jean jacket and long floral skirt.

'Come on,' Lucas said in a voice so soft it barely carried over the sound of the waves. 'What were you talking about, Sissy?'

'Cookies,' she said.

'All right, then.' He glanced at the truck parked at the edge of the hill. 'Into the front, please, Katherine. I'm sure you'd like an opportunity to enjoy the scenery.'

Jessica shot her a desperate look. Kit sensed that she had almost convinced most of the others. Lucas probably guessed as much.

'I don't mind riding back there,' Kit told him.

'And I don't mind if you ride in front.'

Wyatt stood, his black curls blowing across his face and his scarred neck, his hands out, as if asking what he had done. 'What about me?' he asked.

'Join the others. It won't be long now.' Lucas marched toward the truck, and then turned around to face them. 'Everyone in, please. Ike, you help Katherine.'

'Wait,' she said. 'Just a moment.'

'Now, please.' He opened the truck door. 'We need to hurry.'

TWENTY-NINE

On the road again.

Jessica could still hear that country song from the convenience store all those hours ago. Yet she didn't feel on the road moving toward anything better. She felt as if she were strapped to a ticking bomb. That's what this truck was. She needed to talk to Wyatt alone. Good luck with that. The others in the back with them stared at them as if she and Wyatt had done something wrong.

Sissy curled up to Jessica's left and went to sleep. If she ever got away from these people, she would take Sissy with her. Camp gossip had always been that the Weasel had treated Sissy with the drugs and not the placebo, but Sissy had been almost as young as Lucas when her rancher parents had her picked up as a runaway and slammed into the camp with the rest of the Originals. No one had been all that nice to the little blond girl who arrived too late.

Lucas had pretended to be, but Lucas wanted to build his power, and in order to do that, he needed people.

Jessica sat next to Wyatt. He stretched out on the worn carpet beside her where Katherine had sat all of those bumpy miles.

'My butt will never be the same.' He grinned at Jessica.

'Welcome to the rat hole,' Angel said from her place against the back of the cab.

'It's not that bad,' Theo said, without looking up from his card game.

'Didn't mean to complain.' Wyatt leaned closer to her, and Jessica breathed his scent as clean as the ocean, as safe as any shelter she had ever known. She wrapped her arms around his neck.

'Get a room, you two,' Angel said.

Jessica shot her a look. 'Let me know when you find one for us.'

The others laughed, and Jessica placed her lips to Wyatt's ear.

'What?' he asked softly.

'We can't do this,' she whispered.

He pulled back from her and smiled. 'Yes.' That's all he said, but in his eyes Jessica saw something far different.

She leaned into him again. 'What?' she asked.

'Katherine,' he mouthed back. 'She's trying to stir up shit.'

'Pretend you're kissing me.'

He grinned. 'Sounds good to me.'

Arms around his neck, she whispered, 'Katherine's right. If we do this, we'll never be free of Lucas or the compound.'

'Got it.'

Theo removed his earbuds and let the hip hop he'd been playing fill the back of the truck.

'I thought Lucas didn't allow electronics,' Jessica said.

'It's not connected to anything but the music,' Wyatt told her. 'He explained it today. We can't risk being traced.'

Wyatt's hair smelled like the ocean, like rain water, like the security of a past she had lost. Jessica pressed her face against it.

'Turn up the music, Theo,' Angel said, 'and hand me the cards. 'I'm sick of watching these two lovers.'

'We're both smart,' Jessica whispered to Wyatt. 'We don't need to stay with these people. It was never our plan.'

'It's too late to back out.' He shrugged and pulled a sleeping bag over them like a blanket.

'We need to make him stop the truck as soon as we hit town, and then we've got to get help. He's only one little kid.'

'Is that what Katherine's been telling you?' he asked.

'It's the truth,' she said. 'Lucas can't control us any more than the Weasel could.'

Wyatt smiled at her, and Jessica could see that he was considering what she had said.

'We need to talk to Ike,' she said. 'I think he's having second thoughts too.'

'What makes you think that?' he demanded in a too-loud voice. 'Ike's the last person who would cross Lucas.'

'It's not crossing him. It's protecting ourselves. In a way, we'll be protecting him too. Lucas is too young to spend the rest of his life with a police record.'

Wyatt hugged her and rested his head against the camper shell. 'You only get a record if they catch you,' he said.

Jessica didn't reply. She wanted to believe he would do the right thing, but something about Wyatt was different, and she didn't know what or why.

At first, Farley had argued with John Paul about discussing Kit Doyle's disappearance on the air, but John Paul knew he was right. All of the stations were following the story. Nothing they could add would do more than capitalize on it. Richard McCarthy might be a judgmental asshole, but he had been right about John Paul, and he had sensed his uncertainty even before John Paul had figured it out for himself.

John Paul and Farley headed for the gym Saturday afternoon. Later that night, they would sit in on Jasper's weekend gig at the blues club. John Paul drove, and Farley sat silently beside him.

'You still think we should do the segment?' John Paul asked.

'No.' Farley stared out the window. 'I talked to Kit's dad, and he agrees with you. It just sucks is all. One day, she's here, and one day . . .'

'Yeah.'

'You really want to go to the gym?' Farley asked.

'Not really.'

'Neither do I.' Farley turned to face him, pale eyes vacant. 'You feel like a beer?'

John Paul thought about it. 'No. Maybe later. Want me to drop you off at your place?'

Farley nodded, and they drove without speaking. They had pretty much said it all.

As John Paul walked into up the path to his front door, his phone rang, and Jasper's number popped up.

'What's going on?' John Paul asked.

'A girl in a NorCal convenience store,' he said. 'She told the clerk her name was Kit Doyle.'

'Shit.'

'A guy claiming to be her boyfriend threw some cash at the clerk and got her out of there. They took off with some other kids in a pickup.'

John Paul's body tensed, and he headed back toward his truck. 'Description?'

'It matches. And, John Paul, the clerk heard the kids talking about how long it would take them to get to Mendocino.'

'Thanks, man,' John Paul said. 'I'm going.'

'Figured you would. Don't say I'm the one who told you.'

'You know I won't,' he said, and reached for the truck door.

THIRTY

Lucas hadn't assigned Kit to the front seat for the view. He probably sensed that the others were having second thoughts. Even the nervous way Angel avoided eye contact with her meant she didn't want Kit or anyone else to guess her thoughts.

They drove through Mendocino, twisting around the curves of the highway. The truck shook in spite of Ike's expert handling of it. Perspiration broke out on his forehead. He shoved his hoodie down to his shoulders.

'Almost there,' he said in a fake-cheerful voice.

Sitting between him and Lucas, Kit watched the signs for Caspar and Jackson State Forest fly past.

'I've been thinking,' Lucas said.

Kit already knew that when he said thinking, he meant planning, so she didn't reply.

'About what?' Ike asked, taking the bait.

'That woman at the Mexican restaurant.' Lucas smiled, and Kit knew it wasn't because he was thinking about the food.

'Juanita? We can't steal from her,' Ike said. 'She gives us free stuff. She doesn't charge us.'

'You're so funny, Ike. I wasn't suggesting we steal from her.'

'What, then?' Ike asked. 'She doesn't cause us any trouble.'

The road evened out. To their right, Kit saw a motel and then another. Finally, they would be close enough to people who could help her.

'She hasn't caused us any trouble yet that we know of,' Lucas said. 'But she's gotten way too curious about what we do, where we live, that kind of thing.'

Ike bit his lip and stared straight ahead. 'We already agreed to stop using the restaurant as a meeting place.'

'That avoids future problems.' Lucas cracked the window, and sea breeze filled the cab. He took a deep breath of it. 'It doesn't fix what she already knows, though.'

'No, Lucas.' Ike gripped the wheel.

'No, what? I thought we should just discuss it. He's touchy, don't you think, Katherine?'

'What I think is that you're baiting him,' she said, 'trying to goad him into harming that woman, maybe with one of those fires you enjoy so much.'

'I don't bait, and I don't goad.' Although his tone was pleasant enough, his lips tightened. 'I'm not the Weasel.'

'You'd like to be, though. Wouldn't you?'

'That's ridiculous and unkind.' His pale cheeks turned pink. 'I think Ike made a mistake offering you a place to stay with us, Katherine.'

Kit knew she had pushed him too far, but there was no way to backtrack. 'I took you seriously when you said we had free will,' she told him. 'But I didn't have free will about whether or not I came along on this trip. I don't even have free will about where I sit in this truck.'

'I apologize for that.' Lucas quickly regained his composure. 'The rest of us knew each other before, and you're the wild card, so to speak. Until you prove yourself, I have to protect the others in the group.'

'Burning down that woman's home, nearly killing her, didn't do it for you?' she asked.

'It helped.' His smile grew wistful. 'But quite frankly, you can be disrespectful in your speech. For that reason, I'm going to ask Ike to stay with you when we complete what we came here for tonight. If you're truly with us, you shouldn't have a problem with that.'

She looked at Ike, who pretended to be watching the road.

'Does that plan work for you, Ike?' Lucas asked.

'It's fine.' His expression didn't change.

'That's more like it.' They pulled into town, and Lucas cranked the window down farther. 'This is such a pretty place. Once we start back, let's talk about Juanita some more, Ike. If you don't agree that she's a problem, I'm sure Wyatt would be willing to help.'

Ike clutched the steering wheel as if he wanted to rip it out. 'I can handle it,' he said.

'I'm sure you can. And I have a puzzle for you.'

'I'm not in the mood.' Yet Ike raised an eyebrow.

'Two boys are enrolling in a fancy school, and they tell the admissions guy that they have the same father and mother. They also have the same birthday. He asks if they are twins, and they say no. How is this possible?'

'I don't care,' Ike said.

Lucas glanced out the window and began to hum softly.

'They're triplets,' Ike blurted.

'Very good. I can't stump you for long.'

With Ike back under his control, Lucas seemed to relax. Kit hoped that they would stop in town, but he directed Ike down Main Street. Once they passed a Safeway grocery store, they pulled off Main and on to roads that grew only narrower.

'How do you remember how to get here after so many years?' Kit asked.

'Technology can be useful on occasion.' Lucas patted the truck's glove compartment.

'You have a phone in there?'

'Locked in a foil-covered box. Like any convenience, it has a negative side, so we use it rarely. I did check out the social media pages of all our compound members before they joined us. The first rule: *Take no chances.*'

'You checked me out online?' Ike demanded.

'I make use of my technical skills when I need to. The church pics of you with your grandma were cute. And no worries – I deleted your secret stash of porn.'

Ike's cheeks blazed. 'That was a long time ago.'

'If you say so. It's history now, friend, as are those photos of Jessica in her bikini and much less that I never shared with anyone. In a way, I have to thank the Weasel for making me so careful. Otherwise, someone would have already traced us to the compound.'

'You hated that he took pictures of us when we didn't know it,' Ike said. 'Was that when you got the idea to do the same thing?'

'I wanted only to protect us. The Weasel was trying to analyze us. Analysis destroys, Ike. It breaks you down into pieces.'

'That's what he tried to do.' Ike nodded, and his expressive, easy-to-read eyes filled with anger. 'Bastard tried to break us down into pieces so he could look at them under his fucking microscope. Pardon my English.'

'Well put,' Lucas said. 'It felt pretty crappy, didn't it, Ike?'

'Still does. Why would he do that? We were only little kids.'

'Just little kids,' Lucas echoed, and folded his hands over his chest. 'Right down this road, Ike.'

Even in broad daylight, the trees would have dimmed the place. Now, with the setting sun casting only fragments of light through the shadowed branches, Kit knew it would be dark soon.

'How do you plan to get inside?' she asked.

'No worries,' Lucas said. 'Wyatt and I already discussed it.'

'Wyatt?' Ike almost lost control of the truck.

'By now, he's shared our plan with the rest of the group.'

'What about me?' Ike demanded.

'We'll need you at the very start to overpower the Weasel.' Lucas tilted his head as if studying Ike. 'If you think you can handle it, that is.'

'You want overpower, I'll give you overpower.' Ike slowed down as they came to the turnoff leading to Weaver's camp.

'Take a right down this path.' Lucas couldn't hide the excitement in his voice. 'You and Katherine can go to the door together.'

'Why?' Kit and Ike asked at the same time.

'You're in charge of Katherine, remember? Besides, the Weasel doesn't know who she is. You can have her ring the bell. He usually relaxes with a martini by the fire about this time. You might be able to catch him outside.'

'How do you know that?' Kit asked.

Lucas smiled. 'How do I know anything?'

Kit could almost hear the energy bursting from the back. Wyatt was the new Ike. At least, that's what Lucas wanted Ike to believe. He knew these kids better than Weaver ever could have, and he knew how to manipulate all of them. Kit wouldn't have a chance to escape, but maybe she could warn Weaver in time to stop whatever Lucas had planned.

'Stop here,' Lucas told Ike. 'We'll walk the rest of the way.'

They got out of the truck, and Ike took Kit's arm. 'Come on,' he said, and stared straight ahead. 'Lucas. Check it out.'

Kit turned in the direction Ike was looking and caught sight of a tiny flame in the darkness. The fire pit.

'Beautiful,' Lucas said. He took his time getting around to the back. 'We're here,' he said. 'Come on. Let's get him.'

The others piled out of the truck. Wyatt and Jessica led them. Kit tried to catch Jessica's eye, but the girl ignored her and clutched Wyatt's arm. Sissy followed behind with Angel and Theo. All of them held small bags in their hands. Wyatt carried his knife case.

'I said let's go.' Lucas clapped his hands, and Ike pulled Kit ahead. 'You heard him.'

'Not so fast,' she said.

'Shut up. You've gotten enough mileage out of that ankle.'

As they approached through the thick trees, Kit spotted Weaver in a long-sleeved sweater and jeans sitting by the large antique metal fire pit.

'Don't even think about warning him,' Ike said.

'Please stop this,' she begged him. 'You're the only one who can do it.'

'So that Wyatt can take my place? No way.'

They got closer to the camp, and Kit could hear music, classical piano, a Mozart sonata. For a moment, she hoped someone else might be there with Weaver, but she knew better. Lucas was far too careful in his research to allow for slip-ups.

'You go up,' Ike said. 'Tell him your car broke down. I'll be right behind you.'

'I can't,' she whispered, but Ike shoved her ahead.

'Who's out there?' Weaver rose from his chair, and the fire pit lit the fear on his face. Then he spotted Kit. 'Ms Doyle. What are you doing here?'

'Another lie,' Ike said. 'You know the bastard.'

She started to explain, but Ike lunged at Weaver. As if tossing a stuffed toy, he pinned him to the ground. The others ran in, shouting. They ignored Kit, and she wondered if she could sneak back to the truck to the phone in the glove compartment. But Lucas said it was in a locked box. Her only chance was to try to stop what was going on.

'Chain him,' Lucas shouted.

Wyatt dropped his case. 'Chain him to a tree.'

'No. Here.' Ike ignored the huge trunks of the redwoods and, with Wyatt's and Theo's help, chained Weaver to one of the wooden pillars bordering the front of the patio.

Kit stepped back, closer to the knife case. Ike wiped sweat from his face and stood beside her.

Wyatt and Theo ripped Weaver's clothes from him, and he stood in a pair of boxer shorts, weeping.

'Don't do this.' He looked at Lucas, not Ike.

'You didn't spare us,' Lucas said. 'And you said we could only heal by saying goodbye forever to those who had harmed us. We're here to heal from you.'

Angel stepped forward, her small jacket open over her broad chest. She walked up to where Weaver wept. 'You tied me up over there.' She pointed at the trees that hid the camp. 'You called me an animal. I screamed all night. No one heard me, and no one is going to hear you.'

She reached into the bag she carried, took out something, and tossed it toward Weaver. He shrieked, and Kit realized it was a dart, now imbedded in his left shoulder. Angel laughed bitterly and walked back to the others. The dart toppled out, and blood trickled out of Weaver's flesh.

Kit started to move forward, but Ike pulled her back toward the walkway. 'There's nothing you can do,' he whispered. 'You liar.'

'I don't care what you say,' she whispered back. 'You aren't like this, Ike, not really. Don't let him manipulate you.'

'Shut up.'

'Jessica?' Lucas asked.

She clung to Wyatt. 'It's all right, baby,' he told her. 'You know what to do.'

'You punished all of us if one of us did something wrong,' Jessica said, her voice trembling. 'You gave us Bleeds. When I was late to breakfast, you made everyone skip lunch. When I tried to run away, you took away my shoes. Now we have your shoes. She picked them up, walked back toward the house and threw them into the fire pit.'

Everyone cheered.

'Do the rest,' Wyatt urged.

Jessica glanced at him and then marched up to Weaver. 'My feet nearly froze.' She threw a dart at his foot and squeezed her eyes shut.

The dart fell on to the ground inches from him. The kids booed.

'You didn't belong here,' Weaver said, his voice as flat as Lucas's had been. 'I should have refused your mother's request, and I'm sorry for that. Let me go, and I swear I'll make it right.'

Wyatt started to pick up the dart, but Lucas shook his head sharply, as if he wanted no more attention given to Jessica.

'Next is Wyatt,' he announced proudly.

His jacket tied around his waist, Wyatt walked up slowly to Weaver.

Wyatt's long curls, almost to his shoulders, now hid his face from Kit. They didn't hide his naked shoulders, though.

'You created these scars when you tried to burn me to death,' Wyatt said. 'But I survived you, and these scars just remind me how much I hate you.'

'I didn't try to kill you.' Weaver moaned. 'Lucas convinced the others that you were the weakest. What happened to you was because of him. Don't keep repeating that sick violence.'

'Here's what I'll repeat.' Wyatt tossed a dart that hit Weaver in the stomach. 'Suffer, you bastard. This isn't the last you're getting from me.'

Weaver screamed. The dart fell to the ground. A thin stream of blood appeared on his stomach. Kit inched closer to the knife case.

'Good job,' Lucas said, as if speaking to a child or a pet dog.

'Good job, Wyatt. Who wants to go next?' He looked behind him at Sissy in her jeans jacket, clutching Jessica's hand. 'Come on, Sissy. I have one for you.'

'I have one of my own.' Sissy spoke clearly.

'No,' Kit shouted, and ran beside her. 'Don't make her part of this.'

Ike grabbed Kit's wrist in a vise grip and pulled her back. 'How many times do I have to tell you to shut up?'

'Somebody turn up the music,' Lucas said, and Theo sprinted toward the computer on Weaver's patio table.

'Don't make her do this,' Kit begged Ike. But it was too late. Sissy walked up to Weaver, holding her dart the way a child would hold a pencil for the first time.

'You were bad to us,' she said. 'You gave me drugs.'

'I tried to help you,' Weaver sobbed. 'I tried to help all of you.'

'Give him the dart,' Lucas told her.

'Don't do it,' Kit begged Sissy. 'Remember who locked you in that cooler. Remember that Lucas did that do you.'

'Lucas did that?'

'He's worse than the Weasel. You need to break free. You can do it.'

'I can?' She seemed to think about it. Then she turned and hurled her dart into Lucas's chest.

He cried out in pain. Then he grabbed Sissy by the throat. She shrieked and sputtered, trying to catch her breath. Kit went for her just as Jessica did. They pried Lucas's hands free, and Sissy clung to Jessica.

'That's enough.' With one swing, Wyatt knocked Sissy and Jessica to the patio.

'Good,' Lucas said, his voice weak but free of emotion.

'Wyatt, please.' On the rough stones, Jessica lifted up her bloody palms.

He ignored her and turned to Lucas, who was still gasping for breath. 'Are you OK, man?'

Lucas nodded. 'Let's finish it.'

'Wyatt.' Jessica grabbed his leg, but he kicked her free.

Kit reached down and yanked up the knife case. Before anyone realized what she was doing, she ran back toward the house and tossed the case into the fire pit.

For a moment, everyone stopped and stared at her.

'No!' Wyatt ran for the pit. 'My knives!' He fought the flames with his hands, and Jessica screamed. 'My knives!' Wyatt cried again. He perched on the pit's edge as if he didn't feel the heat, digging through the blaze.

Lucas moved closer, not speaking, fascinated.

'Help him,' Kit told Ike.

He didn't budge.

'I said help him.'

Ike ran toward the pit and yanked Wyatt from it. Then he slammed him to the grassy area surrounding the patio. Wyatt looked stunned. He sat watching the flames as the horror of what had almost happened crept into his expression.

'You're done,' Ike said. 'All of you.' Then, as they watched speechless, Ike unchained Weaver.

'Wait,' Lucas said. 'Stop him.'

No one moved.

'Come on,' Kit told Jessica. 'Get Sissy.'

'Where are you going?' Angel demanded.

'To find help.'

'What about us? Theo and me.' She had already distanced both of them from Wyatt and Lucas.

'We'll get you out of here as soon as we can,' Kit told her.

As Wyatt sobbed on the ground, and the flames leapt into the air, Lucas drew nearer the fire, smiling.

'It will be OK,' he said to everyone. To no one.

Ike and Kit led a silent Jessica and Sissy into the woods. Behind them, Kit could hear only Wyatt's moans interspersed with Mozart.

THIRTY-ONE

Ike still couldn't get his thoughts together. Kit, Sissy, and Jessica rode with him to the bus station with Kit's cop friend John Paul. The guy seemed to appear out of nowhere once Lucas had been arrested. Ike had always been the one to handle everything, and now he felt relief when he could do something as simple as take a nap.

That's what he had done this morning, just slept so hard and so heavy in the backseat of Kit's friend's big truck that he felt as if he were floating. *Kit*, not *Katherine*. She had always seemed different to Ike, and now he knew why. Her runaway story was an act. She was really a crime blogger trying to find her ex-husband's niece. She'd found her, all right.

Kit hugged him hard and gestured toward the station and the bus that waited for him. 'You have my contact information. Let me know if you need anything.'

'I will.' He felt as if he should say more, though. 'Police types like my dad – military types – we always have problems with authority. That's where our trouble started. Then I met Lucas, and . . . well, you know.'

'You stay safe, Ike,' Kit said, and looked behind her at Jessica.

Ike put out his hand. Jessica walked up to him, reached out for it, and then hugged him tightly.

'You know how to reach me,' she said.

'I'll be in touch.' He hugged her again. 'All we have now is each other.'

Once he had settled into the stiff small seat of the bus, he realized he'd been wrong about what he had told Jessica. He had almost sounded like the Weasel. It wasn't about having each other. No, it was a lot more complicated than that. It was about trust, about comfort.

He thought about it as he finally felt relaxed enough to sleep.

The bus jerked him back to life so late that he didn't know if the light around the terminal was the blaze of an overhead fixture or the late-afternoon sunshine.

His bag over his back, he let a few people get out ahead of him and stepped down. It was dark, all right. He must have needed the sleep.

Kit had offered him money so that he could find a place to stay if he needed to. He couldn't take it, though – not from a girl – and he confessed to her that he'd kept a little stash of his own. Turned out, Lucas had been so focused on withholding food from them that he hadn't paid enough attention to the money.

Ike started walking toward the taxis.

Then he heard a commotion and saw a couple moving toward him. His dad still wore his uniform. His granny was dressed up in a dark skirt and her church blouse.

Ike made himself as tall and serious as they were, even though the faster he walked, the more he felt the tears try to crowd out of his eyes. Pretty soon he was running, and they ran too, all three of them toward each other. Then, face to face, they stopped, out of breath. None of them seemed able to speak.

Ike pulled back his shoulders. 'Good to see you, sir,' he said.

His dad nodded. 'You too, son.'

'You got back just in time.' His granny's lips were tight, but he could see a trace of a smile there. 'I got a roast in the oven and the makings for that hot chocolate you like,' she said. 'You best hurry up.'

THIRTY-TWO

Richard's house smelled of apples.

'Cider,' he said as he let Kit in. 'Mom thought Jessica might want something warm. She gave me careful instructions. You know how she is when she's on a mission.'

Kit had guessed his mother would drive there as soon as Richard called her with the news. Once the investigators finished speaking with Jessica, one of them would bring her to join her family, and their nightmare would be over. Almost.

'Where's your mom now?' Kit asked Richard.

He glanced toward the front window and its open blinds. 'About ten minutes away, maybe closer. She said to tell you she says thank you, Kit.'

That was a first.

'I'm glad she'll be here to help you and Jessica.' It was the most honest response Kit could muster when all she wanted to do was burst into tears.

'Guess I'd better check up on it. Come on.'

Richard headed into his kitchen, and Kit followed. The usually spotless stove held a large pot of steaming cider. A loaf of partially sliced bread and assorted deli packages littered the tile counter. Richard picked up a spoon, dipped it into the pot, and offered it to her.

The cider tasted as sweet and comforting as it smelled.

'Perfect,' she told him, and wondered how she could possibly explain to him what she and Jessica had just been through.

'How is she?' he asked.

Kit closed her eyes and tried to come up with the most honest answer she could. 'Tired,' she finally said. 'Confused. Scared. She'll need patience, Richard, and I don't know anyone better for that than you.'

She handed the spoon back to him, and they stood there looking at each other. His hair gleamed as if he had just washed it, and Kit could smell the spicy soap he had showered with mingling with the scent of the apples. She would do it again, she knew. She would do all of it just to find that girl and bring her back to him.

'I can't believe this has happened.' He seemed to swallow back whatever else he was going to say and finally added, 'I'll never forget what you did for me, Kit.'

'And I'll never forget how you stood by me last year.'

That's all they could say to each other just then – all either of them was ready to, at this point, she guessed. But Kit knew that when she looked back one day, she would think of this moment in his kitchen – with the smell of cider everywhere – as the end.

'If you like, you can stay and have dinner with us,' he said.

'I need to get some rest, Richard.'

'Of course.' He held out his arms, spoon and all.

Kit hugged him tightly. She pressed her cheek against his beating heart. Then she reached up and took his face in her hands. Richard's eyes were wet, but he was smiling.

A car pulled up in front of the house, motor running.

'Jessica,' he shouted, and his eyes filled with joy. 'She's here!'

He ran for the front door, and Kit followed. Once there, she glanced back for a final look at his home. Later, she would have to sort out her pain from her gratitude. Right now, Kit had only enough energy to follow Richard outside and watch as he and Jessica stood facing each other in the driveway. Until that moment,

Kit had never thought of Jessica as frail. Now, in spite of her height, the young woman looked fragile and delicate.

'Uncle Rich?' In just a few steps, Jessica was in his arms, and all three of them were crying.

As Kit drove away a few minutes later, Richard and Jessica were still hugging and gleefully interrupting each other's sentences. They would be OK now because they both had found what they had lost.

Kit stopped at the corner and looked back at his house, a soft glow of light spilling out on to the street. Too tired. She was too tired to think or feel anymore tonight. First she needed sleep, and then she would take one final step to make sure Richard's family was safe.

The apartment door stood open. Coming outside in her yellow tunic and black tights, Sarah looked like a bright beam of color against the dim sky. The big guy with her carried a white-wicker lawn chair in each hand and carefully placed each one into the back of the waiting truck.

Sarah spotted her and hurried to the sidewalk where Kit stood.

'Thank you for coming. I've been meaning to call you. Let's go inside.'

'You're moving?' Kit asked.

'Dan has a job in Vegas.' She flushed with pride. 'He's my new guy. Produce manager for a supermarket. I might get on part-time, too.'

'You've given up looking for Jessica?'

'I can't wait here forever. Let me know if you hear anything.' She looked up, her expression tense. 'You will, won't you?'

'That's why I'm here.' Kit had thought this would be easy, thought it wouldn't bring back too many memories. 'Actually, I found your daughter.'

'You did?' Sarah's heavily made-up expression went from faked bliss to panic. 'Where is she?'

'Far away from you,' Kit said. 'If you ever try to locate her, we will fight you with everything we have.'

Sarah's dark eyes flickered, and Kit could see her trying to figure out what kind of trouble she was in. 'We?'

'Jessica and I. She told me why you put her in that camp.'

Sarah stepped back as if trying to decide her best way to attack. 'She's lying.'

'And Doctor Weaver? Is he lying too? He knew Jessica didn't belong there.'

'Keep it down.' Sarah jerked her head toward the door. 'Dan doesn't know anything about that.'

'Maybe it's time he knows what kind of woman he's involved with.'

'Don't you judge me.' Tears filled her eyes, but her expression grew even harder. She closed the front door and marched up to Kit until she was inches from her face. 'You have no idea what my life was like, trying to raise that girl on my own, a dead father who never would have helped anyway. Every time I looked at her, I saw that miserable bastard.'

'You don't have to explain to me,' Kit said. 'But if you come around again, I'll make sure everyone knows the truth.'

'Sarah.' The guy pounded on the front door. 'Come on. Hurry up.'

'I've got to go,' she said, in a voice so low she might be talking to herself. 'Don't you ever try to find me. Tell Jessica I'm dead.'

Kit's frantic heartbeat made it difficult to speak. 'Jessica already knows that,' she said.

'Sarah,' the guy yelled again.

She glared at Kit, her eyes a mixture of anger and pain. Then she ran to the door.

Kit knew she needed to tell John Paul about Jessica and Sarah that afternoon as they drove to the shelter, where he would do the final interview for his segment on runaways.

He had turned out to be a natural reporter on the air, probably better than she was. His serious, professional manner, combined with Farley's passion, made the segment snap with energy. His contacts had already come through. In the time Kit had been gone, he had uncovered important information about one of their cases.

Kit turned on the seat beside him and thought how different this truck was from Ike's pickup.

'Whenever you're ready.' His smile lit his light brown eyes, and for the first time since she had entered the world of runaway kids, Kit felt safe.

'I couldn't take Jessica back to her mother, John Paul.'

'So that's it.'

'That's it.'

'Well, you're not law enforcement.' He glanced over at her with that expression she had once feared, the one that always seemed to delve below the surface. 'As long as no crime's being committed.'

'It should be a crime to shove your daughter into a psychologist's study for disturbed kids in order to earn a little cash while you keep her away from your current boyfriend.'

He exhaled and shook his head. 'Jessica's of legal age now, right? Tell me she is.'

Kit started to lie but then met his gaze with a shrug. 'Almost.'

'Like in a year? Two years?'

'Not that bad. Next month.'

'That's a relief.' They drove in silence. Finally, he said, 'So where'd you hide her?'

'You know me pretty well.'

'Not well enough apparently. Where's the girl? Please say she isn't at your place.'

Kit couldn't help grinning because for a moment she had considered it. 'No,' she said.

'Not your mom's?'

'No. Jessica is staying with Richard while he helps her find the resources to live on her own.'

'Just Richard?' he asked.

She nodded and looked away. 'Just Richard. And his mom will be with them for a while.' When John Paul didn't respond, she added, 'He's the only family Jessica has, and he'll take care of her for now.'

'What makes you think the mother won't find out where Jessica is?'

'She doesn't want her.' Kit's voice trembled. 'And you and Farley can cover anything about the camp you want to on the segment as long as you keep the kids' names out of it. I'd love to see Weaver exposed.'

'Why won't you and Farley cover it?' he asked. 'Now that you're back, it's your segment.'

'I think I'm going to take a break from radio.'

'But you and Farley are a team.'

'So are you guys, and you're a good one.' She stared out at the passing cars. 'Besides, writing about these cases isn't enough now. I want to do more.'

'Ah, so you want to be a rescuer.' His expression switched to borderline smug. 'Do you know what all rescuers want more than anything, Doyle?'

'To save themselves?'

He raised an eyebrow. 'So you've figured out that part too.' His tone was softer, almost tender. 'That's a plus.'

'I've had a lot of time to think about it.'

'Yes,' he said. 'I guess you have.'

Kit thought about what Richard had told her that day she met Sarah, about looking at a rose and seeing the garbage, yet looking at the garbage and seeing the rose. That was what had happened to her with these kids. She had seen both sides of that complicated equation, and, if she had a choice, she would never again deal with anything that mattered at arms' length.

By the time John Paul finished his interview with the shelter director, it was close to five o'clock. Clouds had hid the sunlight most of the day, and Kit knew it would be an early night. Again, she thought of the kids staying here, those on the street, and those who were hidden in places she couldn't begin to imagine.

In her bag, she had brought cash that she planned to donate to the shelter, but she felt awkward just pulling it out as if she could pay for having a life that kept her out of places like that. Better and far less emotional just to make an anonymous electronic donation.

They stepped outside and headed for the parking lot. Kit had learned to walk to the rhythm of John Paul's uneven gait, and she could tell he was more at peace than he had been since they met. Perhaps he had come to terms with being unable to work in law enforcement, or maybe he saw the good he could do where he was.

Several homeless girls gathered around a pile of blankets in a storefront. At least they were close to the shelter. If the wind and their luck blew the right direction, they would probably be safe tonight.

'Excuse me, ma'am.' One of the girls approached from her left side. 'Would you have any spare change?'

In the street light, Kit could see the girl's dark skin and black eyes. Under the thick jacket, she glimpsed a red plaid shirt. Virgie. She looked as shocked as Kit felt. For a moment, they stared at each other.

Then, wordlessly, Kit dug into her bag and pulled out the wad of bills intended as a donation to the shelter. She shoved them into Virgie's hand, even though she knew there wasn't enough money in the world to give this girl what she needed or repay her for what she had lost.

Virgie clutched the bills, and Kit gripped her hand so tightly that it shook. Then Virgie blinked, pocketed the cash, and said, 'Thank you, ma'am. Bless you.' She walked back toward the others.

Once Kit and John Paul took a few more steps, he asked, 'Are you all right?'

'Not really.'

'Do you know that girl?'

'In a way.'

'Want to talk about it?'

'Not right now.'

'Maybe later.' He put out his arm.

Kit squeezed it, and he covered her freezing hand with his. Together, they continued down the broken sidewalk, not speaking, heading toward the lights and the city.